STEEL MILL VIKINGS

STEEL MILL VIKINGS

THE KINSLAYER SAGA, BOOK ONE

SARAH JOY ADAMS

Charlotte, NC

FALSTAFF
BOOKS
WWW.FALSTAFFBOOKS.COM

For Noel —
I promise to always be on your side and fight the monsters with you.

FOREWORD

An Affectionate Note to my Fellow Scholars, Medieval Geeks, and Old Norse Nerds

If you are looking for scholarly accuracy you will, I hope, find it in my published scholarship, but you won't find it here. This book is a work of fiction. It is not a scholarly treatise, nor even historical fiction. It is a fantasy of my own, woven from whatever cultural and literary threads most pleased me. I have taken elements from Icelandic sagas, Old English epic, and the Eddas with wanton disregard for language diversity, historical eras, or current scholarship. The characters themselves are not university scholars, nor are they native Icelanders or Swedes or Norwegians or English. Their measure of authenticity is their lived experience and the stories their elders have told them. In my defense, I can only say that it is the nature of myth making and storytelling to reinvent the former things and put the old tales together in new ways.

A Warning to White Supremacists

I love Norse myths. Infuriatingly, those same myths and imagery are often invoked by racists in the US and Europe, so I wish to be very clear. Absolutely nothing in this book is meant to be supportive of white supremacy in any form. The berserks in this book are only heroes if they individually choose to do heroic things, and none of them are superior by blood or heritage to other human beings. Take your racist fantasies elsewhere, there is nothing for you here.

CHAPTER

ONE

As Harvey pulled her ten-year-old Ford pickup into the employee lot at Erie and Midlands Steel, hundreds of ravens descended, settling on every fence top and wire. They faced into the wind off the Niagara River, eyes focused on Harvey. To the north, Grand Isle loomed over the long strip of factories, grain elevators, and warehouses that crowded the riverbank. For every one that was still working three more stood empty, gates chained shut, graffiti scrawled across the No Trespassing signs. Buffalo had seen better days.

Even without her mother Anna's gifts, Harvey knew what the ravens wanted from her. Make food or be food. Either way, her kind always fed them—until she gave up that life. She sighed and slid out of the truck cab. The largest of the ravens landed on the side view mirror on the driver's side, ruffling his feathers and clacking his beak at her.

"Food!" the bird said. "Feed my people, Hervor, daughter of Angantyr."

"Fuck off, Stormcrow. I'm not dead yet." She turned her collar up against the cold as she headed for the factory. In her twenties she would have been wearing a short, cute little jacket that showed off her long legs. Now in her mid-thirties she preferred the comfort of the longest coat Burlington could provide. Even with the coat's protection, the cold crept up her legs. The predawn wind whipped strands of her chestnut brown hair out of its tight braid and into her eyes. Behind her the raven laughed.

Inside the factory smelting fires flared, red and gold. Sweat prickled across her scalp. One minute before shift change. She quickened her pace, stripping off her coat as she headed for the locker room.

"Shit." Harvey jerked her hand back a second too late, her hand damp. The lock dangled, broken and dripping white with jizz. Again. She smacked the door with the flat of her hand and it bounced open. Someone had pissed all over the locker's insides. Sour urine dripped off her fire-resistant work gloves, safety goggles, and hard hat. Even last year's school pictures of her kids, Mal and Caleb were splashed. Instinct roared awake, but she held back the rage.

Stay in control. You need this job.

She turned and scanned the room, damp fingers flexing. A man fussing with his bootlaces caught her eye and decided to be elsewhere. A few loiterers, still bitching about the Bills' latest loss were hustled out of the room by friends. The ones she was looking for clustered across the aisle, waiting with bare toothed grins. Mac and his guppies.

Mac had never been her friend—he'd backed her brother Heidrek for leadership in their clan when their father died—but he'd kept a safe distance between them the last few years. Heidrek put her in the hospital, but her testimony put him jail for attempted murder. Now with Heidrek up for parole, Mac was sending a message. *Keep your mouth shut this time.*

A bench, bolted to the floor, stood between her and them. She kicked it out of her way, sending the wooden seat crashing. The bolt pinged away into the far corner of the locker room, jingling as it rolled across concrete. The men beside Mac crowded closer to him, but he just grinned wider.

She gripped his shirt with her damp hand. As paunchy as he was broad-shouldered, Mac was hardly a small man, but her five foot ten plus heavy-soled work boots gave her the height to lean over him. "You owe me a new lock," she said between gritted teeth.

"So what?"

"So I'm taking yours." She let the berserker madness echo in every word, and a shiver ran through Mac. But behind him the men nudged and whispered.

"You gonna let her talk to you that way?"

"Say something! Go get her."

"Bitch."

Harvey dropped Mac and turned her back on them.

With one hand she yanked open Mac's locker. The padlock snapped and pinged across the room. She dumped out the contents: lunch sack, coat, *Playboy*, and hung her coat inside.

The air moved at her back. Harvey slid sideways, ducking at the last second. Mac's fist slammed into steel with a crunch. He howled in pain as she clamped her hand around his wounded wrist, forcing him to his knees. Bone and tendon shifted under her grip.

Harvey put her mouth next to his ear and whispered, "Just because I don't anymore, doesn't mean I can't. Remember that from now on."

She released his wrist and he staggered to his feet, backing into the arms of his friends who stood there wide-eyed and open-mouthed. No need to fear them—nothing but bullyboys and hangers on, drawn to Mac's bravado, but with no idea what he, or she, really was. They'd probably piss themselves if they ever saw a real berserker in action.

Harvey spat on the broken lock. Dragging her index finger through the spit, she drew the runes for *closed* and *danger* on the flimsy metal door. Not as good as blood, but it would work.

"Break that," she said to the dead silence. The shift whistle drowned out whatever they might have said.

Ken, her shift manager, glared as she punched the time clock with exactly one second to spare and paused to run her goggles and hard hat under the water fountain. Sweat stains already peaked out from the armpits of his short-sleeved button down shirt. "I don't need trouble on my floor."

"No trouble here."

"You're telling me if I go in there, I'm not going to find any reason to write anybody up?"

"No, sir." She held his eyes with her own. "None at all." She may have betrayed the entire berserker community when she stole her father's sword Tyrfing and testified against Heidrek, but that didn't mean she would whine to the authorities every time a member of the community expressed his feelings on the subject. Some things were private. Besides, Mac's wife and kids deserved to eat.

Ken's gaze shifted over her shoulder. "That right, Mac?"

"Yeah." Mac's right hand was curled against his stomach. He punched the clock with his left.

"Then get to your goddamned stations, both of you. We got steel to pour."

Mac glared but said nothing as he slid past Harvey toward his place up the line. Ken grabbed Harvey's arm.

"Look, I don't know what kind of bad blood the two of you have going, but there are laws against harassment for a reason. You just say the word and I'll support you."

She gave him a tight smile. Ken was a good guy, even if he had moved up to wearing a tie and a clipboard. He'd taken more than his own share of bull for being one of the few Black employees at the steel mill to get promoted.

4

"Thanks," Harvey said. "It's fine. I've got it under control. Are you going to approve those two days off I need?"

Ken sighed. "I'd like to, but we need the manpower. And it's not exactly an emergency."

She lowered her voice, pleading. "Ken, it will be if I don't convince the parole board to keep my brother in jail. He's got some prison psychologist convinced he's a changed man. I even got a letter from the guy asking me to come down state and participate in a family reconciliation program—hug it out and make nice. You never met him, so you don't know, but if Heidrek gets out he'll come after me or my kids."

"You don't think the police will protect you?"

Harvey snorted. "You have no idea."

Ken raised his eyebrows.

"Okay, maybe you do. Give me one day. Or hell, move me to the graveyard shift that night. Something. *Anything*." *Anything so I don't have to kill my own brother to save my kids' lives.*

Ken took off his hard hat, rubbing his hand over his short, curly hair. Even at this distance from the forges, sweat glistened on his bald patch. Under Harvey's clothes a bead of sweat ran down her back, the hairs on the back of her neck sticking to her flesh.

He rapped at the clipboard with a pen. "You know the company's always looking for an excuse to cut people."

"Yeah."

"I can't give you the day off. But you call in sick on the day of, I won't count it against your record."

"Thanks, boss. Appreciate it." She smiled and settled her hard hat onto her head as she walked toward her pouring platform.

"Don't get cocky about it," he called after her.

She made it up the platform stairs two at a time. Finally, the day was looking better. "All good?" she asked the man coming off shift. She eyed the giant ladle full of molten steel gliding down the line toward them.

"It's sparky today, so keep an eye out," he said, handing over the logbook and key.

"Are you still able to cover my shift next week?"

"Yeah, I need the hours. Pour safe."

"Thanks." She slid on her goggles and gloves, scanned the bank of gauges controlling the 200-ton ladle of molten steel, added her initials to the log sheet, and took her position.

Golden fire flared around the factory as arc furnaces melted scrap. Great gouts of smoke went up from the furnaces' tap holes. Suspended on giant pulleys, each ladle eased down the line toward a pouring station. Slag, the honey thick scum of burning impurities, rolled across the surface of the molten metal. Up and down the line sparks fountained upward as the purified steel hit the cold molds.

At her elevated platform, Harvey worked her own ladle smoothly, finding a rhythm she could sustain all day. In her head she counted the seconds for each pour, keeping up with the pace of demand, but not rushing. If she went too fast the parts would be full of trapped air bubbles that could crack an engine block under stress. Too slow and the process would grind to a halt, the polishers and grinders down the line losing their own rhythm between pieces. She settled back on her heels, knees unlocked, her wide shoulders centered above her hips. Pouring wasn't muscle work exactly, but posture counted. You couldn't stand all day in the same position without your back locking up if you didn't watch your posture.

Too many sparks. The steel was too hot today. With a flick of her wrist she raised the ladle's lip, cutting off the spill. The mold moved on down the line and a new one slid into place. She twiddled a dial, raising the ladle so that the stream would have a foot farther to travel through the air, cooling a bit on the way down.

She squinted at the red and gold cascade, gauging the stream by the flash and smoke. The pouring rhythm eased the fight in her back and shoulders.

Mama made bread and mead. She made steel chassis and engine blocks.

She let her imagination wander into stories her father-in-law Ivor liked to tell. The forges of the dwarves where the cursed sword Tyrfing was made—were they like this? They said it was her own ancestor who forced the dwarf Dvalin to make the sword with his own hands, and her namesake, Hervor, who wielded it best.

But the steel that made Tyrfing was long cold, buried with her father.

This steel, on the other hand, was a real bitch. It popped and fizzed with burning phosphorous. She squinted, twirling dials. She raised the vat again until its lip was even with her boots. Sparks landed on her toes.

Clenching her teeth against the smell of sizzling metal and boot leather, she thumbed the mic on her station, calling up to the furnace operator. "Hey, cool down the furnaces. I'm at max pouring height already."

Mac's voice crackled over the radio. "You feeling the heat a little too much today? Maybe you should take your top off and you'd feel cooler." Snickers and whoops came through the static. "You need a man to come down there and hold your hand, sweetheart?"

She flipped off the radio. Maybe Ken was right about reporting Mac. Messing with her stuff was one thing. Screwing up the pour process could get the men down the line hurt. But she wasn't going to let a pisshole like Mac turn her into a crybaby. She gritted her teeth and squinted at the spitting stream of molten steel.

A drop of molten steel jumped higher than the others. It struck her cheek, sizzling onto the flesh just below her goggles. She screamed and slapped at the hot metal with her free hand, even as she kept her right hand on the controls. The flash stuck on the edge of her goggles, burning under the silicone seal. She ripped off the goggles to get at the fiery goo.

The ladle jerked and bobbed. A phosphorous bubble broke in the cascading stream. Flash splattered in a fan across her station. It burned through her wool shirt, across her arm, her chest, her neck, her cheek. A single drop of gold sizzled into her eye. Red pain burst across her vision.

She slapped blindly at the emergency off button. Boots rang on the platform steps. All she could see was darkness and red flaring lights. The berserk flooded through her. Fight. Fight the pain.

Someone grabbed her by the shoulders, shoving Harvey toward the emergency shower. She flung them away. Blind, she flailed at the darkness. Arms wrapped around her. Someone grabbed her by the back of the head, holding her face up in a stream of icy water.

"We got you, Harvey," Ken shouted. "Let us help you!"

She gripped fabric, clinging to the arms that held her. Not the enemy. The pain was not their fault. She clenched her teeth against the pain, against the instinct to fight and fight until nothing was left. Hands forced her eye open in the freezing water.

She gasped, choking and coughing. She wrenched her head away, knocking back the helpful person drowning her. A quick breath. A one-eyed glimpse of men crowded around her, fear on their faces. She plunged her face back into the stream. Red and gold pain flooded across her vision, clouds of light bursting in the darkness. Harvey held onto the berserk as hard as she could and let the pain flow on.

CHAPTER
TWO

Halfway across Buffalo, Carl dragged himself up the wooden stairs to the apartment above his garage, Lars' footsteps heavy behind him. He ached in every joint, and the slice in his left arm throbbed. He dragged his fingers through his beard and hair, scraping out the tangled wet braids. Stripping down to his undershorts, he dumped his soggy clothes in the nearby hamper and his chainmail into the plastic tub of oiled sand nearby. His double-bladed axe went neatly on the pegs by the door. He'd already wiped and oiled it before coming home. Shivering, he pulled on the wool bathrobe he always left waiting on the peg and shuffled barefoot into the kitchen.

Behind Carl, Lars's gear clanged onto the floor. Lars's clothes, soaked and stinking of river mud, followed with a wet splat.

"Don't leave that shit there," Carl said over his shoulder. "Rinse it out in the shower and put it in the hamper."

Lars groaned and rolled his eyes, but he gathered the wet clothes and trotted toward the shower. Clotted with river muck, his short blond dreadlocks dripped onto his paper-pale skin. Livid bruises edged in frostbite where the frost demon had clamped down on his shoulder. Thin stripes ran across his lower back onto his backside, relics of a childhood that put him on the streets by age twelve. The nineteen-year-old never seemed to stop eating, but his ribs still showed despite ropy muscles he'd put on in the last year.

"You doing okay?" Carl called after him.

Lars wasn't shivering—anybody should be after spending that long in the cold water. He should make the boy sit by the radiator, check him again for hypothermia or shock.

"You're not my mom," Lars said over his shoulder.

"Thank the gods for that." Carl grinned and turned toward the galley kitchen and the automatic drip that sent coffee fumes through the two-bedroom apartment. In the living-slash-dining room the radiator hissed.

As the ancient pipes banged and bubbled, Carl ran water over the three-inch gash in his arm, clenching and unclenching his fist. He picked at bits of leaf and gravel embedded in the clotting blood. The lukewarm water burned his cold fingers, but he ran it anyway, rubbing his hands over the wiry red hair on his forearms to get the blood flowing again.

Jesus H. Christ, it hurt. Fucking frost demons.

For good measure he poured hydrogen peroxide over the wound, where it foamed and hissed. He breathed hard and sharp through gritted teeth, pouring on more. By the time the bubbling stopped he was bent over the sink, sweating and shaking.

Damn, he was tired. Only November and he was already shit full of fighting the damn river. One of these days, if he lived long enough, he was going to retire to Florida. Somewhere that Winter couldn't reach.

Who was he kidding? Florida was miles of swampland and monsters everybody knew about. The gods only knew what else lived in those waters. He shook away the black thoughts. In the midst of his battle rage, he felt invincible. But it came at a price. He was weak and shaky now and would be for hours, prey to a grim depression that drained the hope and flavor out of the world. Lars was still young and cocky, able to bounce back quicker, but for Carl it seemed every year older he got, the longer the gray aftermath lasted.

Leaning on the sink, he closed his eyes for a second, and in the darkness behind them he saw Lars going down for the third time, the grayish white of the frost demon rolling him over and under in the black water. Lars dead. Gone like Harvey's husband, Jon. All on him. His stomach growled and groaned, his hands trembling as he bent over the sink.

"Hey." Lars, wrapped in a towel, punched him in the shoulder. "You worshiping your old gods there or just passing out?"

Carl forced a laugh, still leaning on the sink. "You doing okay?"

"Me? Hell yeah." Lars poured himself a giant mug of coffee and dumped in half a cup of sugar. "That was a good fight. Did you see me take that big fucker's head right off? Whack!" He mimed the motion of the head flying away into the bushes. "Whoo! I'm good." But his hand holding the mug trembled a bit. He clamped a second hand on the mug and downed the rest.

"You almost died, jackass."

"Almost." Lars saluted him with the empty mug. "Aaaaalmost. And, like the lady said, almost ain't shit except in horseshoes and hand grenades." He yawned so wide that his tonsils showed and shook his head like a dog. "Man, that was some fight."

As Carl poured himself a coffee, Lars took a beer out of the fridge and shotgunned it in one practiced motion. He yawned again, jaw cracking. "When is this friend of yours showing up? It's about time someone came out to help. So far all I'm seeing is you, me, and a whole lot of angry river water."

Carl's jaw twitched with the urge to yawn, but he blinked it off. "He gets here when, and if, he gets here. Dan's hard to get ahold of." Especially since Harvey had turned her back on them. Every once in a blue moon Dan sent a postcard—South Dakota, Maine, Nova Scotia, once even from Hawaii. They never said more than "still riding." Carl had sent an email to the Aroostook Band of the Mi'kmak people, hoping they knew where Dan was but the only answer he'd gotten back was "we do not keep records of our members' movements and cannot provide you with contact information at this time." They probably thought he was a cop.

"I'm going to bed." Lars grabbed a stick of beef jerky out of the jar next to the coffee pot and bit off a hunk. "Screw the garage."

"That's my livelihood you're talking about." Carl slapped Lars on the arm. "Try to get out of bed by noon, would you?" That would at least let the kid have four hours to sleep. He could nap in the evening before they went out again. Probably wouldn't though. Lars would most likely spend the time hunched over a video game, cursing cheerfully into his headset. Asshole. Youth was wasted on the young.

"You got it, boss." Washing his jerky down with another beer, Lars shambled towards his bedroom. Carl watched him go, a half-smile on his face. The boy was full of restless energy, ready for a fight at any second of any day, and certain of his own immortality. A typical berserker, even if Lars hadn't known a damn thing about it before he met Carl. Hiring Lars fresh out of juvenile hall two years ago had been more pity than good sense. He owed a kind of debt as well—if not for Harvey and Jon's families, he might have ended up as bad off as Lars. Or worse.

The post berserk gray darkened inside him, settling like a lead weight over his soul. When the berserk was on him, the world took on a bright, pinhole focus, a clarity of purpose—destroy the monster in front of him. Pain or cold or doubt didn't matter in the berserk, but when it faded all those things rushed in with a vengeance. Having a family hadn't saved Heidrek from himself. If Lars went that way...

He shook himself hard, like a dog shaking off water. Lars would never have Heidrek's cruel streak. He was more likely to go Jon's route and get himself killed young, hunting for cheap thrills and glory.

"It's not going to happen," Carl said. "Not while I'm here." The muscles in his arms twitched and jumped, his hand shaking with exhaustion.

How much longer do you think you're going to be here exactly? Pushing the wrong side of forty, working all day and fighting monsters all night with no one but a skinny teenager with more balls than brains as back up. You think you'll last forever?

"Knock it off," he said out loud. He grabbed the coffee pot and gulped, singeing his tongue, but pouring the heat down into his core. While the second pot brewed he squeezed ointment onto his wound and wrapped his arm with the last of the gauze from the first-aid kit.

He really should go down to the garage now to check the payroll invoice, get started on the paperwork before they opened for business. He swigged more coffee, but it didn't help.

With a sigh, he gave in. Two hours, he told himself, as he padded toward his bedroom. He'd take two hours and then he'd get to work. He yawned again, hard enough that his jaw popped.

He hoped to whatever gods might listen that Dan got his message and still cared enough to come back.

CHAPTER

THREE

A hundred miles downstate, Heidrek stretched out on his yoga mat and thought of Harvey. The runes etched into his wrists with a sharpened paperclip tugged and stung as he pressed his hands into a sun salute.

Around him in the prison meeting room other prisoners huffed and grunted with the effort of the pose. Heidrek relished the calm, the sense of contained power the movements brought him. The instructor, a volunteer from outside, pressed a hand against his back. *Touch me again, bitch, and I'll snap your neck.* But he nodded meekly and said nothing.

The woman walked between the prisoners, correcting a stance here, giving a word of encouragement there. "Remember," she said. "True freedom comes from inside you."

Other men nodded along or voiced their agreement. Heidrek smiled to himself. *Oh, you have no idea.*

"Let everything else go. Just be in the moment," the instructor said.

Heidrek closed his eyes and shifted smoothly into the next pose. Even through the yoga mat he felt the ground beneath his feet, the layers of dark earth stretching beneath him. He breathed from his diaphragm and brushed a finger over one of the runes on his wrist. Revenge. Blood. Winter. His body held its position, but his spirit flowed down into the earth, to the roots of the world where dark things slept. *Wake up. Listen to the call of my voice. Wake and hunger. Find her for me.*

He smiled to himself and shifted into warrior pose. A drop of blood fell from his wrist onto the mat.

CHAPTER

FOUR

Mal lay in bed, listening to the blood rush through her head. She could feel it in her jaw, in her shoulders and back, every muscle taut the moment she woke. She should have gotten up to go running when Mom left for the steel mill, but she'd already hit snooze five times. It wasn't that she didn't want to run. She wanted it too much—wanted to hit the horizon and keep going until the road left everyone behind. Everyone had told her that junior year of high school would be hard. No one mentioned feeling like this.

She curled into a tight ball, hugging her core. Her hands clenched into fists, ready to punch anyone dumb enough to get in her face. If she went to school, she'd be lucky if she made it to lunch without getting detention. She should stay here, lock herself into a cocoon of bed covers until she could stand humanity again. But Grampa or Caleb would tell on her. Or the school would call. Mom would find out.

Maybe she could make it through to third period and then ditch out the back of the gym. Maybe find some weed and smoke it down by the river, spend the day alone until she didn't need to pick a fight with the world.

Downstairs, the kitchen timer went off. Her brother Caleb's feet thumped down the hall, then the shower hissed in the bathroom next to her room. The sound grated on every one of her nerves. The kitchen timer downstairs kept screaming.

Grampa's cane banged on the stairs. "Time to get up, kids. Hurry up!"

Gritting her teeth, Mal hurled herself out of bed and into her clothes. Dressed in leggings and a plaid flannel shirt dress, she vaulted the bannister from the second floor, landing by the entryway. She popped back up, scraping her blonde hair out of her eyes into a ponytail.

The stairs to the second floor divided the first floor in half with the living room on one side, and the kitchen and Grampa Ivor's room on the other. Caleb's homework was still spread out all over the computer desk in the living room. Mal gathered his papers together and stuffed them into his backpack for him, before grabbing her own pack and taking both into the kitchen with her.

In the kitchen, Grampa Ivor stared out the window at nothing, his white mustache and muttonchop whiskers quivering. He wore boxers and a wifebeater that barely covered his barrel chest, his hand around his cane.

Jesus, old man. Put on a robe or something. She scrubbed her hands over her face. *Just don't talk to anybody until after gym and you'll get through.* Bypassing her grandfather, she shoveled oatmeal out of the waiting crockpot into a bowl and dumped in enough brown sugar to darken the mush two shades.

Caleb came in a minute later, dressed in his usual jeans and band t-shirt. His long, dark bangs, still damp from the shower, dripped into his eyes. They were hollow and bruised looking. At fourteen he'd shot up in height but had yet to fill out in any other direction. He had a habit of folding his gangly limbs into odd pretzels whenever he sat.

"You okay?" Mal asked, breaking her own self-imposed rule.

He shrugged and sat down with his own bowl. "The ravens won't shut up. And there's a weird wolf-looking dog in the front yard."

She glanced out the window—nothing there. She gave him a side eyed glance, old worry churning her stomach.

"What?" he snarled at her.

"You're being weird," she said.

"You're being a bitch."

"Knock it off, you two." Grampa Ivor's hand slammed down on the table, shocking them both out of their locked gaze. "Family fights together, not against each other."

Caleb deflated first. "Sorry," he muttered.

Mal tried to say, "me too," but it came out as a mumble.

"So, it's time." Grampa pulled out a chair and sat across from them. "Listen to me."

Not now. Not more mystic shit. Just leave me alone. She shoveled more oatmeal into her mouth, hoping he'd stop if he didn't have an audience. But Caleb was leaning forward eagerly, oatmeal untouched. Mal glanced from her grandpa to her brother and back. Neither one of them was going to let it go, and if she was late again she'd get a detention. She dropped her spoon in her bowl and said, "Fine. What is it?"

Ivor rapped his knuckles on the table, as if calling a meeting to order. "I have seen my fetch. The wolf has come for me. Now, after I die, I want the two of you—"

"No." Mal shoved her chair back hard enough to knock it over onto the linoleum. "You are not dying. Take your heart pills and shut up about that crap."

But Caleb leaned forward, his face creased with worry. "Is that what the ravens are talking about? I thought...I thought they were saying bad things, but I can't ever make it out."

Ivor laid his hand on Caleb's shoulder. "It's just bird chatter to me. But ask your mother—she has the gift from her mother."

Mal clutched her head in frustration. Grampa's stories about monsters in the water and animals that talked were fun when she was a kid, but she and Caleb were too old for that kind of nonsense now. Except Caleb still believed every word.

Caleb frowned. "I feel like I could understand them if I just listened harder. Like they're in another room and I can almost make out what they're saying, you know?"

"Perhaps you will someday," Ivor said. "But don't be surprised if you can't. That kind of skill...it's a woman thing. Now, about my death. As I said, I have seen my fetch—I was hoping for a beautiful woman, but an animal will do. When I die I want you to scatter my remains on the ocean. Send me back to the waters our ancestors crossed."

"Okay," Mal broke in, grabbing bowls off the table, "Got it. Good old Viking funeral for Grampa. But it's time for us to go to school now and learn about stuff that's not total crap. Come on, Merlin." She hauled Caleb out of his chair by one arm and shoved his jacket and backpack at him. "Grampa, you sit tight and call 911 if any more dogs come into the yard, okay? Great. See you tonight."

She shoved a resisting Caleb out the kitchen door and slammed it behind her. He tried to slide past her, back into the kitchen, but she hooked an arm around his ribs and swung him off the steps like he was still a little kid. He was light in her arms. Almost as tall as she was, but he weighed next to nothing.

He ran after her as she jogged toward the high school, but soon fell behind, panting. She slowed to a walk until he caught up.

Without looking at him, she said, "We've been over this! You have got to stop talking to animals."

"But..."

"No, buts." Wind whipped strands of her hair across her eyes and into her mouth. The air tasted like fallen oak leaves and overnight frost. Ahead of them a raven landed on a street sign and croaked. Caleb turned his head toward it.

"Stop." She reached out and turned his face back toward hers. "No more talking to birds."

"I don't talk to them. They talk to me!"

19

"Then don't talk back."

They glared at each other, fists dug deep into their pockets. Mal's shoulders tightened the more she looked at her brother's sharp face. Half the fights she'd gotten into over the years started with "Hey Mal! Your kid brother's a freaking weirdo" and ended with the teachers hauling her off to the principal's office. He knew she'd always stand up for him, but dammit why did he have to make it so hard?

Caleb blinked first, shrinking back inside his hoodie. "Sorry."

Mal sighed and let her shoulder's slump. Poor kid. She kind of wanted to hug him, but he'd probably shove her away. The closest he came to hugging anybody since he turned thirteen was letting Mom put one arm around his shoulder, and even then, only at home. He seemed to be all sharp knees and elbows and hunched shoulder blades these days.

She punched him in the shoulder instead. Something about the smile he gave her in response felt like a counter to the gut. It was like the way Dad used to smile when he and Mom argued and she forgave him.

That was it—Caleb might have Mom's dark hair, but he had Dad's pale blue eyes and his smile. People had commented over the years about how she got her dad's blond waves, but she didn't really see his face when she looked in the mirror. When Caleb smiled, that's when she could see her dad again.

"What?" he said, suspicious.

"Nothing. Come on. We're going to be late." She stretched her legs toward the school. The heavy gray dome of cloud overhead felt like a pot lid, closing off any chance of climbing up and out to sunnier places.

Her sprint wasn't good enough. The last bell rang as she crossed the parking lot. Principal Padowski already stood in the doorway, pink detention slips in hand. "Late again, Mallory," she said. "For a member of the track team, you seem to have a lot of trouble getting off the mark in the morning."

Mal planted her feet and rolled her eyes. "The bell is still ringing!"

Principal Padowski pursed her lips and held out a pink slip. "And I'll see you in detention this afternoon."

With Mal blocking the principal's view, Caleb scooted past without catching any snarky comments or a pink slip. When his sneakers squeaked off down the hall, Mal gave the principal one last sigh and took her detention slip before trudging off toward her own locker.

CHAPTER
FIVE

Frozen to the bone, Harvey lay in the ER bed with her cotton gown open over her chest to let the burns breathe. Silvery dots of burn cream speckled her skin wherever the flecks of molten flash had hit. The nurses draped heated blankets over her, but she couldn't stand the pressure on her chest, so she lay in the bed and shivered. The smell of molten steel, burned wool, and charred flesh seared her nose. Every movement sent a burst of pain through her face and chest. The gauze over her eye puckered and the tape tugged at her skin.

"Is there somebody we can call? We tried your husband, but he's not answering," a nurse said, paging through a stack of papers.

"He's dead," Harvey croaked. Eight years. How did she not manage to update that one piece of paperwork? She stared at the fluorescent bulbs overhead. Ivor, her father-in-law, couldn't drive anymore, not with his eyesight and his bad hip. And no car. Mal had been nagging her for months about getting a second car.

Dammit. There was one person.

"Call Carl. His number's in my cell phone." She gestured at the plastic bag at the foot of the bed. Ken had made sure her coat and purse went with her in the ambulance.

While the nurse dug out her cell phone, Harvey focused on the pain, trying to herd it back to its place, compress it until it no longer mattered. She focused on the pressure on her finger from the oxygen monitor.

The pain medication made the lights overhead drift and sway. She flung an arm over her good eye, blocking out the white glare, until she fell down into the darkness.

"Harvey?" Carl's voice woke her. Pain stabbed out again.

She lifted her elbow to peer at him with one eye. On anyone else the warrior braids, red beard, and copper torc with Thor's hammer would have looked stupid. A grown man playing dress up. On Carl, it was the jeans and Diebold t-shirt that seemed out of place.

She swallowed hard around the dryness in her throat. "They won't let me drive home and there wasn't anyone else to call. And my truck is still at the factory."

"Don't worry about it." He held out a pair of garage coveralls. "They said you needed a change of clothes."

"Thanks."

He nodded and laid the coveralls over the foot of the bed. He shoved his hands, the knuckles red from fighting and fixing cars, into his pockets then jerked them out again. "Do you need help? Probably not, right? I'll just...I'll let you get dressed. Yell if you need anything." He backed out of the ER bay and dragged the curtain shut.

"I'm good. Thanks," she said to the empty bay.

She sat up. Shit, her arm hurt. Hissing through clenched teeth, she shrugged out of the hospital gown. Every movement dragged at the burned skin on her chest. Slowly, she eased herself down to the foot of the bed and swung her feet onto the cold linoleum floor.

She looked down at herself, assessing the damage. Under the silvery cream the nurse spread on her chest, ten white blisters rose where the bursting bubble splattered her. They hurt like the devil, but there was no charring that she could see. She owed the guys at work for shoving her under the shower so fast.

It was her eye that worried her. For a moment she cupped her hand over the patch, letting the cold tips of her fingers cool the heat that radiated and throbbed from her injured eye.

Now for the coveralls. Resting her butt on the bed, Harvey shook out the coveralls and stepped into them one leg at a time, the flannel lining sliding easily over her legs. Good so far. She dug her arms into the sleeves and hissed in pain as the fabric dragged at the bandage over her arm. In her head, she ran through half the curse words in her vocabulary.

She took a deeper breath and shrugged her shoulders into the coveralls. Now for the zipper. It stuck right over her belly button. She gritted her teeth. Every time she tried to yank on the zipper the motion of her arm pulled at the burns on her chest.

She closed her eyes in resignation. "Carl. Can you help me?"

The cubicle's curtain rattled as he threw it back. "What do you need?"

She pointed to the zipper. "It's jammed."

"No problem. I'll just...um." His already wind reddened face burned darker red as he bent over the zipper.

Up close, he still smelled the way she remembered him—lava soap, engine grease, and the strangely clean smell of metal tools. She turned her head to one side, ears burning as he wrestled the zipper into submission. He pulled the zipper up as high as it would go—barely cleavage height.

"Sorry," he said. "That's the best I can do."

"No problem," she said. Just as well—the burns on her chest throbbed and pulled every time she breathed.

A trickle of water ran out of her hair and down her back, sending hard shivers through her body again. Automatically she put her hand up to pat her thick braid of dark hair. "At least I've still got my hair." She chuckled weakly.

"Didn't your mom used to say that?"

"Every time one of us came home hurt. I didn't think she meant it quite so literally." She sagged back against the bed. "Can you help me with my boots?"

"No problem."

"Thanks."

As he retrieved her boots, she reached up to adjust the gauze patch taped over her eye. The tape was pulling at her eyebrow and driving her crazy. Taking it off for just a second wouldn't hurt. She bent her head down to shield her eye from the light as she pulled off the gauze. Carl knelt at her feet.

And she saw him. She saw him with her burned eye, sharper than she ever had with two good eyes. Instead of flannel and jeans he wore chainmail and woolen breeches. The silver lines of the mail ran and writhed across his chest, turning themselves into battle runes and snarling animals. Beside him on the ground lay his axe, notched and bloody. The light gleamed gold off his red-blond hair. Blood crusted around his temple and ran down the side of his face. More blood oozed through a wound in his left side.

Gray noise, like the aftermath of the berserk, cold like an ocean wave roared up over her and sucked her down. Her knees buckled and she fell hard, fighting to breathe. Hands pressed into the cold hospital linoleum, she squeezed her eyes shut, but the vision remained, painted on the backs of her eyelids.

"Harvey! What's wrong?" Carl grabbed her, hauling her back to her feet, but she shoved him away. She clapped her hand over her burned eye, panting. The bloody vision faded.

"Harvey. Harvey, honey, what is it? Talk to me." He grabbed her by the shoulders, his face pale.

"Let me go."

"Do you need the nurse? What's wrong?"

"Let. Go!" She shoved him away from her one handed, the other hand still holding her eye shut. "I can't do this," she said to the darkness behind her eyes. "Not again."

He reached for her, but she blocked the hug. "Get my things and take me home." She shoved past him to where the nurse was waiting with piles of paperwork.

CHAPTER
SIX

Mal sprawled in her seat at the back of second period math while Mrs. Dunnow's marker squeaked across the whiteboard. Three seats over, Taylor Padowski, decathlon star and all-around douchebag, tried to get her attention.

"Me." Taylor whispered and pointed at himself. "You." He pointed at her and writhed in his chair, hips pumping. She gave him the finger. His grin only got bigger and he mimed a bump and grind as best he could in the plastic desk.

"Taylor!" Mrs. Dunnow snapped from the front of the room. "Are you having a seizure? No? Then I suggest you turn around and take notes. Unless your passion for me is so intense that you want to spend all summer in my remedial algebra class."

The class sniggered and Mrs. Dunnow went back to explaining polynomials. *Polly wanna cracker?* Mal wrote in her notebook.

Outside the classroom ravens circled above the empty track around the football field. She pictured herself running, faster and faster until she left everything behind. Running over the far playing fields, hurdling the chain link fence. Chasing the horizon in a land she'd never seen. The only thing that seemed real today was the urge to run, to find an enemy big enough.

In the stories her grandfather told there were islands full of fire, sea monsters that would drag a boat down. Reality told her the ocean was full of trash, big floating islands of it. That she could believe. All of it. This class she was forced to take but would never need; this city with its seven thousand empty buildings, its crumbling grain silos and hipster coffee bars; Taylor and his rule the school attitude—garbage. She slid farther down in her seat, eyes on the circling ravens outside until the bell rang for third period.

In the locker room Mal stripped off her shirt and bra together in one motion. Metal doors slammed all around her, echoing off the tile floor and walls.

"Hey Mal, look what I got!" Brittnee flashed a brand-new belly button piercing. "My mom is totally going to kill me."

"Oh yeah, you're a badass alright." Mal wriggled her sports bra on, scooping her boobs into place. The girl beside her hunched her shoulders toward the bank of lockers, trying to change without showing an inch of skin. Freak.

As soon as she thought it, she regretted it. Shelly wasn't a bad kid. She didn't deserve Mal being a bitch to her. Mal pulled on her shorts and bent to tie her sneakers.

Shrieks erupted from the far end of the locker room. Male whoops and cheers echoed around the tile and metal room, and a yodeling call of "Titty Inspector!"

Mal whipped around as Shelly gasped and clutched her shirt to her chest. Taylor Padowski jogged toward them at the head of a pack, slapping asses as he went, a shit eating grin plastered across his face. He raised his hand in salute. "Whoo! High five, Mal! Track team rules!"

She straddled the way in front of him. "Get the fuck out of here,

Taylor." He lunged at her, hands groping for her chest, and she knocked him back with one arm.

He darted past her and made a grab for the shrinking girl in front of him. Mouth open, Shelly stumbled backward into her open locker door, clutching her shirt. He lunged at her, making honking noises.

Mal grabbed him with both hands and hurled him into a bank of lockers. The crash of shoulder on metal echoed through the locker room. Taylor's knees buckled.

"Bitch!" He staggered upright. His boys formed a solid wall behind him.

But they didn't matter. Nothing mattered. The lockers, the onlookers, the sound of a whistle blowing—all of it faded into a distant, dreamy background hazed with red. Only her bare feet on the cool tile floor told her she wasn't dreaming. "Call me that again. Please, call me that again."

"You're a fucking bitch, Mal."

Joy surged through her as she said it. Her eyes widened, heart pounded, lungs expanded as if she had hit her stride in a 10K. She grabbed Taylor by the front of his shirt and swung, hurling him shoulder first into a wall. His temple bounced off the cinderblock. She let him go, dancing, arms wide. "Come on, football boy! Come and get me!"

Taylor staggered, catching his balance. He lowered his head and charged at her, but she reared back and planted her bare foot in his stomach. Onlookers gasped as Taylor went sprawling on his ass, skidding backwards on the narrow aisle between the lockers.

Mal dove after him. Taylor threw up his arms to protect himself from the attack, but she landed on him with her full weight. Knees and arms and ribs tangled together. Something hit her in the back of the head. Like she gave a damn. She straddled Taylor and punched him square in the nose. He kicked and writhed, flailing to protect his face as she rained blows on him. Someone kicked her in the ribs.

Hands dragged her off Taylor, out of the fight. They gripped her arms. Mal laughed from deep inside herself. A hot wellspring of life and power erupted inside her as the efforts to hold her back only heightened her joy. She breathed deep lungfuls of air, gulping as if hitting the best runner's high she'd ever known. She punched whoever was holding her arm and they let go. With a whoop she seized the person grappling her from behind and flipped them over her shoulder onto the heap that was Taylor.

Girls screamed. Mal laughed more. The wailing of women and the cry of ravens could come after. Now for battle joys, for red blood and bright swords. She bellowed and whooped, laughing the more Taylor writhed, and threw off the hands that reached for her.

Pain like lightning shot through her body.

Every muscle contracted. As quickly as it came, the red haze disappeared, leaving her gray and cold, writhing on the locker room floor.

"Enough." Coach Well's voice broke through the haze. "She's not resisting. Stop."

Little darts with wires stuck out of her chest. Coach Wells yanked them out of her. She dragged Mal to her feet. "Are you high? What is wrong with you?"

She swallowed hard. Blood. She'd bitten her tongue. "I don't know." Her eyes didn't want to stay in one place or to focus on one thing. The room rolled and she giggled.

Coach Wells shook her. "Look at me. Look me in the eye." Mal did her best. "What did you take? So help me Mallory if you're using meth, I will slap you myself."

Mal blinked and focused hard. Just as fast a they'd come, the giggles faded and a gray emptiness filled her. "I just...I just got sick of his shit." Her knees buckled and she started to shake. Black fog pressed the edges of her vision. She was starving and nauseous at the same time. It was like the time she'd done a cross country 10K after skipping lunch. "What...what did I do?"

Coach did not relax her grip. A slender Black woman, she stood at least a head shorter than Mal, but there was power in her gymnast's build. She held Mal close with one hand, turning her head

30

away from the whispering crowd. "Look at me, Mal. Look me in the eye."

Mal tried. She swayed on her feet. "My mom is going to kill me. Did you tase me?"

Coach Wells gestured at the school Resource Officer standing nearby, Taser still raised. His badge hung from a torn strip of cloth on his blue uniform. Taylor was crying, huddled on the floor. Blood dripped off his face. A couple of his boys were bruised, their clothes torn. Everyone stared at her—girls, guys, a couple teachers—their eyes and mouths round.

Coach Wells shook Mal again. "Look at me. What happened?"

"I don't know. But I want it back."

High heels clattered on the locker room tile. Principal Padowski swooped down on Taylor. "Oh my God! My baby!"

Shoving Mal down onto a bench, Coach Wells turned on the crowd, her hands raised. "That's it, show's over. Everybody out. You heard me, get out of here, all of you. Come on." Wails and yells about it being too cold outside and weren't they supposed to play volley-ball were drowned out with shrill whistles. "The rest of you want to be suspended too? 'Cause I've got the time. Outside and on the track. Now!"

The security guard shouldered his way past Coach Wells to grab Mal by the arm. "Hands behind your back." Before she could comply, he yanked her arms so tight her shoulder popped, and he zip tied her hands together.

On the other side of her, Coach Wells stood on tiptoe to whisper in Mal's ear. Her hundreds of long tiny braids pattered against Mal's cheek. "Don't say anything. You want a lawyer and your mom. Nothing else. Understand?"

Mal nodded as she was hauled to her feet. Gray fog clouded her brain; her legs twisting around each other as the RSO lead her away. The buzz faded and rose again, pulsing, fighting to come back. Cold settled in her bones. She shivered in the RSO's grip as he dragged her out of the locker room toward the principal's office.

CHAPTER
SEVEN

By the time Carl got to her house, Harvey had stopped shivering, but the drunken merry-go-round in her stomach whirled and wobbled. Even in her good eye, the edges of her vision kept fuzzing out. She promised herself not to take any more of the pills the hospital doctor prescribed. Whatever was in the medicine cabinet at home would have to be enough. She didn't need hallucinations on top of everything else.

As Carl parked the tow truck beside the curb, he yawned hard. When he put his hand up to cover his mouth his sleeve pulled back to show a clumsy bandage with blood seeping through.

"Jesus, Carl. Did you get knifed?"

He shook his head, blinking hard against a second yawn. "A frostie bit me."

"Did you go to the ER?"

"It'll be fine." He hopped out of the cab and headed back toward the winch to lower her truck.

"Bullshit," she yelled after him. The burst of anger cleared her head somewhat. Muttering "goddamn stubborn men," she came around the truck's side. "Get in the house and let me stitch that up. Come on, I owe you."

"You're high and I'm fine. You don't owe me anything. Why don't you go on inside and lay down?"

She crossed her arms and gave him the eye until her truck was unhitched from the tow. His hand still on the control lever, he returned her steady look. She raised an eyebrow at him. "Do you want gangrene?"

"I cleaned it," he said.

She raised her eyebrow a fraction of an inch higher.

"Fine." He slammed the lever off and went to get his keys from the truck cab.

"Thank you, honey," she said, hopefully too quiet for him to hear.

Once inside the house, she yelled, "Ivor! I'm home early" and kicked her boots onto the mat before bending down to retrieve the EMT-sized first-aid kit from under the sink. She snuck a look with her good eye at Carl as he hung up his coat by the door. Nothing noticeable about him this time. Except, had his backside always been that nice? She mentally slapped herself. She was high. The drugs they gave her at the hospital were making her high. Obviously. No other explanation.

While Carl unbuttoned his shirt sleeve and rolled it up past the bandage, Harvey sterilized and threaded a curved needle. She hardly ever used it, though her mother had insisted she learn. The only parts of the kit she really needed these days were the rubbing alcohol, the tweezers, and Band-Aids for the occasional road rash when Caleb fell off his bike or Mal took a tumble doing cross country.

"I already cleaned it out," Carl said.

"I believe you." She put a tea towel under his arm and dumped hydrogen peroxide over the wound. Carl hissed, ground his teeth, and looked away as the peroxide fizzed and bubbled. She cradled his arm in her hand while she swabbed dried blood off the wound with a cotton ball.

His skin was rougher than when they were young, dotted with

more freckles, but the inside of his wrist was still veined in blue river deltas. "Sorry. I know it hurts."

"It's fine." He still didn't meet her eye as he said it.

"That's the bad part. We're almost done. I promise," she said. As quick as she could, she whipstitched the edges of the wound closed. It was the only needlework she'd let her mom teach her.

As she stitched, Ivor limped into the kitchen, his cane thumping on the floor in counterpoint to the shuffle of his house slippers. "Carl! Haven't seen you around here in a dog's age. You frostbitten this early in the year?"

Carl's face was pale around the edges, but he laughed. "River's full of them. Worst I've ever seen. You want to come hunting with us? We could use an extra hand."

Harvey shot him a glare, but he ignored her. She bent back over her work.

Ivor settled into a chair at the table. "Those things are foul in the mouth. I got bit in the leg one time—turned all yellow and full of pus."

"This is nothing," Carl said. "Lars, the new kid I've got working for me, he almost went down for the third time last night. Stupid fucker waded right into the river after a frostie." He said it the way another man might say 'hit the game winning home run.'

Harvey tied off the thread and snipped it. The burns dotted across her chest stung and throbbed with every motion. She steeled herself against the pain and said, "You're recruiting old men and kids now? What are you going to tell this kid's mother when he buys it, huh?"

Carl turned back toward her, his eyes narrowed. "His mother's a meth addict actually. He hasn't seen her in years."

"Oh well, that's fine then. Nobody will miss him when he dies." For a second the berserk fizzed through her veins, but tears welled up and drowned the anger. She buried her face in her hands. "Dammit, Carl. Don't go getting yourself killed. Or this kid."

Pain furrowed Carl's brow and he opened his mouth to speak,

but then shut it again. His arm lay on the table as his shoulders sagged. "I'm doing the best I know how."

Harvey didn't look up. She breathed in deep through her nose and held her breath to keep back the tears.

His voice low, Carl said, "Someone has to keep the river clear. We can't all hide at home."

She didn't answer, except to shake her head. The knot in her throat ached. Finally, she said, "I'm not having this fight again."

"You started it!"

Ivor heaved himself to his feet to limp over to the fridge. He took out a six pack and set it on the table between them. "Everyone calm down and have a drink. Better a glass in your hand than a weapon. There's no need for hard words. We're all friends here."

Carl clenched and unclenched the hand on his wounded arm, staring at the stitches.

"Go on. Both of you," Ivor snapped.

Snorting through his nose, Carl grabbed a beer and twisted the cap off like he was wringing its neck. "Be well," he said, in the old language before raising the bottle and taking a long drink.

Harvey pried the top off a bottle and raised it in a salute, but she kept her sip small. She didn't need beer on top of whatever the pain meds were doing to her. Neither she nor Carl met each other's eyes.

Nodding in contentment, Ivor opened a bottle for himself and took a drink. He settled into a chair on the other side of the table. "Ah, now that's better. Be well, each of you. Who wants to tell me the story of their wounds first?"

Shrugging, Harvey said, "I got burned at work. It's no big deal. Just a random accident." She shoved her chair away from the table and began packing tools back into the first-aid kit as Carl described the fight with the river demon that dragged his friend Lars under the water. He made a good story of it.

With her back to Carl and Ivor, Harvey pretended to be drying the breakfast dishes in the drainer. It gave her a chance to wipe her eyes and fix her face. Now she understood her own mom's sudden, violent need to clean something back when her husband and his friends, and later Harvey and her friends, sat swapping tales around the kitchen table, comparing bruises and near-death escapes.

"—if you're willing to come, we could use your help," Carl said.

Harvey whipped around. "What?"

But Ivor was rubbing his chin and smacking his lips. "It's been too long. I just might join you. It'd limber up the old joints."

"No," Harvey said. "Don't you dare."

The two men stared at her. She turned on Carl, seething. "You don't come into my house and try to get my family killed. You hear me?"

"I'll make my own decisions, Hervor, daughter." Ivor rested his hands on his cane. To Carl he said, "It's bad this year, is it?"

Carl nodded, his eyes still locked with Harvey's. He swallowed and looked away. To Ivor he said, "It's not just the number. They're bigger, smarter somehow. More directed. I don't know why, but it's worse than I've ever seen it."

Ivor rubbed the stubble on his chin, sucking on his teeth. "Maybe this is the way then. I'm ready. When do you go hunting next?"

"Tonight, if you'll go with us. I've got a call out for reinforcements—Dan's coming back. I hope."

Harvey threw up her hands. "Oh, just fuck me sideways! You can have old home week with the whole gang. Why don't you go down and break Heidrek out while you're at it?"

Carl pounded his fist on the table. "I need help, Harvey! People are going to die if we don't fight this."

"That's what the police are for!" It was a stupid argument and she knew it, but she let the words fly anyway.

Of course, Carl called her on it. "You know that's bull. The police don't even know the monsters exist." Carl slid his chair back and stood. "We're the ones who stand between the hearth and the darkness. It's what we're made for. If not, we're nothing. Worse than nothing. We're just violent men looking for a fight."

Pushing off from the fridge, she locked eyes with him. "I am not a man. And when every one of you men are dead or in jail, I'll still be here."

Their faces inches apart, he spoke, his voice hoarse. "We need you, Harvey."

"My children need me more."

"You children need training. What are you going to do when the berserk comes out in them? Mal's sixteen—it's a miracle she hasn't gotten arrested for assault and battery yet. Caleb is thirteen. He could mature any day now. You can't pretend they're normal." Shaking his head, he dug his keys out of his pocket and headed for the door. "Ivor, I'll pick you up around nine."

The screen door slammed behind him.

Harvey's hands shook so hard she clamped them under her elbows. She swallowed against the painful dryness in her throat. "Don't go out with him tonight," she said to Ivor. "Please. We need you."

Ivor sighed, a deep, gravelly sound more like a growl. "Hervor daughter. Fate goes as it must. You know that."

Through blurred eyes, Harvey nodded. Her burns throbbed, her burned eye pulsing with every heartbeat. Ivor patted her on the shoulder and went off to his room, whistling a tune.

She grabbed Carl's beer off the table and swigged it before pressing the cold glass against her face. The cold made her shiver but didn't do much for the flaring fires behind her eyes. She stood alone in the kitchen, locked in her swirling thoughts until her phone rang.

Mal's school.

"Fuck."

CHAPTER
EIGHT

She was in no condition to drive, so she walked the half mile to North Tonawanda High School. Stormcrow and his flock leapfrogged over her through the trees the whole way. Before she crossed the road into the school parking lot, Stormcrow spiraled down out of the sky to land on the stop sign beside her. Harvey pretended not to see him, looking left and right for cars.

"Your sword is missing," Stormcrow said. "Why are you not ready?"

She struck out into the road without responding.

"The battle is coming. The feast! The feast is coming! Your own flesh and blood will feed us. Oh yes, they will!" Stormcrow called after her.

Harvey speed walked into the school lobby, slamming the door behind her. She must have looked as bad as Ivor said because kids and teachers alike flinched as she stamped by them down the school hall to the office.

Mal sat in a sports bra and shorts on a bench outside the office, handcuffed and shivering. Twin trickles of dried blood ran down her chest. A bruise shone red on her temple and another on her cheekbone.

Harvey dug her hands into her jacket pocket and looked down at her daughter. Mal had been in scuffles before, but none that left her bleeding and tied up.

"Who did you hurt?" Harvey said.

Mal looked up. "Jesus, Mom. What happened to you?"

She sat down beside Mal and unzipped her jacket, letting the burns air. "Accident at work. Hurts like hell, and I'll probably have a few scars, but I'll be fine. How are you doing?"

"I'm so screwed. I hurt Taylor." Mal's head hung down again and the shiver returned. Harvey took off her jacket and tucked it around Mal's shoulders. "Mom, they called the cops. And an ambulance."

Oh God. Of all the kids in school to take on. Deep breath.

"Okay, you're still a minor. Maybe you can get off with community service."

Mal sniffed hard and swiped at her nose with her bound hands. "When he came in the locker room he was grabbing people's tits. And he went after this girl, Shelly, she's such a little mouse. Somebody had to stop him...you know?"

"Yeah, I know." Harvey hugged Mal with one arm, mind racing. Bonnie Padowski was going to nail Mal to the wall on this. All she wanted to do was lie down in a dark room with some ice on her face, but she needed to get it together and think straight. She stared at the floor, mind scrambling in every direction and none.

Sneakered feet appeared in her line of sight. Harvey looked up to see Mal's coach standing over her. "Mrs. Otvar, could I speak to you for a moment?"

"Sure." She stood and walked a few feet away to huddle with Coach Wells. "Did you see what happened?"

"The last bit, yes. Which makes me a witness. I shouldn't even be talking to you. But the other girls told me the whole story. I want you to know—Mal was defending another girl from Taylor. She didn't start the fight. And he had it coming." Coach Wells kept her voice quiet in the echoing green tiled hallway. "What worries me isn't that Mal fought back. It's the way she did it. It was way beyond anything I've seen in a high school fight before. I think she may be on something."

"She's not."

Coach Wells's eyebrows went up. "They had to tTaser her before she could be pulled off him."

Harvey swallowed hard. "It runs in the family."

Coach Wells's eyes grew a bit wider and she looked Harvey up and down, then looked over Harvey's shoulder at Mal as if reevaluating what she knew about her best cross-country girl. What calculations were going on in the other woman's head Harvey couldn't be sure, but the coach took a long minute before she spoke again.

"Principal Padowski tells me that the two of you have a history as well." She paused and fixed Harvey with a stern look that made her seem every bit as tall as Harvey herself. "I've said this to Mal more than once, Mrs. Otvar, and now I'm saying it to you—I can't help if you won't talk to me. And Mal needs help. She's been heading for some kind of blow up for months."

Harvey nodded and licked dry lips. "I know. I—" she shot a glance over at Mal. "I haven't done a good enough job keeping on top of her. It's my fault this happened."

"No, it's not." Coach Wells pointed a finger at Harvey's face, her voice stern. "I've seen you at every home track meet Mal has run. I've seen you every parent's night since Mal started high school. She is not a bad kid and you are not a bad parent. And that's why I'm confused. Because something bad is happening inside her and I think you know what it is. You need to trust me."

Harvey bit her lower lip. She'd trusted the cops to handle Heidrek and now not a day went by that she didn't wonder if she'd done the right thing. But letting Bonnie send Mal to jail wasn't an option. "What do you think I should do?" she asked.

"The best defense is a good offense. Paint Mal as a victim and Taylor as the aggressor. Threaten to get a lawyer."

"I don't have lawyer money."

"Who does these days? Now, go in there and threaten her like you've got lawyer money to burn."

Harvey cracked a grudging smile. "I hate those kind of moms."

Coach Wells smiled back. "Don't we all?"

Someone cleared their throat behind the two women. The school secretary stood there. "Mrs. Otvar? Mrs. Padowski will see you now."

Harvey straightened—Bonnie might still be fitting into her high school jeans, but Harvey still had bigger boobs and at least six inches of height on her rival—and followed the secretary into the office. Her mind raced, assembling details into a plan of attack. Think like a PTA bitch. Think like someone who thought the rules worked for her. A sly smile quirked the corners of her mouth. That was it—she'd used the rules to bring down her brother, she could do the same with Taylor.

Bonnie, fingernails perfectly filed and manicured, sat on the other side of the desk. She didn't stand or offer Harvey one of the chairs in front of the desk. Harvey sat anyway, grateful for anything that helped the room not sway and swirl. Those pain medicines weren't kidding when they said not to be taken with alcohol. A police officer stood behind the desk with the principal.

As Harvey sat, Bonnie's eyes widened in horror, fixed on the burns across Harvey's chest.

Harvey took a deep breath, looked the police officer in the eye, and said, "I'm glad you're here, officer. This woman's son sexually assaulted my daughter. I want him arrested."

Bonnie's mouth fell open. Her perfectly glazed nails skidded on the arms of her chair. Harvey sat back in her own chair and crossed her arms in what she hoped was a confident gesture. The police officer looked back and forth between the two women, confused.

Bonnie's mouth was still wide open, gasping. "My son has a broken jaw thanks to your thug of a daughter," she squeaked.

Harvey narrowed her eyes at Bonnie and gripped the armrests. "Your son was in the girls' locker room grabbing girl's tits. Mal was defending herself and the girl next to her. From where I sit, Taylor's is the one who should be in cuffs."

Behind Bonnie, the RSO shifted uncomfortably. "Ma'am, when I got to the locker room your daughter was on top of Mrs. Padowski's son."

Harvey glared at him. "So it's not sexual assault unless the girl just lays back and takes it? I hope you don't have a daughter if that's the way you think. But," she shrugged and reached for her purse, "I'm no lawyer. Maybe I'm wrong. Let me just phone the Assistant District Attorney and find out what he thinks. I think I've still got him in my favorites list." She had her phone halfway out of her purse before Bonnie caved.

"Fine," Bonnie snapped. "But Mal serves a month suspension for fighting and she's off the track team for the rest of the year."

"I can live with that. If Taylor gets the same penalty."

Bonnie's nostril's flared and her chest heaved. They glared at each other across the desk. The police officer's hand hovered by his belt as the tension in the room loomed.

Bonnie wilted first. "A week's suspension for both of them. And they can both return to their teams. After the suspension."

Harvey slid her phone back in her purse and leveled a shit-eating grin at Bonnie. "We wouldn't want the kids to lose their scholarship eligibility, would we, Bonnie?"

Bonnie glared daggers at Harvey, but she clamped her mouth shut and gripped the arms of her chair. Harvey stood, still smiling, and nodded at Bonnie and the police officer. "Have a nice day."

She turned to walk away when Bonnie threw one parting shot. "Mal is going to end up just like her father if you don't do something about her," she spat.

Harvey's hand gripped the office doorknob till her knuckles turned white, but she held down the roar inside her. She'd learned years ago not to lose her temper at the Bonnies of the world.

Either way, Harvey turned to look over her shoulder. "We both know Jon was a good enough man that you wanted him for yourself once upon a time. If Mal turns out like her dad, she'll be miles ahead of your little rapist in training."

Forcing herself to breathe slowly and keep her back straight, Harvey made her way out to the waiting area. Coach Wells was gone, but she had brought Mal her backpack and coat.

"Come on. We're going home." Harvey said. She reached down and snapped the plastic ties that held Mal's wrists.

"What happened?"

"I'll tell you all about it outside." One hand gripping Mal's upper arm, Harvey steered her daughter toward the doors, fighting the urge to look back over her shoulder. *Never turn your back on the monsters.*

CHAPTER
NINE

Mal trudged along the side of the road beside her mom, feet dragging, arms hugged around her jacket. The back of her head throbbed. Her blood still ran too fast through her veins, whizzing and rushing over every nerve ending. She felt like she'd run a marathon and drank a whole pack of energy drinks at the same time—too tired to think, too wired to hold still.

The sun was too bright, the air too sharp. Starving, she ached all over. Every time the wind blew it went straight up the legs of her gym shorts. Her feet kept moving, but her eyelids kept shutting against her will. She shook her head hard enough to rattle, trying to knock away the fog.

"You need sleep," her mom said. "Then we have to talk about what happened."

Mal nodded, mouth too thick to say anything. After a few hundred more yards she said, "Where's the truck?"

"That's a long story too. Just keep walking."

"Am I going to jail?"

"Not today. You are suspended though. It was the best I could do."

Mal hunched into her coat and muttered, "Your best sucks."

Her mother turned on her. "Do you have any idea how close you came to losing everything? You ought to be thanking me right now. And your coach."

"Fine! I'm sorry."

Her mom snorted and kept walking, her pace angry fast. Mal rubbed a hand over her face as she followed. She wanted to go home, lock her door and go to bed, but the thought of having a 'talk' with her mom right now made home the last place she wanted to be. There was a spot down by the river off the Seabee Memorial Park where the hemlocks made a kind of cave out of the wind. She and the other members of the cross country team built campfires down there sometimes. If she got lucky, there would be matches under one of the milk crates and she could get warm. Her stomach growled.

As they came up to the house, her mom grabbed her elbow. Mal came up out of her mental fog enough to register where she was.

A lone Harley sat in the driveway, its rider leaning against the seat, chewing a stick of beef jerky. The bear claw necklace around his neck stirred memories, but she couldn't place him. A webbing of cracks ran all over his black leather jacket. Gray streaked the two black braids hanging down his back. His faded black t-shirt bore an eight-pointed star in black, red, yellow, and white.

The bike was in better condition. Even in the wet and mud of late November the black paint and chrome gleamed. The high set handlebars kept the rider upright, positioned to sit back in the seat, ready to ride all day and into the night.

"Hey," the guy said. "It's been a long time, Harvey."

Her mom's grip tightened on Mal's elbow. "I didn't know you were back in town."

Mal turned to look at her mom. "You know this guy?" she whispered. As she said it, memory came creeping back. The bike. A guy in black jeans and leathers who let her sit on his bike in her funeral dress and make *vroom, vroom* noises while her mom and uncle screamed at each other in the house.

"You're Dan," she said.

"That's right." He smiled at her. "You're a lot taller than you were before, Mal. Got your dad's look though. I knew you the minute you crossed the road." Being told she looked like her dad relit the fading candle inside her and made her stand up a little taller.

"What are you doing here?" Harvey said.

He shrugged. "Carl asked for help. Thought I'd stop by and see if you were still playing suburban mom or if you'd come back to us yet."

"This is not a game. Now get out of my way."

He didn't move. Instead, he looked Mal over, a line of worry showing between his brows. "You're looking pretty gray around the edges there, girl. You let the berserk out at school or something?"

"I got into a fight."

He chuckled. "Yeah, I can see that. But not every fight is a berserk. You ought to know that by now."

Mal shot her mom a look, but all she could see in her mom's face was fear. "I don't know what you're talking about."

"Don't listen to him," her mom said. "He's not the right person to be teaching you anything. Come on. We're going in the house." She dragged Mal by the elbow past Dan. He didn't move to stop them.

As they made it inside the kitchen too many questions swirled around in Mal's brain. She tried to force one to the front, but instead she just yawned wide enough to make her jaw creak. Mom gave her a gentle shove. "Go take a nap. We'll talk about it later."

Numbly, she stumbled past the staircase and into the living room. The last thing she remembered before sleep took over was Mom pulling off her sneakers and a sound like a knife being sharpened down the hall.

CHAPTER

TEN

On his way home, Carl admitted that his arm hurt less with the stitches in it. Maybe with Harvey's help it would heal up better too—there'd be a smaller scar that didn't catch when he moved his wrist. Lars might still be at the "pain is temporary, and chicks dig scars" stage of life, but he was more at the "my knee says it's going to rain" stage.

About a mile below Fisherman's Park, he pulled off the road where the jogging path squeezed between the river and the bridge supports. For a minute he sat, tapping his fingers on the steering wheel. He didn't have to go out again tonight. But Ivor had agreed to come along and Dan should be back by now. It would be better tonight.

With a sigh, he hopped out and took a sack of charcoal briquettes from the truck bed. Hoisting it over his shoulder, he headed for the path that ran under the bridge. A steep concrete slope rose up from the path to the base of the bridge, but the pigeons flying in and out of the darkness showed the opening between concrete and the bridge's underside. He set down the bag and called. "Anybody home?"

A Black man in fatigues, a combination of Gulf War and Vietnam cast offs layered over wool sweaters, emerged and slid down the slope. His clothes might not be regulation, but his shoulder still bore the gold chevrons. Other heads, more ragged, peered down.

"Hey, Sarge. Good to see you," Carl said.

"Good to see you too, man. Pretty early in the day for you to be out hunting, isn't it?" Sarge offered his hand and they shook. He had a persistent twitch that made it seem as if he was just on the point of turning away mid-conversation, but his smile remained friendly.

"I was in the area and thought I'd stop in for some information. You seen anything lately?"

Sarge nodded, his lips pursed in thought. "Joey's missing."

"Are you sure he didn't just go somewhere else?" Carl asked.

"He's not much of a wanderer, you know?"" Sarge said. "I thought maybe the police got him for loitering, but he's gone. A guy I know at the Mission said he saw Joey get dragged under. I didn't quite believe him at first, but Joey ain't been back since."

"It's them government robots," another man up the slope shouted. "One of them got Joey. Dragged him under." He nodded several times to himself, the motion turning into a nervous rocking. Others muttered confirmation that they had seen it too, or heard that they had seen it, or that someone else had seen it.

"I'm really sorry, man," Carl said. "You know where it happened?"

Sarge pointed up the river. "Just off Fisherman's Park. There's some nice shelter up there under the trees right by the riverbank. Kids leave beer and campfire stuff sometimes. I was up there yesterday and there were footprints all around the water's edge. Like bare feet, but with claws on the toes. I'd say there were at least four different ones by the sizes. There was something else too. A godawful almighty smell, like dead weeds and river muck dredged out of the bottom. Those frost things don't usually smell of anything."

Carl whistled. "That's not more than a mile and a half from here. You guys probably ought to think about moving somewhere safer. Can you go up to the Mission for a few days? Or move somewhere off the river, at least?" Not a hundred feet away the river lapped at the bank. The jogging trail on which they stood threaded a narrow path between the water's edge and the concrete embankment holding up the bridge.

"No damn govmint robots are gonna drive me out," one of the men shouted. He hawked a tremendous gob of mucus onto the ground.

Sarge crossed his arms. "A man's got to defend his home. I'm not letting some piece of ice with an attitude push me and my boys around." He pointed up the steep embankment to the three-foot gap between the bridge bottom and the concrete slope. "We'll be alright, as long as we've got each other's backs. We can keep a fire going up there. Cops'll take you in for lighting fires, but they don't come by here much. There's more room back there than you'd think. Kind of like a cave, only we got pigeons instead of bats."

Carl laughed. "Good man. Keep the fire going and keep an eye on each other."

"You know it." Sarge reached into his jacket and took out a Ka-Bar, the handle worn with use, but the edge still bright. "It's been a while since I saw any real combat, but I figure I still remember a thing or two. You and Lars need some help, you let me know."

"Thanks, man. I will." Carl clapped the man on the shoulder. "Be safe now."

"Good hunting." Sarge hefted the bag of charcoal over one shoulder and clambered back up the slope.

Carl gave a last wave to the men under the bridge and headed back to his truck. A mountain of paperwork was waiting on his desk at the shop. If he got it done by four he'd have time to take a nap before supper. By the sound of it there'd be plenty of work for all of them that night.

The morning was half gone by the time Carl got to the garage. Lars had a car up on the lift. At least he didn't have to go upstairs and drag the kid out of bed.

Shutting the door to the office, he flicked on the little space heater that kept the room bearable and sat down to do paperwork. Thank God Harvey had convinced him years ago to hire an accountant. The man might be expensive, but he was worth his weight in silk ties just for the aggravation he saved every month. Not to mention the fines, fees, and possible jail time for not having a clue what the feds' miles of rules meant. Carl checked over the final numbers, confirmed that the garage was still running in the black, and signed the pay ledger. Done and done.

Next order of business, restock basic parts. He tapped his pen against his teeth, studying the parts catalogue. The roar of a badly tuned motorcycle and Lars's shout broke his concentration.

Dan, a small duffel hooked over his shoulder, walked in, Lars close behind him. Carl rose to pull him into a one-armed hug as they pounded each other on the back.

"Hey man, how you been?" Sleeping in a ditch by the look of him. Ever since Heidrek went downstate. "Where have you been?"

Dan shrugged in response before dropping into the green and gold thrift store armchair. "Canada mostly. Maine. Been up to Newfoundland. Got into a couple scuffles over the Trans-Canada pipeline."

Lars leaned against the wall, flipping a wrench back and forth in one hand, a huge grin on his face. "You're Canadian? What are you going to do, say sorry to the frosties? Back off hosers, eh?"

Without turning toward Lars, Dan said, "I'm First Nations. But you wouldn't know what that means, would you?"

Carl said, "Lars, apologize."

Lars started to laugh, caught Dan's look and lost his grin. "Sorry. I guess. I mean, what's so bad about being Canadian?"

Dan gestured to his shirt with the red, white, black, and yellow star on it. "This mean anything to you?"

"Not really," Lars admitted.

Dan pinched the bridge of his nose and looked at Carl. "I'm here. What'd you want me for?"

Carl settled back into his desk chair. "Man, I'm glad you came. We need you bad. Lars and me, we're up to our ears in frosties and it's way too early in the year."

"Tons," Lars said. "More than you can count. We could fight for days if we really tried." He spun the gleaming wrench around his wrist. "It's been great."

A frown tugged the corners of Dan's mouth down. His eyes flicked from one to the other. "You going to pull that leader shit again?"

"Someone's got to," Carl said. Jon died, Heidrek got himself a ten-year sentence, and Harvey expected everybody to stay home and play nice. Somebody fucking needed to step up and lead. A buzz of anger flickered along his arms and he passed a hand over his face to keep from making a fist.

Harvey was right to protect her kids. He had to keep telling himself that. But God Almighty, they needed her. "I'll let you lead if you want to, Dan," he said, "but you know damn well you can't see straight, let alone think, when the berserk's on you. Hell, I'll let young Lars here lead if it'll make you happy. But whatever we do, we've got to work together."

Dan sniffed. He crossed his arms and leaned back in the chair, leather jacket creaking. "I don't need you to tell me how to fight. Or when."

"I know that, man." Carl settled into his chair, hands loose on his knees. "We need you."

"Come on, man," Lars said. "I've heard all kinds of shit about what you can do in a fight. Carl says you've been living on the road. Don't you want to get back in the game?"

Dan pointed at Carl. "You have no idea what I've been doing the last few years. You think this little corner of the world is the only one that matters? There are bigger monsters out there than the ones in

51

the Niagara River, and some of them ride around in fancy cars in three-piece suits."

A beat. Carl nodded. "I can't save the whole world, Dan. I'm just trying to keep this corner of it safe."

Dan leaned forward, his elbows on his knees. "I'll help. But I'm not taking any crap from Harvey."

"You won't have to." Carl kept his voice flat. "She's out. You know that."

Dan raised an eyebrow. "She stuck to that?"

Carl nodded. "She hasn't been in a fight that I know of since Heidrek went downstate."

"God, are all you old guys obsessed with this babe?" Lars said. "She must be one sweet piece of ass."

Dan rose out of his chair and slammed Lars up against the wall, the wrench cutting off his windpipe. "You shut your mouth before I shut it permanently. Do you hear me?" he growled. Lars squeaked in agreement and tried to nod. Dan gave him one more shove for emphasis and let him go.

Lars stayed against the wall, rubbing his throat. "Sorry, man."

Dan glared at Carl, daring him to say something. "Thought she'd be back eventually." He shrugged again. "If that's the way it is."

"That's the way it is." Carl stepped toward him, hand out. "Come on, man. I'm offering you a warm place for the winter and all the frostie ass-kicking you can take. Are you in or not?"

Dan nodded slowly, his eyes still on the floor. "Was thinking about getting down south. Somewhere warm."

"One of these days," Carl said and laughed.

Dan snorted deep in his sinuses and spat across the room to hit the wastebasket. "I'm going to sleep. Wake me up when there's something to kill." Hunch-shouldered with his collar turned up, he walked away, letting the glass-paned office door slam behind him.

Against the wall, Lars rubbed his throat. "What's up with that guy?"

"He's lost a lot of people over the years. Harvey and Jon and me

—we were like Dan's family in high school. And don't say dumb stuff about his nationality. He's an American citizen just like you are. But he's also Native and that's more important to him. His people were here a long time before Columbus or even Leif Erikson."

"He's an Indian? I didn't know they had berserkers."

Carl scratched at his beard. "You call him that and see if you can still eat solid food afterward. You think we're fierce? His people were the reason the Vikings didn't stay long the first time they landed on this continent. Skraelings, the sagas called them. They called themselves the Beothuk though, before they were basically killed off. Officially his people don't exist anymore. Dan says they didn't die out— they came south and joined up with the Mi'kmaq. You keep your mouth shut and don't piss him off, he might tell you more some time. Or not. He doesn't talk about himself much."

"Huh."

Carl looked back at the avalanche of paperwork on his desk. "Go fix something, would you? Make me not regret keeping you on payroll."

Lars saluted with the wrench and sauntered back to the work bays. Carl returned to his paperwork. They were a sorry excuse for a warband, but better that than no warband at all.

At least he hoped.

ELEVEN

T he forced idleness lasted through lunch before Harvey decided she needed to get out of the house. When she called the workers' comp doctor and they offered her an appointment that day she jumped on it. Mal was still sleeping off the effects of her first berserk and Ivor was "polishing his armor" in the comfy, rose patterned armchair in his room. His snores rumbled through the house.

Getting on the highway was a bit tricky with one eye, but she made it to the ophthalmologist in one piece and only got honked at once. The ravens that followed her truck downtown and perched along the wires outside the doctor's office could caw all they wanted. *I'll be back on my feet in no time.* She ignored the wincing looks of the other patients as she waited to be seen.

Eventually the nurse called her back and a smiling man in a white coat shook her hand and ushered her into an exam chair. But his smile faded as he shone a light in her eye. "This isn't good, Mrs. Otvar. You're going to be out for at least six weeks. I'm not sure you'll ever fully recover your sight in this eye."

"What? No, it can't be that bad. I can already see a little bit." She pushed back in her chair, trying to see him with both eyes.

The doctor grimaced. "Maybe with surgery to remove scarring, you'll get some light recognition back, but right now you've got a hundred percent sight loss on that side. For now, keep the eye covered except in the dimmest light and keep putting this salve in it to prevent infection. No strenuous exercise and don't cry for at least three weeks. The tears will only irritate the wound. I'll get the disability paperwork started for you."

After that he'd fitted her with an eye patch and wished her the best of luck.

For an hour afterward she drove around aimlessly, easing down surface streets with no plan except to keep moving and concentrate on something that wasn't the future of her job. The word "disability" kept running through her head, no matter how many times she pushed it away. She couldn't be disabled. Disabled meant car tags and wheelchairs. It meant pitying stares and checks from the government that didn't cover the bills. Disabled meant sitting at home doing nothing with her life. She swallowed hard and turned the truck north toward St. Stanislaus cemetery.

The family graves were in the far back near the river, away from the polished stones and monuments, alone in an area of plain markers flush with the grass. Most of the stones were nothing but names and dates. In the center stood a pillar as tall as she was, its surface unpolished. The ochre outline of a dragon wound around the stone, its sides etched with runes like broken twigs. She stopped on the stone's far side, reading their names.

Ingvi, Arnar, Thrain. Robert, Ben, Allen. Svein, Will, Thorrar. Angantyr Andersson.

Jon Otvar.

"Hi hon," she said. "I really wish you'd bought that life insurance policy before you died. I know. I didn't think we needed it either." The wind rattled the brown oak leaves that still clung to the trees. For a moment the ravens were silent, their glossy black bodies filling the branches. She closed her eyes, trying to remember how to pray. All that came to her was the word "please," and the ghost of the standing stone, each rune floating above its surface.

The alarm on her phone chimed. Time for school to be out.

"Okay," she said. As signs went, it wasn't much. But she'd take it. *Go home and take care of your kids.* That's all she did these days anyway—work and kids, work and kids. She got out her keys and trudged over the wet grass to her truck. Mal was at home, but Caleb would just be getting out.

When she arrived outside the school kids were beginning to hit the sidewalk, the occasional loner walking purposefully by clusters of friends. She parked on the opposite side of the road, under the "No Parking" sign, to avoid getting into the line of busses and cars inching past the school doors.

Stormcrow landed with a thump on her roof. The click of his feet punctuated the caws from the others in the trees.

Buses filled and left. Teachers went back inside or edged off around the building for a smoke. Eventually the last minivan pulled away. Had she missed Caleb?

Caleb trudged out of school, thumbs hooked in his pack straps, and the hood of his sweatshirt low over his head. Stormcrow launched himself off the truck and flew toward Caleb with two of his lieutenants. Harvey stood up on the brake pedal, craning to see Caleb's face. Her right eye saw the ordinary world—empty schoolyard under empty sky, her son stretching his long legs. But her left eye insisted on laying a ghostly image over the scene, like a camera negative.

Screw the eye doctor. It wasn't that bright out and this patch was making her crazy. She pushed the patch up on her forehead. For a second it was a relief to see with both at once.

Then she blinked.

Caleb straightened, seeming taller, though not much broader in the shoulders. His hood was thrown back. Blue runes circled his neck and ran down under his collarbone, the lines edged with dried blood. He held out bloody hands to the ravens, and flickering blue grave fire surrounded his body, as if he marked the burial place of the unquiet dead.

She fell back in her seat, scrambling to pull the patch back in place, her heart hammering in her chest.

Outside the ravens circled her son, cawing louder and louder, until he broke into a run, hands clamped over his ears. They followed, dive bombing him, wings grazing his head.

Harvey threw the truck into park and jumped out, running toward him. "Caleb! This way!"

Caleb stooped at the road edge and rose with a rock in his hand. "Shut up!" He hurled the rock straight at Stormcrow, barely missing him. "Shut up! Shut up!"

Harvey ran across the road, wincing past the tug and pull of the burns. "Stop!" She grabbed his arm. "You can't hurt crows!"

He jerked his arm away. "They won't leave me alone!"

She hustled them across the road and into the truck, where he slouched in a corner of the cab.

"Are you okay?"

"Yeah."

Harvey swept the bangs out of his eyes, looking for scratches or cuts on his face. Dark shadows rimmed his eyes.

"Did you sleep at all last night?" she said.

He shook his head. "The birds kept me up."

She sighed and put the truck in gear. "Why were you so late getting out of school?"

He hunched further down in his seat.

She gave him the side eye and eased out into the road, tires crunching on gravel. "I can wait."

The words came out in a sullen mumble. "I got detention."

"What? What the hell, Caleb?"

He exploded from a silent heap, red faced and shouting. "What the hell? Mal gets detentions all the time. She can't go two days without mouthing off to somebody or ditching a class and you're mad at me for getting one detention?"

"Okay, calm down. I'm not mad, just surprised. You're right— you're owed a few passes on detentions. What happened?"

He slouched back into the far corner of the truck cab. Inaudible mumble.

"I can't hear you."

"I skipped gym class!" He shouted so loudly her ears rang. In a more normal tone of voice, chin sunk on his chest, he said, "It was track day. I didn't want to go outside so I hid in the library."

"Because of the crows?"

"Yeah."

If she hadn't been driving, she would have banged her head on the steering wheel. "Look, I know they're annoying—"

"They're everywhere! They won't leave me alone."

"You have to ignore them. Nothing good comes out of listening to ravens." She turned into the driveway and put the truck in park with a *thunk*. She sighed again. "Trust me on this."

Caleb crossed his arms. "You think I'm crazy like everybody else."

Her seatbelt pressing painfully against her chest, Harvey turned to look at him. "I don't think you're crazy." She reached out to push the hood off his face. "They just don't have anything useful to say, that's all."

"They want me for something."

"They want you to feed them. That's all. It's all they ever want."

"No. It's not. I know it's not. It's like I already know what they're saying, I just can't hear it."

"That's because you haven't fed them," she said.

58

Harvey shivered at the unwelcome memory. Mom, taking the sword out of her twelve-year-old hand, promising to show her what women could do. The two of them, standing in the yard, Mom pressing a chunk of raw hamburger into her hand. The half-understood caws and squawks blurring into speech. "Don't ever hurt a raven," Mom always said. "They remember the ones who hurt them."

Caleb's hollow eyes stared at her from under a shock of bangs—blond like his father's. But she'd never seen Jon looking so worn. She brushed the hair out of his eyes. "Please trust me. You don't need to listen to them."

"But you do. You just admitted it. You understand them. You know what they're saying."

"Only because I can't help it."

He snorted and flung himself out of the cab, racing into the house ahead of her. She followed slowly, her feet heavy.

CHAPTER
TWELVE

Dinner started with Ivor putting a whetstone on the table by his plate.

"Really?" Harvey glared at him. He moved the whetstone to the kitchen counter. One-handed, Harvey scooped spaghetti onto plates. Thank whatever gods might be for bulk size bags of frozen meatballs. Outside the night pressed in on the house and the ravens rustled in the oak tree, but in the kitchen the light was warm, pressing back against the darkness.

"Where's the garlic bread?" Caleb said as he sat.

"In case you haven't noticed, I got burned at work today and both you and your sister got into trouble," Harvey said. "I apologize for not having the time to make you garlic bread. If you want some, make it yourself."

Caleb muttered something that might have been an apology.

Mal walked into the kitchen, rubbing her eyes and yawning. "Spaghetti. Cool. I'm starving." She grabbed the loaf of bread off the counter and the garlic salt out of the cupboard before sitting and buttering three slices of bread. Harvey gave her a double helping of spaghetti.

"Eat up," Harvey said. "It'll help you recover."

Mal yawned again. "Why do I feel like I got run over by a truck? And can I have a beer?"

Harvey opened her mouth to say no, then shut it again. She exchanged looks with Ivor, pursed her mouth, nodded. "Sure. Just one though."

"You're letting her drink?" Caleb's yelp echoed off the ceiling. "She's not even an adult."

Harvey gingerly rested her face on one hand. "She is now. Sort of."

"Get me one too," Ivor said. Harvey nodded and held out a hand for a bottle.

Caleb seethed. "You are such a hypocrite. You tell us all the time not to get into fights and now you're rewarding her? This is bullshit."

Mal returned to the table with three beers and a shit-eating grin. She wiggled her eyebrows at Caleb over the top of her bottle.

"Can we just eat our food in peace? Please," Harvey said. She took a bite and winced as the jaw movement pulled at the burned spots on her cheek. The rest chewed in silence. Mal shoveled pasta into her face twice as fast as the others and reloaded her plate. Caleb pushed a meatball around his plate, making tracks in the sauce.

"I need to explain some things to you both," Harvey said. She took a drink from her beer and stared at the ceiling. "You remember the stories your grandfather told you about our ancestors in the old country being berserkers? How the bear spirit would come up on them and they'd be able to fight like no one else, with no pain, no fear, no stopping?"

Both kids nodded.

"It's not just a story," Harvey went on. "It still runs in the family. Your dad and I both have it. Had it. Whatever. So does your grampa. And your uncle. And after today, now we know Mal does too."

"What about me?" Caleb said.

"Probably, you too. Eventually," Harvey said. "There's no way to know until it happens. Or doesn't."

Ivor patted the boy on the shoulder. "You've got the blood on both sides. You'll have your time sooner or later."

Harvey sighed. "I'd rather you didn't. I was hoping neither one of you would have it."

Mal reached for another slice of bread, her eyes narrowing. "So that's what happened to me today? I was possessed by bears?"

Ivor nodded, but Harvey shook her head. "I don't believe that part. It's something that runs in our blood, but we can control it. It's not an excuse to run wild and do whatever you want."

Ivor chuckled. "In the old days, berserkers were the most feared of warriors. They worked for kings. Some of them *were* kings. Like your mother's father."

"Kings?" Mal said. "We're royalty?"

Caleb leaned forward, pale eyes burning. "Could they talk to animals?"

"No," Ivor said. "That was mostly warlocks and witchy women. You want to stay away from warlocks, boy—the berserk runs in the blood. But warlocks, they use other people's blood to get what they want." Caleb sank back into his chair, bangs falling to shadow his eyes as his shoulders closed in on themselves. He pushed his fork slowly through the red sauce on his plate.

Mal's eyes were bright with questions. She pointed with her beer bottle. "If it hadn't happened to me today, I'd think you were both crazy. Why didn't you tell us this before? Why didn't you warn us?"

Ivor gave Harvey a pointed look.

Harvey mopped at the remaining sauce on her plate with a piece of bread. "That was my decision. Maybe it was the wrong one. I thought I could raise you two to be different, to be peaceable people. Being a berserker—it's pain and loss. It's fighting for control over your own body so you don't kill someone. It's seeing the people you love lose jobs or go to jail or die young fighting monsters. I wanted you two to be safe. To have something better in life. I'm sorry I didn't tell you."

Silence. Harvey stared at her plate while Ivor drained the last of his beer. Mal nodded slowly, her eyes distant. Caleb crumbled bread balls onto his plate. No one spoke for a long time. A single raven cawed outside. Stormcrow. Harvey got up and locked the kitchen door.

"Are there others out there like us? Caleb said, his voice quiet.

Harvey returned to the table and set her hands on the back of her chair. "Not many. But a few." Carl was probably getting his gear together right now. Him and Dan against whatever waited in the dark. And now Ivor too. She'd thought he'd die in his bed, safe at home with his family, but tonight might be the night he didn't come back. Her throat tightened and ached.

"Tell us about it," Mal said. "Did you guys fight monsters? Were you and dad like a superhero team? Come on—we need details!"

"Not tonight," Harvey said. "I can't. Will you two clear the table?" She pushed away from her chair and left the room.

Harvey sat in the living room, her head in her hands, the light from the kitchen spilling into the gloom, until the dishes were washed and put away. For some reason, Ivor's words about warlocks and witchy women kept running through her mind. He hadn't meant anything by it, she knew that. But her mom had been one of those "witchy" women. It had been her mother who drew runes of protection on the bottoms of Harvey's shoes before she went to her first day of kindergarten, who stuffed bits of flowers and herbs into windowsills and the edges of doors while muttering under her breath or spat between her fingers to ward off the evil eye. Her mother who talked to ravens.

"The Allfather may have been a man," her mother once shouted during an argument with Harvey's dad. "But it was women who taught him magic!"

Harvey's burned eye throbbed, lights flashing behind it. If she closed her good eye the lights threatened to resolve themselves into images. She pushed the cold tips of her fingers under the edge of the bandage, trying to soothe the burning.

In the kitchen the noises of dishwashing and sibling bickering stopped. Ivor's footsteps retreated down the first-floor hallway to his room. Soon she heard the rhythmic scrape of a blade on a whetstone. Mal jogged upstairs to her bedroom, slamming her door.

Caleb came into the living room, flipping on the light, and slung himself down at the computer, clicking open half a dozen tabs. He hunched over the keyboard, eyes close to the screen and put his headphones on.

"What are you up to, honey?" Harvey said, shaking herself out of her funk.

He pointed to the course portal suddenly taking up the whole screen. "Math! Complex polynomials, okay? See? Geez!" He hunched in on himself even more, glaring at the screen.

"Okay. I was just asking."

She rose from the couch and stood behind him, her hands resting on his shoulders, but he ignored her. The thump of the bass line filtered out of his earbuds. She watched for half a minute more while he scribbled equations on scratch paper and clicked answers on the screen. Fine. God knew what he was going to open up after she left, but she couldn't hover over him all night. His grades were good enough anyway.

"Love you, Caleb."

He grunted.

She went upstairs to check on Mal but found her daughter's door locked. "I'm getting the homework from Jessa, Mom! Jesus," Mal yelled when Harvey knocked. Her voice continued on the phone, but still audible. "Gawd, parents, right? Is Coach Wells super pissed at me?"

Harvey rolled her eyes and instantly regretted it. *Pick your battles,* she told herself. *Pick your battles.* "I love you!" she shouted through the door. She got a pause and a "love you too, Mom!"

Harvey's grip on the door handle locked for a split second. She took a deep breath and let it out slowly. "Pick your battles," she told herself before releasing her grip on the knob.

Not sure what to do with herself, Harvey traipsed downstairs again. In the living room, Caleb was typing like the keyboard was his personal enemy. Harvey wandered into the kitchen. Nothing to do there—everything was cleaned and put away. She should probably go down in the basement, do a load of laundry. Instead, she got herself a cup of coffee. The mug had a rainbow on it and "World's Best Mom." She snorted and dumped in a slosh of whiskey into the coffee.

Her phone buzzed—Coach Wells. For a second Harvey's thumb hovered over the green dot. What would it be like to tell someone else, an outsider, the truth? She hit decline and put the phone face down on the counter.

Her burns throbbed, the heat and pain becoming sharper. She eyed her purse, where the pills from the hospital lurked. The pills had dulled the pain earlier, but she didn't need any more bloody hallucinations tonight. Ibuprofen it was. She reached for the mega bottle Ivor kept over the sink and used her coffee to wash down two capsules. Hopefully the whiskey would give them enough kick that she wouldn't be up all night worrying about Ivor.

By the time she'd finished her coffee, the world was feeling a little bit softer, a little less painful. She poured herself half a cup more and padded down the hall to Ivor's room.

His door stood half open. He half raised his head and smiled when Harvey entered. A chainmail byrnie waited, draped over the footboard. Ivor sat in the rose-patterned armchair, tucking the cuffs of his wool pants into the heavy wool socks that came up over the tops of his hunting boots. His cane was propped against the bed next to his sword.

Stupid things, like "you don't have to do this" and "what will I do if I never see you again?" came to mind, but she kept her mouth shut and leaned on the doorway as she watched him lace up the boots and resume stroking the whetstone over his sword's blade. His hands, gnarled by years of work, still kept a firm, even grip.

"Is that Jon's byrnie?" she asked. The knee length chainmail shirt had survived many battles. More importantly Jon had survived them while wearing it. Except that last one. But then it was the cold that got him, not teeth or claws. Woven steel rings couldn't do everything.

"It is," Ivor said.

"Good. He always did have the best gear." Harvey swirled the dregs at the bottom of her mug. "How are you going to handle a cane and a sword at the same time?"

"Eh, I don't really need the cane," he said. "Just plant my feet and let them come to me."

"In the woods. In the dark."

He shot her a mischievous grin. "Hell of a lot more exciting than playing shuffleboard down at the VFW."

She reached out to take his hand. "Please don't get killed. Not tonight anyway."

"Every man has to die some time." He wiped the sword down and slid it home in its scabbard. Leaning forward in his chair, he put his hands on his knees. "You are one eyed now. Perhaps it will let you see more clearly."

Her hands tightened around the mug. She swallowed hard.

"So I'm right," he said.

"I thought it was the drugs the hospital gave me."

Ivor tilted his head at her like a schoolteacher with an obstinate student.

"Yeah." She could feel her words slowing down a bit. Pressing the warm mug to her forehead said, "I saw...I saw something when I looked at Carl with my burned eye. And Caleb too."

"Go look at Mal. See what that tells you."

"I'm afraid to."

Ivor raised an eyebrow.

"Don't give me that look." She sipped from her mug again. The stomach-churning anger and fear of not being able to protect the ones she loved began to push back the soft edges of the whiskey and pills. "I notice you didn't ask me to look at you."

"I'm old. What would there be to see?" He shrugged. He also didn't meet her eyes. "But you aren't. You need to stop hiding and face reality."

Harvey glared back, straightening from her place by the door. The tightening of muscles in her face tugged at the burns under the eyepatch, but she squared up to her father-in-law. "I am facing reality, old man. Every damn day I get up and spend twelve hours over a pool of burning steel so my kids have a roof and food and running shoes and all the other million and one things kids need. That's reality. It doesn't get realer than that."

He nodded solemnly and pushed himself out of the chair, his hip creaking. "It's not easy. When I die, have me burned. Scatter my ashes at sea."

"Dammit Ivor, the doctor said I'm not supposed to cry for at least three weeks" She pressed a hand over her burned eye and bit her lower lip.

The doorbell rang. Seconds later Mal thundered down the stairs and Caleb yelled, "Hey Mom! There's a guy like a *Lord of the Rings* extra outside with a tow truck. He's wearing chainmail!"

Harvey took a deep, shuddering breath. Setting down her mug, she picked up the byrnie and helped Ivor slide it over his head. His armor in place, she hugged him tight, despite the pain in her chest.

He hugged her back, his arms still iron strong. "Hervor, daughter of my heart. Don't wait up for me."

She should walk him to the door, wave goodbye. Something. Like her mother used to do. But she couldn't muster the strength. Loss weighted her arms and legs like a lead apron. She stayed, standing in Ivor's room, listening to the Mal and Caleb's chatter. What was he going to do exactly? Where was he going? Who was the guy with the red beard outside? The kitchen door opened and closed again.

Jeez, Harvey thought. *All those times Mom waved goodbye from the front step with a smile on her face. No wonder she dropped dead of a heart attack at sixty-three.*

She stood in the empty room, listening for the sound of the truck pulling away, thinking about the last thing she'd said to Jon.

Please, don't get killed. Not tonight, anyway.

He'd laughed and promised he wouldn't.

CHAPTER
THIRTEEN

The night wind rattled the empty branches around Fisherman's park, but Carl, snug in his wool-lined steel, sipped coffee from his thermos and nodded at his choice of location. Good open ground for a skirmish. A rim of trees guarded the river, deep enough that frosties might already be coming up from the water unseen, but another, thinner, screen of trees shielded the parking lot from the road's view.

In gray pants and steel shirt, he was the color of a shadow, but even if they were seen it wasn't likely to cause a problem. Thanks to all the gaming and fantasy groups around nowadays, a bunch of grown men sneaking down bike paths and running through abandoned buildings in the middle of the night were less likely to spook the cops if they wore chainmail and swords. Better a harmless kook than a suspected drug dealer. Beside him Lars juggled a crowbar from hand to hand. Carl hadn't convinced him yet to try a more refined weapon. Ivor stood quietly with his hands on his sword, eyes on the distant trees.

"Your girlfriend is not going to help us, but her gimpy old dad is?" Lars said. "That's fucked up."

"Father-in-law," Ivor corrected him without turning. "Her father was Angantyr and he was a king among us in his time. She was queen after him, until her brother's anger and her husband's death drove her away from us."

Lars snorted deep in his sinuses and spit. "You are one weird old man, you know that. You talk like something on TV."

Carl screwed the cap back on the thermos and set it on the truck's seat. "And you talk way too much. One of these days someone's going to take your tongue home as a souvenir."

Lars grinned and did a little jig. "Let 'em try. You should have seen this guy I took on in juvie. He was big—like elephant big. So one day he started talking shit and—"

Without turning his gaze, Ivor said, "Young men make big boasts to cover their lack of great deeds."

The crowbar flashed. "Watch your mouth, old man."

A flicker of steel in moonlight and Ivor's blade rested under Lars's chin.

Lars's mouth clicked shut. Slowly, he raised his hands, letting the crowbar drop. Ivor held his gaze for a second longer and nodded before sheathing his sword.

The puttering roar of a Harley with a bad spark announced Dan's arrival. He skidded to a circling halt in front of them, laying down rubber as his back wheel pivoted around the front.

Lars whooped and bounded over to slap him on the back. Carl sauntered over to shake Dan's hand. "Glad you didn't change your mind."

Dan gave him a half smile. His smile faded as he jerked his head back toward the road. "She coming?"

Carl shook his head. "I told you, she's out."

Dan narrowed his eyes. "Then what are we doing here, three miles from her house? There are better places to find a fight."

"The river is right there," Carl said, all too aware of how close Harvey's house lay to the water that ran along the park's far edge. Not that there were many places in Buffalo that were far from water.

Between the river, the great lakes, and the canal each with its streams, tributaries, and spring ponds, it remained a city of water all year round. "We're sure to find frosties here. It's got nothing to do with her."

He turned his back on the others and strode toward the truck, yanked open the driver's door harder than he needed to, and took his double-bladed axe off the modified gun rack. Out of sheer habit, he ran his thumb along the sweep of each blade. He knew perfectly well he'd sharpened it properly, but the cold steel in his hand and the gleam of the edge awoke the berserk inside him. He had designed and forged it himself, a double-headed version of the bearded war axes his ancestors might have carried, light, but with long cutting edges. Rubbing his thumb over the leather wrapped handle, he took three deep breaths.

"Alright," he said, his back still turned to the others. "Let's gear up and do this."

"Helmet?" Lars said, holding it out.

"Thanks."

"Pussy." Lars grinned at him and wriggled into the thigh-length chainmail shirt Carl had made him.

"Troll fucker. I like my ears where they are, thanks." Carl slid the helmet onto his head, giving it a tap to settle it into place. "Of course, you're already ugly. Who cares if you lose an ear?"

Lars laughed and feinted at him with the crowbar. Carl whirled his axe, loosening up his arm and shoulder. He'd left his shield in the truck tonight, covering his hurt arm with a long gauntlet. If he made it through the night without popping a stitch in his arm it would be a miracle.

Fuck it. Fuck her. Fuck all of it. He raised his axe overhead and bellowed at the stars.

Lars danced where he stood, drumming the ground with his feet and shaking his head back and forth. The growing berserk widened his eyes, drew his grin back into a mad man's laugh.

Dan stood stock still, arms at his sides. His fists clenched and unclenched around his brass knuckles. His clouded eyes brightened and he breathed rough and hard.

Ivor limped forward, leaning on his sword for support until he was alone in the center of the field. He raised his sword high over his head, brandishing it at the woods. He called out in the old language, daring the frosties to come to him.

Carl planted his feet, facing the river. "Come shadows! Come and find your death." He thumped his chest with his fist. At each blow the battle rose within him. Battle joy filled his limbs, ran along every nerve. He whirled his axe one handed, making the air silver with the flashing blades. His breath whitened the air. "Come Winter!"

The river echoed with his battle cry. Behind him, Lars whooped.

White shapes moved between the black tree trunks.

"No need for bait tonight," Carl said. "Space out and take 'em as they come. But watch each other's backs." He advanced up the grass, keeping Lars and Dan in his peripheral vision. The song rose in his blood and he bounced on his toes. Frost crackled underfoot.

The first frost demon emerged from the trees. Shaped like a man, but not a man, the slick ice of its body gleamed in the moonlight. Its shoulders hunched, head swinging side to side as it hunted for warm life to prey on. The monster's clawed hands, like living icicles, curled and uncurled as it searched. Each footstep left behind a rime of ice, the grass withered by its passage. Low-hanging branches snapped and crackled, their sap flash frozen by the frost demon's touch. Carl bent his knees, beckoning to it.

The creature stopped its slow searching, eyes focused on Carl. Its mouth spread in an icicle fanged grin, wider than any human mouth could spread. Its clawed hands rose. It sprang forward, hands reaching.

With a whoop, Carl released the berserk inside him. No fear, no loss, no cold—just joy. He charged, axe swinging, feet pounding over the half-frozen ground. Steel blade bit ice, shattering it to pieces. The frost demon cracked in half, split from head to shoulder. A wrench, a twist and he freed his blade. He hacked at the body until it was lifeless hunks of ice, singing its death song with each blow.

Another monster to his right. A tawny blur, dreadlocks flying, Lars sliced it to pieces.

Carl swung his head from side to side, shoulders swaying like a bear searching the waters for its next fish.

Ivor planted his feet, weight on his good leg. He barely seemed to move, but his sword's edge always found its target. Heads and limbs piled up around him.

A frost demon, taller than the first, charged from Carl's right. He spun to meet it. His backhanded blow sunk the axe's blade into its chest. The spike stuck and they danced together, turning and turning, linked by the sharp steel. It raked him with its claws, nails catching in the fine mesh of his shirt. He reared back, kicked hard, and the creature popped free. Reversing the axe, he swung in a wide arc. The frost demon's arm fell to the ground.

It lowered its white gleaming head and charged. Instinctively, he brought his shield arm up to block its rush. But he carried no shield tonight.

The monster's head caught his arm and plowed into his chest. It wrapped its remaining arm around him and they both went down.

Laughing at the pain, Carl fell, his enemy on top of him. His fingers slipped, the axe skittering away over the damp grass. Icy teeth tore at his mail shirt and it was all battle joy, all fierce heat and death. He punched at the living ice on top of him. Hooked one leg around his opponent and twisted, rolling. He straddled the ice demon, seized it by the wrist with both hands. The demon screamed like tree branches rubbing together in a high wind.

Carl hung on and laughed. Beneath his thighs the demon writhed, keening a death song. He hung on, ripping, twisting, tearing upward until the demon's arm broke free. It shrieked in pain and he silenced it, beating its head into gray slush with its own arm.

He threw back his head and roared, bellowed his triumph at the stars.

Nothing answered him. He scrambled to his feet, shoulders low, searching for the next opponent. Nothing came. No reaching claws, no rending teeth.

"Hey man, we're done," Lars called. "Not a frostie in sight."

The rolling vibration in his blood still ran fast and hot, urging him on into the darkness. He closed his eyes and remembered the light. The sun drops dancing on Lake Erie in the summer. The rocking of a rowboat as he fished the open waters, the sun's heat warm across his shoulders. Silence and light and the weight of a rod in his hand.

The joyful roaring inside him subsided like waters calming, falling back into its place. He let his arms drop to his sides. He opened his eyes to Lars and Ivor, both sweat drenched, but smiling. "That's it?" he said. "We got all of them?"

"Yeah. Dan's still working on his." The younger man pointed. "But I think he's just showing off."

"Oy!" Carl shouted. "Dan, it's dead. Let it go. You're pounding slush there, man."

On all fours, Dan swung towards them, growling. He half rose, fists out, but Carl held up his empty hands. "We're your friends. Your enemies are dead," he called, keeping his voice low and gentle. "Come back to us, my friend. Come back from battle strife."

The green spark faded from Dan's eyes. He sagged, down on all fours.

Carl signaled to Lars to stay put and walked cautiously toward Dan. "Hey man," he said. He reached down, right hand open. "Let me help you."

Dan's grip was still berserker strong, but he didn't strike or pull Carl off balance. As he levered himself to his feet, bars of pain shot through Carl's ribcage where the demon's head had hit. Dan swayed on his feet, still clutching Carl's hand.

"You doing all right?" Carl asked him. His stomach growled. "How about some food. You hungry?"

"I want a drink," Dan threw away Carl's hand. "Somewhere warm."

"Yeah! I like the way you think." Lars danced up, carrying Carl's axe. "You dropped this, Grandma. Come on. Let's go down to Arn's, get hammered, and maybe pick up some skirt."

Carl started to laugh, cut off by the pain in his ribs. He was going to have to tape those. He took a cautious breath and said, "There aren't any women at Arn's, stupid."

Not since Harvey left. Now the women stayed home or went better places with their girlfriends. Half the light went out when she left. The cold wind whistled down his collar and along his ribs. He was a fool.

"But they still have beer," Ivor said. "And I deserve a drink. Or four."

Carl clapped him on the back. "You're right. Let's go. I'm going to drink all three of you under the table." He threw an arm around Lars's shoulder as the four departed, ignoring the sharp pain in his ribs, and hefted his axe over his shoulder.

FOURTEEN

"Lights out!" the guards shouted. Nightsticks beat rhythmically on the cell doors in time with the tramp of their feet. "Get to bed."

Heidrek lay on his bunk, eyes closed, hands folded over his stomach. He waited until the main lights went out with an audible *kachunk* of breakers flipping. Only the dim emergency lights pocketed the darkness.

The prison's night noises began—the slide of contraband across the concrete floor from cell to cell. Groans and sighs. Far off at the end of the cell block someone cursed in broken grunts. A man wept and called for God. Heidrek savored the darkness all around him and a smile grew on his face.

Silent and barefoot, he hopped off the top bunk to stand on the spiral of runes etched into the concrete. His cellmate lay curled in his bed, pretending to sleep. Heidrek threw back his head, shaking off the remnants of the day. He breathed deep and slow, reaching for the calm center, his inner eye searching the darkness. *If only Dr. Collins could imagine the real power in the calming techniques he taught.*

When he had focused his mind, he slid the sharpened paper clip out of his pants' hem. Too small to make an effective weapon, but perfect for his task—another thing he had Dr. Collins to thank for, though this time it was Collins's inattention to small details like the number of paper clips he had brought in rather than conscious effort.

More by feel than sight, he re-carved rune after rune around the circumference of his wrists. Drop by drop, his blood fell onto the pattern around his feet. Pale blue fire sprang from the spotted floor. With his feet planted firmly, he felt himself expand, stretching down into the earth, into the lightless halls underground. His footsteps echoed through caverns with no passage to the world above.

Water trickled—water that connected everything, touching every part of the earth in its time. Things moved in the darkness.

Aha. There you are. His spirit found another that hungered like he did, that hated the sound of human voices and hid in the shadows. It slept, undisturbed for ages, dreaming. He called to it in his sister's voice, breaking into its slumber. *This is who disturbs your sleep. This is who wakes you in pain.*

He fed it on his blood. The loss drained him, but the pain was worth it. Beneath the earth and water, the creature stirred, hungering and angry, seeking revenge on the bloodline that disturbed it. In his cell, Heidrek strained every nerve to speak to the creature's mind, showing it his sister's house. *Go here. Here is where you will find your enemy.*

FIFTEEN

The kitchen clock ticked toward midnight. Harvey shivered. She could have let the pain meds from the hospital knock her out hours ago. Or at least laid down in bed. Instead she'd opted for padding around the first floor in her bare feet, sipping whiskey and black coffee. Upstairs, the kids slept, or at least were quiet. Ivor was still out.

She hoped he was having fun. She checked her phone. Nothing from Ivor. One voicemail from Coach Wells. She tapped it.

"Hi Mrs. Otvar. This is Lily Wells. I heard about the deal you worked out with Bonnie to keep Mal in school." A pause like someone choosing their words. A small puff of breath. "Whatever's going on with Mal right now—it's serious. I think you already know that. I'm not calling you because I represent the school. I'm calling because I care about Mal. If you ever want to talk about it outside school, just woman to woman, let me know. Anyway, you've got my number. Let me know if I can help."

Harvey rubbed her forehead. A smile quirked one corner of her mouth as she let herself imagine the conversation. "Mal's just going through that difficult stage when a young woman gets possessed by the bear spirit. You know how it is, right? When your hormones are surging and you want to pick fights with the sky itself just to prove you're strong. Oh, it's a magical time, isn't it?" And Coach Wells would laugh and nod and they'd swap stories about their first time while Mal writhed in teenage embarrassment.

Harvey laughed out loud in the empty kitchen. It'd be nice. Impossible, but nice. She deleted the message. Her burned eye throbbed in time to her heartbeat. Whenever she closed it, red and gold flares swirled.

She wished she could just take some pills and go to sleep. But the later it got, the more the berserk thrummed inside her, prowling back and forth across her blood. *Fear. Danger. Get up and watch.* She began to circle the house, going from window to window, watching for some nameless trouble outside. Something was out there. Something that hated her, something that wanted her children. Harvey knew it in her blood.

So she watched. In moments like this she wished she'd listened to her mother more and her father less. Dad knew how to use a sword, but Mom knew how to keep evil things from the door.

"How do you know it works?" she'd asked as a child, trailing her mother through the house.

"Trust me," Mom said. "It works." A drop of blood, a little spit, and a word. It had all seemed a bit pathetic compared to fists and swords. Now she'd give anything to understand how it worked. Or if it worked. How much danger had her mother really kept from the door all those years? Perhaps her mother was the stronger parent all along.

Harvey sipped the last of her spiked coffee. A drop rolled over the rim onto her finger. Taking a shot in the dark, she dragged her damp finger across the windowpane, tracing the same rune she'd used on her locker at work. Spit and coffee. And booze. Would whatever was out their even register the ward she was putting up?

Not as satisfying as a sword in her hand. For the hundredth time she thought about the chest upstairs under her bed where she'd locked away her weapons. It would be nice to be holding something sharper than a visitor's pass the next time she saw her brother. But she'd promised—she'd leave them there.

Something on the window flickered. A wiggle of blue light, like the flame on a gas stove, but paler. Harvey squinted. She could see it and not see it at the same time. Ghost fires, her mother called them. The light flickered again. Blue flames that danced over haunted graves and the homes of evil things.

Ivor called her One-Eyed. She put a hand over her burned eye. Nothing. Not a spark. Her heart racing, hands aching with tension, she moved aside her eye patch and closed her good eye.

Blue light flared from every window.

The battle inside urged her to rush out into the darkness, to seize whatever it was, but she held back. Harvey watched the glitter of light off the frost on the windowpanes, tried to concentrate on the practices of control Carl taught her years ago. Breathe. Don't fight. Feel the battle inside and let it pass through you. Find the light and watch it until the rage is yours to control. Breathe. He had the most control of any berserker she knew.

Her husband Jon's berserk had always been like a big, unruly dog, leashed but ready to jump up and play at a moment's notice. Her own, before she'd put it away for good, had been a hibernating bear, slow to wake but ready to tear the head off anything that angered it, impossible to escape once its attention was fixed. And now the bear spirit inside her was awake, certain that something or someone outside was hunting her cubs.

She kept her eyes closed, concentrating. *Listen to your own heartbeat. Feel the silence holding you up. Watch the light. If there is none, find the light behind your eyes. Be aware and you will be in control.* Inside her, the heat from the whiskey rolled outward from her stomach, spread along the nerve ends into her thighs and up her rib cage. The light in her burned eye was a hot, constant glow, as if she were staring straight into the blast furnace at the mill.

A shudder ran along her body, a nameless horror rising up inside her. Her eyes flew open and she peered out into the darkness. She leaned closer to the window until her breath fogged it. Cold radiated off the pane.

Shadows crowded around the house. She circled the first floor, marking each window and door with the few runes she knew. *Nauthiz* for survival. *Eihwaz* for defense. *Fehu* for luck.

The runes writhed with cold fire. She scanned the room with her burned eye. On every window the protective sigils glowed like candle flames. Outside the darkness moved—not a figure in the dark, but a creature made of darkness itself. She got a glimpse of eyes like yellow flames, but even the streetlight couldn't pierce the shade around it. A hand, black and wet with river mud, slammed into the window. Harvey jumped back, her heart pounding, mug raised to throw at whatever was coming through the glass. But the runelight rose, blue-white, and the glass held.

Heavy feet thudded on the wet ground outside, moving away from the window. Another blow, another window. Each time the walls of the house shook. Wooden windowsills creaked and groaned with the impact. The glass crackled as if it was shattering, but the panes stayed intact. The runes held.

A smell like stagnant mud, a polluted ooze full of fish bones and industrial runoff seeped into the house. She knew the sharp cold, like bitter water, of frost demons. This creature was nothing like them. Harvey panted, pressing the back of her hand to her nose.

Gritting her teeth, she lifted the eye patch and stared hard into the darkness, but she saw nothing unless the darkness itself was what she saw. She ran into the kitchen and flicked on the outside light. The thing reached up and shattered the bulb. It slammed against the kitchen door. The frame groaned but held.

She threw herself against the door. Outside, the shadowy creature tried again, shaking the entire house. Cold seeped under the doorframe, burning her feet, but somehow she could almost feel the creature's hot breath on the back of her neck.

Harvey braced her feet and leaned her whole weight into the door.

Her hand tightened on the doorknob. *Don't berserk. Don't berserk.* She closed her eyes and took deep breaths. *Stay calm. Don't lose it. Think.*

She racked her brain, running through Ivor's stories, the legends she'd grown up with, for some clue as to what this thing was. Eyes like flame. Shadowy, but physical enough to beat down a door. It hated the light. *Shadow-walker.* Her stomach turned to acid at the thought. Far worse than a frost demon, a creature from the depths of the water and earth, with an endless hunger for human flesh.

The shadow-walker struck again. The door shook so hard that Harvey bounced, her head slamming backward into the wood. Inside her, the berserk rose up at the pain. *Attack me, will you?*

"Don't open the door, you moron," she said out loud to herself. "You'll break the ward." She gritted her teeth and held on to the door and her temper.

"Mom! Mom." Caleb yelled from upstairs. "There's something out there."

"It's okay, honey," Harvey yelled back. "I got this." At her back the door creaked and groaned.

Caleb and Mal thundered down the stairs, Mal with a baseball bat.

"What the hell is that?" Mal shouted.

"Shadow-walker. I think." Harvey grunted with the effort of holding the door.

Caleb stood on tiptoe, peering out the window in the kitchen door. "You mean a *sceaduganga*?" he said, using its name in the old language. "How do we kill it?"

"I. Don't. Know," Harvey panted.

In front of her, Mal bounced on the balls of her feet, bat ready to swing, her eyes too wide. "Come on—open the door. Let's do this."

"No. It will eat you!" Another thud against the door. Harvey's bare feet slipped an inch on the linoleum. "Help me, dammit," she said, relenting.

Mal dropped the bat and threw her shoulder against the door.

Caleb hesitated. "We need something heavy. Put the fridge in front of the door."

Harvey dug in her toes. "Wouldn't work. I need you, not a heavy thing. I think...I think it's mostly my blood and my will holding the door shut, not my weight." She panted and pressed harder on the door as massive hands clawed at the windowpane. "Okay, it's a little bit my weight."

Caleb hunkered down on the floor between Harvey and Mal, bracing his back against the door and his feet against the kitchen cabinet. A breath like rotten marsh weeds spread through the kitchen. The doorframe creaked and splintered.

"Maybe we need more blood," Caleb said. The door shuddered again.

Mal laughed, leaning her weight on the door. "Sure. I'll make more right now."

"I'm just saying!"

Harvey squeezed her eyes shut, trying to think.

The berserk inside fought back. *No thinking. Fight.*

Every instinct in her wanted to rip the door off its hinges and beat the shadow-walker to death with it. But she'd never gone up against one before. Hell, she'd never even seen one before. They were supposed to be nearly unbeatable. What did Ivor say in the stories? They hated humans and their songs. Hated the light of a hearth and the sun. No weapons. Human weapons couldn't hurt them. None of this helped. A rush of feet outside and a crash against the door. The wood cracked down the center. They wouldn't make it to dawn. One more big crack like that and they wouldn't make it another ten seconds.

Think! If she failed, the kids died. Okay then, what had Mom tried to teach her when she was young and thought ignoring her mother a good idea? Blood and bread for life. Salt and liquor and sunlight for cleansing.

"Caleb, go get the salt, the whiskey, and the honey. Dump it all in a mixing bowl with some bread." Mom used to make her own loaves from scratch. *Please god, let store-bought bread be good enough.*

Caleb scrambled through the kitchen cabinets, dumping items on the counter as he found them. A metal mixing bowl clanged as he set it down. "How much do I use?" Caleb yelled.

"All of it," Harvey said between gritted teeth.

"You can't just dump things together," he protested. "What if the ratios are wrong?"

"Jesus, Caleb! Don't be such a nerd!" Mal yelled back.

"Do what I tell you, Caleb!" Harvey shouted.

"Okay, okay. Caleb upended the bread bag over the bowl. Whiskey glugged into the bowl, followed by the honey and salt. With his bare hands, Caleb mashed it all up into a grainy slurry. His face took on an animation Harvey hadn't seen in a long time. He dug his hands into the mixture, squeezing it through his fingers, eyes on the ceiling. "Needs blood."

Before Harvey could ask him how he knew, he fumbled in a drawer for a paring knife.

"Caleb! What are you doing?" Harvey shouted. He stabbed the knife into the palm of his hand and squeezed the blood into bowl. Harvey felt as if her heart and lungs were being squeezed in a vice. "Caleb..." But her child's name came out in a strangled whisper, her throat knotted in pain. Blood magic—that was the stuff of warlocks.

Caleb was squeezing the wound on his hand with a towel, the bowl tucked under his arm as he came back to the door. "Now what?" he said.

Harvey gasped for breath, her mouth too dry.

"Mom, come on!" Caleb snapped. "Is there a secret word or something? A sign? Do I throw this shit on the shadow-walker or what?"

Harvey swallowed hard and forced the words out. "Paint the doorframe with it. Seal all the edges." The pounding on the door jostled her hard enough to bruise. Beside her, Mal panted. Already her muscles ached. Without the berserker strength, she couldn't

84

hold the door for much longer. But if she berserked, the urge to run out and fight the creature could overwhelm her and her gut knew that the minute she opened the door Mal and Caleb would be goners. If this makeshift kitchen magic didn't work, none of them would make it to morning.

Climbing up on a chair to reach the highest parts, Caleb smeared the goop into the doorframe, spackling in every crack with his fingers. The edges sealed, glimmering with blue grave fire. Every time the shadow-walker hurled itself against the door, the ghost light flared. But the door held.

As Caleb finished the door the sound of the shadow-walker's breathing muffled, as if a bowl had dropped over the room. It gave a frustrated roar and a last blow to the door. Heavy footsteps shuffled away.

Harvey sank down onto the floor, every muscle twitching and jumping. Mal stood peering through the window in the door into the dark. Muffled sounds of destruction filtered through the sealed door —branches snapping and crashing from trees, bush roots being ripped from the ground, and a rolling metallic crunch along with splintering glass that made Harvey wince. Her poor truck was probably a goner.

Caleb ran to the front door and then from window to window dabbing blood goop on them, reinforcing the runes of protection Harvey had already put there, chanting something that sounded like "Monster, monster go away."

"We should go out there and kick its ass," Mal said.

From the floor, Harvey said, "What part of 'It will eat you' do you not understand?"

Mal pressed her face against the window, straining to see. "You maybe. You're old and out of shape. Look at you. You're all sweaty and gray. I could handle it."

Harvey closed her eyes and counted to ten. *Nope. Still angry.* Fortunately for Mal she was too tired to do anything about it. "Please don't make me slap you."

Caleb returned, fingers sticky and eyes bright. "That was a shadow-walker, huh?"

"I think so. That's my best guess anyway." She held out an arm to him and he settled down next to her. His face was paler than normal and his eyes glittered like a fever. She took his hand in hers and examined the cut. "How much blood did you lose?"

He shrugged. "I just kind of winged it. Next time I'll take notes so I know how much to use."

The idea of a next time made her stomach go cold. She hugged him closer, tucking his head against her shoulder. Mal stayed at the window, breathing hard as she peered out.

"Mal, I know how you feel," Harvey said. "But you can't give in to it. You have to control it, or it will control you."

Caleb yawned hugely. Mal muttered something that might have been another argument, her eyes fixed on the dark outside the window. Glass splintered. A car alarm blared. Harvey closed her eyes, ears straining, hoping not to hear human screams. The far wall of the house shuddered.

Caleb fell into a daze, his head cradled in the crook of her shoulder. Mal paced from window to window, bouncing on the tips of her toes. Harvey sat awake by the door and tried to think.

Shadow-walkers didn't form with the onset of winter like frost demons. They had to be called out of the darkness. They were vengeful, focused. She had no proof, not even a good reason—but she knew her brother was behind this. And that meant it was her job to deal with him.

Outside the shadow-walker rampaged around the house. Siding splintered and cracked. Branches ripped off the oak tree. Metal screamed as the screen door was ripped off its hinges. Glass splintered. The lights flickered and went out.

CHAPTER
SIXTEEN

C arl parked in front of an alley between two empty warehouses in the factory district. A few other cars were parked up and down the sidewalk, but otherwise the area was deserted. The city's efforts at revival had put a few people back to work, renovated a few empty buildings down by the waterfront as fancy lofts, but blocks like this were still easy to find. Lars and Ivor got out of the truck with him, the slams of their doors echoing off the buildings.

Dan's motorcycle whipped past him and skidded in a tight turn into the alley. Carl followed on foot with Lars and Ivor behind.

The alley opened up into a wide, square space that was once the loading dock at the back of a warehouse, until the warehouse itself was abandoned and newer buildings blocked it off from traffic, leaving a wide square yard enclosed on four sides and open to the sky. Now it was only reachable by a narrow slit between competing buildings, barely big enough to ease the handlebars of a Harley through. This suited Arn and his customers just fine. A few other motorcycles were lined up beside the dock. The wind howling down the alley's narrow slot stirred scraps of trash clustered in the corners of the space. The air tasted of snow.

No neon lights or clever signs marked the door at the top of the dock steps, only a single rune in white paint. With Lars at his shoulder and Dan trailing behind, Carl flexed his fingers a few times, drumming them against the air as if adjusting his grip on his axe handle, and popped the door open.

The chorus of "Born to Be Wild" spilled out with the smell of new beer. Shouts, cheers, insults, and smatterings in the old language echoed off the steel warehouse rafters where pigeons roosted. Probably a few bats too.

The "bar" was actually two long wooden doors laid on sawhorses in front of Arn's kegs and brewing equipment. He'd managed to scrounge up, haul in, and jury rig together quite the brewing operation over the years, even getting his hands on one of those giant stainless-steel brewing vats once the craze for locally sourced microbrews came to Buffalo. Came and went, leaving some legal businesses bankrupt. Not a drop of Arn's ever saw a health inspector or a tax stamp.

Against one wall, a wood stove created a circle of firelight and warmth, though it left the far reaches of the space cold. In the fall and winter, Arn could use the way back of the warehouse for cold storage without paying a dime in electric costs. Not that he paid for electricity anyway. A few cleverly spliced and strung wires ran in through a high window from the street, dripping pools of yellow light over the mismatched kitchen chairs, tables, and church pews. Arranged more or less between the stove and bar, the seating looked like the world's biggest thrift shop furniture section.

Carl took a deep breath and let out a contented sigh. His cold fingers were already tingling with returning warmth. He rolled his neck, shoulders loosening. He slung an arm around Dan, urging his friend in with him toward the bar.

In the corner opposite the bar, an arm-wrestling match went on, circled by men with money in their hands. As Carl walked to the bar, a few men turned to see who intruded on their hall. Fewer than he'd hoped—there were no more than twenty in the whole place.

"Arn," he called to the bartender, pulling Dan forward. "Look who's back."

Behind the bar, Arn stopped polishing a glass and put it down. As he fixed his gaze on Dan, one hand dropped below the bar where he kept a Louisville slugger propped against a sawhorse leg. At the far table, the armwrestling match concluded with a jerk and a clatter of glasses as the loser lost his concentration.

"What a bunch of pussies," Lars said, loud enough for the whole room to hear. "It's only been a week since you saw me last. You'd think you'd have recovered by now. Not that I couldn't whip all your asses one handed, but that's not what I'm here for tonight. He slung an arm across Dan's shoulder. "What're you drinking? Carl's paying."

Carl grinned and reached for his wallet as the other men laughed. Even Dan cracked half a smile as he shoved Lars off him.

"Beer," Carl said to Arn, who nodded and put a bowl of peanuts on the bar. His entirely unlicensed and under the table operation worked only by word of mouth, but it worked. No one who drank a pint of Arn's homebrew or a mouthful of his liquor dreamt of reporting him to the police.

"Good to you in one piece," Arn said. "About time you took a night off." He nodded at the bandage on Carl's arm.

"Not tonight, though," Carl said. "We got done early, is all." He scanned the room. Lars was already the center of a laughing circle of men at a table, telling the story of his near drowning in heroic terms. Mac and a few of his cronies scowled as Lars talked.

"The boy's got talent," Ivor said as he joined them at the bar. "He'd have made a good teller of tales in the old days. Maybe even a king's *thyle*."

"Who needs a king?" Dan said, on the other side of Carl. He

leaned his elbow on the bar, one hand wrapped around the bear claw that hung from his neck. His thumb stroked along the three-inch curve of the claw. "It's not like the last king did any good."

He's right, Carl thought—that was the problem right there.

Old Angantyr ruled by an old-fashioned sense of honor and a punch that could stun an ox. Even in his prime, he never asked for much—respect, a place to drink, and an audience to keep alive some memory of their ancestors. Easy and simple. But he'd left behind a cursed sword, two grown children, and no clear heir. Both Heidrek and Hervor were stubborn and proud, but one thought the world owed him allegiance and the other had abandoned her post.

He took a long drink of his beer. *Give it up, man. Stop thinking like this. She made her decision.* And he'd made his. Someone needed to stand between the darkness and the firelight, between the monsters and the humans. Otherwise she was right—he was nothing but a thug who liked hurting people.

Dan rolled his eyes, but he did it with a smile. "That kid never shuts up."

"First requirement for a *thyle,* isn't it?" Carl said. He finished his pint and strode over to the crowd gathered around Lars.

Carl hooked his thumbs into his belt loops. "Who wants to join us tomorrow?" The laughter at the table faded. Men studied their glasses. "Come on," he said. "You're not going to let us have all the fun and glory, are you? When was the last time you guys got into a fight worth telling about?"

A few grinned and shrugged. Some of the younger ones looked up. Arn, a broom in hand, worked his way within earshot.

So many good men. So much potential, wasted. They could be a people worthy of the old songs, if only they had a leader who would lead them. But all they had was him. Just an axe swinger who didn't know when to give up.

Carl scanned their faces, men he'd known for years. "Where else in the city would I find men like you? Men with power in their arms and fire in their guts. Men who can fight the dark. It's real Winter out there this time, not just a frostie here and there, but whole troops of them and you're the only ones who can stop them."

A few met his eyes, standing straighter at his words. Others shuffled their feet and eyed each other. Across the table, Mac tipped back in his chair, made eye contact with Carl, and spat on the floor. A few more faces dropped, refused to meet his eyes.

The berserk thrummed through Carl's words. He leaned in, placing a hand on the table and fixing Mac with his stare. "People are going to die if we just sit here. People we could save. Street people have already died."

Mac snorted. "Happens every winter. You live outdoors in upstate New York, eventually you're going to freeze to death."

Murmurs and nods answered Mac.

Carl shook his head in disgust. "And that's okay with the rest of you? You're happy to just close your doors and ignore what happens beyond them?" He snorted in disgust. "Well maybe you are, but this is no ordinary cold. You'd know that if you'd crawl off your couches every once in a while." Carl swept his gaze around the circle, making eye contact with as many as he could. "It's only November and we're already seeing more frost demons than I've ever seen before. The ravens are gathering for a feast. Something has freed the darkness."

More uncomfortable shuffling. A few nervous laughs. "You don't really believe in that superstitious shit, do you?" one of the younger ones said.

"Believe in it?" Lars said. "I don't know if I believe in it, but it sure as hell believes in me. It wasn't the bogeyman that tried to eat my head in the park tonight." He pointed to the bandage poking out from under the rolled-up sleeve on Carl's arm. "You think Tinkerbell did that shit? Fuck no. That was the Niagara River with teeth."

Eyes widened as Carl stripped back the gauze to show the healing gash. "This is nothing," he said. "A scratch. I paid the bastard back ten times. Split him from head to crotch with my axe. You come out with us, boys, and you'll have better stories to tell on a Saturday night than how you struck out with the waitress at Denny's."

He looked at the group again. A few were nodding, dreams of glory growing in their eyes. Dan, glass in hand, joined the circle at Carl's elbow.

"We can't all clock in to work when we feel like it," Mac said. "There's no sick leave for monster bites."

"My boss thinks I'm out getting in bar fights, he'll fire me," another one said, toying with his glass.

"Some of us have families to think about," Arn said.

"Fuck you, fat ass," Dan said, looking back at the barkeep. The room froze.

Arn's hands tightened on the broom and he raised it level with the floor to quarterstaff height. "You want to try me?" he said, his voice quiet.

Dan slammed his empty glass down on the table and stepped forward, fists already raised. The nearest men scrambled to get out of the way, their chairs tumbling as they went. Only Lars, Ivor, and Mac stayed seated.

Carl intercepted Dan with an arm across the chest. "Save it for the frosties, man."

Dan swung around for a haymaker punch, but Carl blocked it with his free hand, holding Dan's fist in his own. Locked, they pushed against each other, Dan seething, Carl breathing hard against his berserk, neither one able to move the other an inch.

Gray clouds swirled in Dan's eyes. Immobile, every muscle in Carl's body strained. In his arm, a stitch popped. Warm blood trickled down his forearm to his elbow.

"Trust me. Please," he said.

Dan's breath shuddered. His jaw worked for a moment. Then he relaxed his grip, letting Carl push him back a quarter inch.

Carl dropped Dan's fist and put his hand on his friend's shoulder. "You're a good man, brother," he said, his voice low.

"I don't need you to tell me that," Dan said. But the tension eased out of his shoulders. He stepped back and nodded once to Arn, who nodded back, broom lowering as he did so.

The room breathed again. "Arn, how about another round?" Carl said. "On me."

"Sure thing." Arn slung his broom over his shoulder and headed toward the bar.

Carl gave the room a big smile. "Well?" Men laughed or smiled back, laughter a touch shaky with relief. He laughed with them, grabbing two chairs and pulling them up to the table. He offered one to Dan, who took it.

The men who bolted out of the way sheepishly picked up their chairs and rejoined the table. Carl turned his chair backwards and sat across the seat, arms propped on the back, making himself one of them.

"Arn has a point," Carl said. "But who's going to protect your kids from the dark and the winter if you don't? He scanned the crowd, catching as many of their eyes as possible. "Most people don't even know these things exist. They wouldn't believe it if we told them. If we don't fight together, we'll end up fighting alone. You want to take on a frostie by yourself? How about a dozen of them? What if it's a shadow-walker? Those babies'll walk right through the wards around your houses. Those of you that even have them."

"Bullshit," Mac said. "There ain't been a shadow-walker around here in..." he waved his hands, groping in the air for a time long enough, "ever. Even Heidrek didn't find one when he took you guys up north looking for one. They're just a story."

As Mac said it, Arn returned to the table with a new round of beers. He slid the tray onto the table for each man to take a glass and then pulled up a chair for himself. Dan raised his glass to Arn and took a long drink. Arn returned the salute with his own glass.

After a few minutes, Ivor raised his head, his eyes distant. "Stories can be true. I saw a shadow-walker once in my youth. Far up in the pine barrens of Maine."

"And you're still here?" Mac said. "They say those things eat people. You're either lying or you ran away."

"Fuck you," Lars said. "You should have seen this old guy tonight. He doesn't run from nothing."

Ivor slapped a hand on the table and laughed. "Of course, I ran," he said, his mustache bristling. "I didn't live this long by being a fool. It was no less real for all that. Even young Lars here wouldn't be foolish enough to attack a shadow-walker."

"What did it look like?" another man asked.

"Like the swamp muck found the form of a man and clothed itself in shadow. Wet and solid at the same time. It had arms like tree trunks and a bale light like swamp fire in its eyes. Stank like all hell too. I watched it eat a live moose."

Sitting beside Dan, Carl nudged him. "Your people live up around there. You ever see a shadow-walker?"

"No," Dan said. "But that doesn't mean much. There are parts of those woods we know better than to mess with. People go missing up there for all sorts of reasons."

As Ivor talked, Carl tugged on his beard and watched the men's faces mingle skepticism, fear, laughter, and intrigue.

When Ivor wound down, Carl said, "The winter is moving in on us and that means it's moving in on everyone around us. We're the only ones who can stop it."

A few nodded, but Mac tossed back the last of his beer and said, "Can't stop winter. Happens every year and always will." The others laughed and relaxed, taking the escape Mac opened for them.

Carl slammed his fist down on the table. "What if it doesn't? This isn't natural winter. It's hateful and full of purpose. Something is making it happen this time."

Even before Arn said, "Oh, come on, now," he knew he'd pushed them too far. Some laughed outright.

"Guess we'll have to rely on global warming," Mac said, and it was all over. People pushed back their chairs, said their good nights. Arn slapped him on the shoulder as he passed and muttered something about going out hunting with them some other time, but that was it.

"Fuck 'em," Dan said. "I fight better alone." He turned and walked away, boots crunching on broken peanut shells. Carl dumped a few bills on the bar and followed Lars and Ivor out to the truck.

CHAPTER
SEVENTEEN

Gray predawn light crept into the kitchen. Sick to her stomach from the pain of her burns and lack of sleep, Harvey sat on the floor, her arm around Caleb. Her burned eye throbbed. Her butt was numb from sitting on the hard linoleum. She looked up at Mal, who stood slumped against the kitchen window, arms hugged tight around herself.

Their eyes met. Mal turned away, returning to her vigil.

Harvey shook Caleb and kissed his forehead. "It's over," she said. "You can go to bed. Go on."

Mute, his eyes heavy, Caleb got up off the floor and shuffled off toward the stairs. He cradled his cut hand against his stomach. Groaning, Harvey pulled herself upright. She yawned until her jaw ached, and leaned on the counter for a second.

"You too, honey," she said to Mal. "You need your rest."

"We could have gone out there," Mal said, not turning from the window. "We could have at least tried. Now look."

Harvey joined her daughter at the window. The front yard looked as if a tractor had been cutting doughnuts on it all night. The oak tree's lower branches were stripped and strewn around the yard among pieces of siding. A huge splintered gash in the tree showed raw wood. The screen door lay twisted among the branches.

Harvey sighed and opened the kitchen door. The metal railings hung on either side of the steps in mangled pretzels. She stepped gingerly onto the concrete steps, Mal close behind her. The truck lay on its side, every window smashed. On the sidewalk, the electrical pole leaned at crazy angle, snapped wires dangling into the yard and sending up fitful sparks.

"Well...shit," Harvey said. She crossed her arms, hugging her elbows.

"No kidding," Mal said beside her.

Barefoot on the house steps, they stared at the yard, taking it all in. Not a one of the neighbors' houses were touched.

They were still standing like that when Carl's truck arrived with Dan close behind on his motorcycle. Lars, Ivor, and Carl piled out of the truck with whistles and exclamations. Dan took off his helmet and looked slowly around, his helmet resting on his lap.

Carl was the first to approach Harvey. "What the...?" "Shadow-walker," she said.

"Why the hell didn't you call for help, woman?" he said.

She gestured around the yard at the destruction. "What could you have done?"

His wind reddened cheeks flushed like a lobster in a boiling pot. He glared at her and turned away on his heel. "Lars, Dan, get over here and help me with this." He pointed to the truck on its side. Together with Ivor, they heaved and rocked the truck back onto its wheels. Squares of broken glass glittered on the driveway all around it.

She almost opened her mouth to shout, "You guys want breakfast?" That's what her mother would have done. Welcome the men home. Feed them full and listen to their boasts of great deeds. Instead, she yelled, "Thanks. I appreciate it."

Carl approached her again, Ivor coming with him. Lars and Dan hung back by the truck. "You want us to stay and help with all this?" Carl said.

"I can handle it."

"But you don't have to. We'll help," Carl said.

"I can handle it. Besides," she pointed with her chin. "You can't do anything until the power company deals with those lines."

Carl gave her a disapproving headshake. "If you say so." He clapped Ivor on the shoulder. "Have a good one, old man. It was great having you back again."

Ivor returned the pat on the back and waved jauntily to his other two companions before pushing his way past Harvey and Mal into the house.

Harvey's eyes met Carl's. He raised his eyebrows at her.

"Thanks for bringing him back in one piece," she said. Then she turned and walked into the house, pulling Mal with her.

As she closed the door, she caught the roar of Dan's motorcycle starting up, and a second after that, the truck driving away.

Mal grabbed Harvey's upper arm. "Mom, I think something's wrong with Grampa!"

Ivor's wheezing filled the kitchen. His shoulders drooped, the jaunty smile gone. He plopped into the nearest chair, panting. His face was flushed and sweating, his breath harsh as he pressed a hand over his chest.

"Ivor!" She grabbed him by the shoulders, shoving him upright in the chair. "Talk to me. Are you having a heart attack?"

He waved her off, wincing. "Angina. Nothing to worry about. I just need some rest."

He struggled to get up, but she shoved him back into the chair. "Sit still. Stay there. Mal, watch him." She ran down the hall to his bedroom for the pills in his bedside table. Half a minute later, she shoved a nitroglycerin pill under his tongue and pressed her fingers to his neck, feeling for the heartbeat. After his first heart attack they'd tried to teach her how to take a pulse on his wrist, but she could never get the hang of it.

She stood beside him, fingertips digging into his neck, listening for every wheezing breath as she watched the clock. *Tick. Tick. Tick.* Seconds turned into minutes. Mal hovered in the doorway between the hall and the kitchen, her cell phone in her hand. Ivor's heart rate slowed, the pulse still strong and regular. The light in the kitchen wasn't gray anymore.

At last, Ivor heaved a deep sigh and rubbed his chest. "That's better. Help me out of this, would you?" He held up his mail clad arms.

"Sure." She and Mal eased his stiff arms out of the chainmail sleeves, falling into the phrases she'd used when the kids were babies and she tugged little arms out of coat sleeves or into pajamas. Arms up. Arms down. Easy there. Okay. Almost done. Good job.

"Thank you," he said. A hint of wheeze remained in his voice.

She shook out the chainmail so that it chimed and hung it with the coats.

"How was it? You have fun?" Hands on hips, she watched him as he answered, still looking for a sign she should call 911. But the grayness was gone from his face and he'd stopped rubbing his chest, though his eyelids drooped.

"More fun than I've had in years." Ivor said and yawned hugely. He heaved himself out of his chair.

Mal laughed, her voice shaky. "Geez, Grampa. Don't scare us like that."

Ivor patted her on the cheek before shuffling down the hall toward his bedroom. His discarded sword lay behind him on the kitchen floor.

"Goddammit, I am not your maid," Harvey said. But she picked up the weapon. She went over to Mal and folded her daughter into a tight hug. "Thank you. You were great tonight. Really brave."

In her arms, Mal shuddered and hugged her back. After a long moment, Mal heaved a sigh and pushed away. "How come the guys get all the fun and we get—" she pointed out the window. "This shit?"

"Sucks, doesn't it?" Harvey said.

Mal nodded hard. "Yeah!"

Harvey chuckled and kissed her on the forehead. "Go to bed."

"You should too."

"I will." She brandished the sword in her hand. "Just have to take care of a couple things first. Go on." She gave Mal a little shove toward the stairs.

She watched Mal clump up the stairs and into her bedroom. Then she hefted the sword and followed Ivor down the hall to his room. He was asleep already, sprawled on the bed with one boot untied.

"I ought to let you lie there," she said. Instead, she tugged off his boots and wet wool socks before she tucked his legs into bed and drew up the covers. She wiped down his sword and stowed it in his closet.

The stairs up to bed loomed overhead like Jacob's ladder. Too much to handle. Harvey rolled herself up in the afghan and collapsed onto the living room couch. She could be angry at him later. And she would be, but for now, at least, her family was still alive. Not even the full sunlight could keep her awake any longer.

Around noon, Harvey stood at the living room window, arms crossed, watching the NYPA put the power lines back together. The November sky, a sharp, clear blue, promised a hard frost in the night. Their truck was gouging up what little was left of her lawn. Her own truck looked like used tinfoil, but the glass replacement guy had come and gone, so at least now it was drivable. The ravens were back in their places, filling the oak tree's branches, but for now they were silent, facing the house with glittering black eyes.

Ivor still snored in his room, but the kids were finally up and lounging behind her. Mal, barefoot, in warm up pants and a hoodie, had her feet up on the back of the couch, eyes glued to her phone.

Caleb, hunched over the computer, still wore his pajamas. A quick glance told Harvey he was looking up runes and scribbling notes in a blank book.

She rubbed a hand over her face, not knowing if this was better or worse than him trying to learn how to berserk. Most of what he'd find on the net was probably garbage, right? Bored housewives pretending to be witches with crystal suncatchers and a few exciting sounding herbs. At worst he'd learn a few useful things that her mother might have taught him anyway if she'd lived.

Except. Harvey stood in the middle of the living room, eyes still fixed on the back of Caleb's head. Except her mother never used blood that she knew of. Caleb seemed to know all on his own that blood was needed. That was warlock magic—offerings of blood to the powers under the earth and in the earth. Even in the old stories Ivor told, warlocks were spoken of rarely and with caution. There was the deer-footed man who stole his own brother's blood, sapping his warrior sibling's strength to make up for his own weakness.

Hugging herself, she frowned, her stare growing distant as she tried to remember the details. Had there been a point to that story or was it just one of the ones that got told from time to time, no one remembering why?

"Mom!" Caleb snapped.

Harvey started. "What? Yes? What do you need?"

"Why are you staring at me?"

"I'm not. I was just... I was just thinking about something else."

Caleb narrowed his eyes at her and shut his notebook, snapping the elastic around the cover before he left the room, still glaring at her. A second later, his feet thudded up the stairs to his room.

"Weirdo," Mal said, casually, not taking her eyes off her phone.

"Him or me?" Harvey said, her voice edged. Mal, still upside down on the couch, shrugged. Harvey gave a sigh that was almost a growl and stalked into the kitchen to make more coffee.

Her fingers itched for a weapon. She ought to be running a whetstone across a blade right now. All she needed to do was go upstairs and drag the old army footlocker out of her closet and pop the lid with a screwdriver. Maybe it was time. Maybe she kept that sword and armor for more than memory's sake and now was the time to get them out again. Because sure as she was standing in her own kitchen, that thing out there wanted her and her children for a reason. She didn't know how, but she would bet her pinky finger it tied back to her brother. No one else in the world hated her like that.

She pulled the butcher knife out of the block on the counter and examined its edge—the same knife set she and Jon got for their wedding. Oh, people made so many jokes about her turning in her sword for a cook's apron and kitchen knife. She chuckled and began sliding it across the steel sharpening rod, each stroke like metal through silk. Pity the monster that tried to invade her kitchen. A smile spread over her face as she honed the already sharp steel to a glinting edge.

Someone banged on the kitchen door. Coach Wells's voice called, "Mrs. Otvar? Can I come in for a minute? I brought Mal's homework."

Harvey jerked around, knife out in front of her. On the other side of the door window, Coach Wells put up her hands. Harvey sagged, panting, her hand pressed over her chest. Lowering the knife, she went to answer the door.

"I'm so sorry. I'm...um...I'm a bit on edge today." She stepped aside, gesturing with her knife hand. "Please, come on in."

Coach Wells stayed where she was, weight balanced back as if to dodge a blow. "You going to put that knife down?"

"Oh geez. Shit. Sorry." Harvey returned to the knife to its block, leaving the kitchen door open. "I'm sorry. Coffee?"

"No. I'm good." Coach Wells came into the kitchen, though not too far, closing the door behind her. Harvey leaned her butt against the counter and pressed a palm into her forehead.

"Looks like you guys had your own personal hurricane here last night," Wells said.

"Something like that," Harvey said.

"What's really going on?"

"Nothing."

"Bull. Shit." Wells took a deep breath and said, "I have heard weird stories about your whole family ever since I moved to this town five years ago. It is not nothing. Whatever tore up your outside there last night was trying to get into this house, wasn't it? And you're trying to handle it all by your damn self because you're either too stubborn to admit you need help or because it's too wild for anyone to believe you."

The two women stared at each other, arms crossed. Various responses crossed Harvey's mind.

Who do you think you are coming into my kitchen and talking about my family?

Yes, please help me. Take my kids and hide them.

I don't know what you're talking about.

Okay that last one was the dumbest idea of the three. But maybe she had a better one. Harvey raised her chin and licked dry lips. "Hold still, will you? I want to see something."

Coach Wells nodded once, but kept her straight-backed, crossed arm stance. To a man she might have looked petite. Delicate even. But every line of her body spoke of quiet strength, a readiness without tension or fear. Harvey took a deep breath and lifted her eye patch.

A hot sun shone on Coach Wells's dark skin. Her long braids were coiled tightly against her head, held back by bands of cowrie shells. More white shells gleamed in double rows down the front of her sleeveless, ochre red dress and a sash or striped red and blue wound around her waist. In one hand she held a spear, and in the other a blade with a curved and hooked edge that made Harvey's butcher knife look like a nail file.

Harvey pulled her patch back into place and let out a shuddering breath. "You're going to think I'm weird for asking, but do you own a sword about yay long with a curved edge?"

Coach Wells lifted her chin, suspiciously. "How did you know that? I don't think I've ever mentioned it to the girls on the track team."

"I saw it when I looked at you." Harvey said. She crossed her arms, looking down at the linoleum floor. "Um...were there fighters in your family? Way back when?"

Coach Wells drew herself up, a stern look on her face. "My people were stolen from their homeland and brought to this country as slaves. We are all fighters." After a minute, she said, "My mother's side of the family always said they came from Dahomey. It's called Benin now. They told stories about the women warriors of Dahomey."

Harvey winced in embarrassment. She wasn't sure what to say. "I'm sorry" seemed inadequate to the point of being insulting. "Okay, well," she said. "Maybe you will understand." She pulled out a chair and offered it to Coach Wells, who unslung her purse from her shoulder and hung it carefully on the back of her chair, unzipping her coat and folding her hands to listen.

Taking a seat herself, Harvey said, "I come from a long line of berserkers."

As Harvey was winding up her explanation of what a berserker was and what she thought attacked the house the night before, Mal wandered into the kitchen, her fingers dancing over her phone. She stopped short as her coach waved hello.

"Whoa. Hey, Coach Wells," she said. Her eyes lit up and she threw her arms around her coach's neck. Coach Wells hugged her back.

As Mal stood up from the hug, her eyes darted back and forth between Harvey and her coach. "Am I in trouble?"

Coach Wells laughed. "Not with me. Your mom was telling me what's going on with your family."

"Mom!" Mal shrieked.

"Relax," Harvey said. "She believes me. You do believe me, right?"

Coach Wells nodded. "Yeah. I've heard weirder stories from my Granny, honestly. Not this stuff specifically, but you know...stuff. We've got our own traditions in my family. Mal, what are you doing to keep this new skill of yours under control?"

Mal shrugged with both shoulders going in different directions.

"Mal, use your words," Harvey said. "It's an important question."

"I don't know," Mal said. "I don't really know what it all means yet. Am I supposed to meditate or something?"

Coach Wells spread her hands. "Not a bad idea actually. Like I tell you girls all season—you need a sound mind in a sound body." She tapped her forehead. "Running is mental work. Fighting is mental work. You can lose a battle by psyching yourself out."

Harvey cocked her head at Coach Wells in surprise. "Have you... fought in any battles?"

"Nah. Not real ones. I can defend myself though. A little melee training. But don't worry about it. What are we going to do about your monster?"

Harvey laughed. "Nothing? I don't even know where to begin. I assume it'll be back at some point, but I don't know what to do besides strengthening the wards again. Maybe I'll park my truck down the street so it stays safe. When my father-in-law wakes up, I'll ask him if he has any advice." She turned toward Mal. Coach Wells brought your homework so you don't fall behind."

Mal grabbed her sneakers from the mat by the kitchen door. "Thanks. I'll do it later!" She was out the door before Harvey could get halfway out of her chair.

"Where are you going?" Harvey yelled after her. "You've got schoolwork to do!"

"Think of this as gym class!" Mal yelled before she hit speed and tore off down the sidewalk. Harvey rolled her eyes toward heaven and instantly regretted it as her burned eye spasmed in pain. Coach Wells shook her head.

EIGHTEEN

Mal pushed through the trees until she reached the narrow little track by the water's edge. Her feet pounded over the ground, mud splashing up her legs as she ducked and wove between low hanging tree branches. The rhythm of running took over. *Relax, let go. Shoulders back, head up, breathe deep.* She shook out her hands, letting go of the tight fists. She ran until the weight lifted off her shoulders.

"We run because we like it." Coach Well's favorite saying echoed in her head. It was from a poem or something.

Slowly, slowly, her pace eased into a jog. The trees thinned overhead. The sun shone down into the path. A wisp of tobacco and wood smoke reached her. She smiled as she rounded the bend.

Just off the path, Jessa, Brittnee, and a few others from the team sat around a campfire, beers in their hands.

"Hey, guys." Mal plopped down on a log next to Claire, who ran the hundred meters. "What's up?"

Jessa smiled and waved at her, but no one else spoke. They stared, faces frozen. Claire leaned away, huddling into her coat.

"What?" Mal asked.

Britnee elbowed Jessa, hissing, "You told her where we were?"

"Yeah," Jessa said. "Why not?" Britnee gave Jessa a wide-eyed glare. Others shuffled their feet, eyes darting back and forth.

"Aren't you, like, supposed to be in jail?" Todd said.

"We don't want any trouble," Britnee said. "Or drugs."

"I'm not on drugs, Britnee." *Bitch.*

Eyebrows raised. Mouths pursed. A few huddled closer to each other.

"What?" Mal repeated, an edge in her voice.

No one spoke. She looked at each of their faces in turn. Fear on every one of them—even the guys. Especially the guys.

"You were laughing," Britnee said. "You were laughing while you were hurting him."

"Are you kidding me?" Mal spat back. "Taylor deserved what he got."

People looked away. Girls hung onto their boyfriends who didn't hug them back, as if afraid the movement would catch her eye.

"It was just a joke," Todd muttered.

"To you maybe. You're not the one who was getting grabbed, were you?" she shot back.

"He didn't grab *you*," Britnee said.

"Oh, that's what matters, right?" Mal glared at Britnee. "As long as I'm not the one getting hurt, I can stand by and laugh with everybody else?"

Claire shifted on the log next to Mal and hunched her shoulders. "Shelley's a freak anyway. She needs to lighten up." Nods and murmurs of agreement went up around the fire.

"Oh, fuck you. Fuck all of you." Mal flipped them the double-handed bird and took off, tearing through the trees. Forget the path. She hit the road on the far side of the park and kept on going, head down.

She made it over the railroad tracks when the roar of a motorcycle coming up behind her broke through the babble in her head.

Dan roared past her and whipped around, spraying gravel as he slewed to a halt in front of her.

Mal narrowed her eyes against the stinging wind and dug her hands into her jacket pockets. "What do you want?"

Dan braced his feet on the road and took off his helmet. "I want to talk to you. Get a better look at you."

She stuck out her chin. "Why?" Instinctively she hunched her shoulders, hiding her breasts from the sweeping gaze she expected. But Dan's eyes stayed fixed on her face.

"Don't worry, little sister," he said. "I'm not here to hurt you." A sad smile creased his face. "You look like your dad. 'Cept your eyes. You get those from your mom."

He sat back in the bike's saddle, keeping his hands where she could see them.

Cocking her head to one side, Mal eyed him for a long time, daring him to leer at her. He returned her look steadily, with no sign of embarrassment. Eventually she let herself look over the bike too, though still from a safe distance.

"That's a really nice bike," she said. "Classic. Is it the same one I sat on as a kid?"

"Yep." He beamed at the bike. "Lotta miles on this horse."

She listened to the idle, letting a bit of a smile crack her 'don't fuck with me' stance. "It sounds like one of your sparks is going bad though."

A bigger smile split his face. "You know about bikes? Where'd you learn?"

"I like anything with an engine, but Harleys are my favorite thing in the world. I took engine repair instead of home ec in 10th grade."

Dan rubbed a hand over his chin. "It was Mustangs with your dad. He was crazy about them." He revved the engine at her. "You remember that silver one he drove?"

She rolled her eyes at him, her smile fading. "You mean the one he died in? Yeah, I remember. It was all smashed up like tinfoil." She sighed. "God, that was a beautiful car."

Dan laughed. "Yeah, you're just like your dad. But when you're angry I can see your mom."

Mal shook off the comparison. "What was my dad like?"

"Don't you remember?"

"Yeah, but..." Mal held up her hands, grabbing for words she didn't have. "I remember him as my dad. He was goofy and he tickled me and..." For no goddamn reason tears pricked at her eyes and she had to stare straight ahead into the gray and pink sunset without blinking to keep them from spilling out and making her look like a pussy. But Dan said nothing, just sat quietly on the bike, looking off into the sky with his own thoughts like he might not even know she was there anymore.

"He painted my nails pink," she said. "And he always wore a knife in his belt and he had snake tattoos and he gave piggyback rides and he let me get the Hello Kitty backpack that cost too much when I was eight. And I miss him."

She scrubbed hard at her face. "I thought he was just my dad. I didn't know he was special."

Dan breathed in slow and steady, mouth shut, and nodded, still looking off at the sky. Somehow his silence and lack of eye contact was more comforting than any school counselor's earnest "how are you *really* doing?" had ever been.

Mal sniffed, her nose running in the cold air. "What was he like when you were around and I wasn't? What did you guys do? Like, I remember sometimes he and Mom would go out at night and leave Caleb and me with Gramma. Then a bunch of you would come home late and have beers in the kitchen. What were you out doing? Being berserkers?"

Dan nodded, looked down at the bike once. He opened his mouth to speak, but the sound of car tires bouncing over the train tracks interrupted them. Dan glanced past her, his eyes narrowing, and she turned to see what drew his attention. A police car pulled over to the side and rolled down its window. The officer put one arm out. He was a red face with a buzz cut, his protein powder neck wider than his jaw. "Aren't you supposed to be in school, young lady?"

"I got suspended."

The cop looked at his partner, who frowned. He held out a hand. "IDs."

Mal reached into her jacket pocket, heart suddenly racing. She'd left the house without her wallet. She glanced at Dan, appealing to him for help. Dan caught her look and gave her a near invisible nod of assurance. He leaned back on his bike. "We don't have to give you IDs."

"You see this badge?" The cop pointed to his chest. "This says when I ask you for ID, you hand it over."

Mal swallowed hard. Little thrills ran up and down her arms. She flattened her palms against her legs to keep from clenching them, but Dan didn't so much as blink. He locked eyes with the cop, face impassive.

"Nope," he said. "State law says it's not a requirement for any citizen to carry ID on them, unless they're a student using a metro card in New York City. This look like a metro stop to you?"

The cop's face twisted in rage. He pushed open his squad car door and stepped out. His partner, an older woman bulging in all the wrong places in her uniform, her hair pulled into a painfully tight bun at the nape of her neck, got out from the other side of the car and came around to stand behind her partner. She rested her hand on her gun.

Her fingers shaking, Mal fumbled in her pocket, bobbling her cell phone as she struggled to hold it upright and push the record button.

Face turning even redder, the first cop said, "Who the hell you think you are, quoting the law to me?"

Dan lifted his chin. "Card carrying ACLU member, that's who. Now are we free to go, Officer..."" he glanced at the man's badge, "Bradley."

Bradley took a step forward. Mal held up her cell phone, gulping hard, her mouth suddenly dry. The second cop eyed her up and down, then grabbed her partner by the arm, leaning in to speak in his ear. Mal heard her muttering, something like "went to school with that little bitch's mom... Not worth it. Let him have her."

The first cop stepped back, his hand still resting on his gun, his face an ugly mask. "You just watch yourself. You hear me?" he said to Dan.

Dan nodded. Casting glances over their shoulders, the two cops got back into their car. They peeled out, gravel spraying off the car's back tires.

Mal watched the squad car disappear over the hill as she panted in relief. "Oh my God! That was awesome!"

But there was no smile on Dan's face as he watched the cops disappear. "Don't play chicken with the cops unless you need to, okay? Come on." He patted the back seat of the bike. "They may change their minds and come back."

For half a second every warning she'd ever heard about trusting strangers whipped through her brain. *Fuck 'em.* He'd known her dad. She took out her phone and disabled "last location" before shutting it off. "Now we're good."

"Where are we going?" she asked, as she flung a leg over the back of the bike.

Dan handed her the helmet and revved his bike awake. "Where the monsters are."

CHAPTER NINETEEN

Dan's bike whipped down an alley so close that Mal squeezed her knees tighter against the bike, afraid she'd lose them to a brick wall. The alley opened up into a loading dock closed off from the world by windowless brick walls. As Dan eased the bike to a stop, she looked up. It was like looking up from the bottom of a square well, capped with gray sky. Overhead a single black bird circled.

Dan led her to a door with an angular white mark spray painted on it. "What does that mean?"

He chuckled. "It means beer and fire. Kind of like saying come on in and drink where it's warm. Ask your grandpa. He knows those kinds of things."

"This is a bar?" She hadn't seen the inside of a bar yet, but this looked nothing like the outsides she'd seen. Her eyes lit up. "Is this a rave? Like a warehouse party?"

Dan chuckled and opened the door. Warm air and beer smell wrapped around her face. A great, shadowy, cavernous space opened in front of her with a pool of flickering yellow light in the middle distance. The last drops of sunset were already blocked from the grayed out windows by the buildings crowded too close outside. Something about country roads played on a radio—the echoing space gave it a mournful reverb. A pigeon flapped away into the rafters.

"Wow." Her voice came out in a whisper. Stuffing the phone back into her pocket, she followed Dan into the warehouse. Peanut shells crunched underfoot.

Whistles and cheers greeted Dan.

"Who's the babe?" someone yelled.

A man nearest Mal patted his lap. "Hey jailbait, want a beer?"

Like a snake striking, Dan's fist connected with the man's temple. His jaw sagged and he toppled out of his chair. The other men at his table watched him fall, looked at Dan, and said nothing.

"This is Mal," he said. "She's with me." He jerked his head at her and stamped up to the bar. Mal followed, trying to take it all in without looking impressed or anything.

A guy with a healthy beer gut, wide biceps, and a short, sandy gray beard polished a glass behind a table on sawhorses. He spoke without taking his eyes off Mal. "Am I going blind or is that who I think it is?"

"Yup. This is Jon and Harvey's girl," Dan said.

"Get out." The man slammed the glass down and pointed. Dan motioned Mal to join him. The bartender leaned both fists on his table. "I mean it, Dan. I don't care what you do, but I'm not having Harvey come down here looking for her kid."

Mal laughed. "Mom's not going to do anything. She'll just get mad and yell."

"You think so, little girl?" the bartender pointed at her. "Have you ever seen your mom mad? Cuz I have, and it was not pretty."

Mal blinked. It was hard to picture mom doing anything except counting to ten and taking away her phone. She couldn't even stand up to Mrs. Padowski.

"Relax, Arn," Dan said. "Harvey doesn't know where she is."

"Yeah, and how long will that last?" Muttering about bears and their cubs, Arn grabbed a broom and went off to move the peanut shells around. Dan walked around behind the bar, filling two mugs with beer and adding a shot of whiskey for himself. He handed the second mug to Mal.

"Thanks." Trying to look cool and casual, like a cowboy in a movie, she put her back to the bar, leaning on it with one elbow, face watching the room, her foot propped on the rail. Since there was no rail, she stumbled backwards, hitting her back on the bar and sloshing her beer. Dan snorted into his drink.

Mal pulled herself back upright and tried for a nonchalant tone. "So, is this place even legal?"

"Not a bit." A grinning man wearing a shirt from the plant where her mom worked held out his hand. "I'm Mac. I know your uncle Heidrek." She stuck her hand out in response before her brain could catch up to the words he'd said. He knew her uncle, not her mom. Her uncle—the guy who had strangled her mom on the floor of their kitchen at Grampa Angantyr's wake. Mal pulled her hand back as Mac tried to shake it.

"You're friends with my uncle?" she said.

"We go way back," Mac said. "Hey, don't believe everything you hear. There are two sides to every story, you know?"

Other men drifted up, many of them nodding along with Mac. Mal scanned their faces, uncomfortably aware that she was standing with her back to a rickety bar, facing a half circle of strange men in a building that probably didn't even have a street address. And if the cops did ask any questions later it would probably be: "You went there voluntarily, didn't you? What did you think was going to happen?"

She risked a quick glance at Dan to see his reaction. He didn't seem to have one. She pulled her shoulders a little straighter and forced a cheerful smile, even as she white-knuckled her mug. "Some of you guys were at my Grampa's funeral, right?" she said. "And my dad's."

Most of them nodded. "He was a good man, your dad," Arn said.

He'd joined the outer ring of the circle, leaning on his broom. Head nods and agreement all around.

Mal licked her lips, "How come my mom doesn't want anything to do with you guys anymore?"

Some of them shuffled their feet. Others studied their beer or tugged on their belt buckles. Why did guys always do that? Did touching their dick help them think or something? "Well?" she said.

"She knows better than to show her face around here," Mac said. "After what she did to her brother."

A few others murmured and nodded.

Dan laughed and ran his tongue around his teeth. "If you think Harvey's afraid of you, it's time to stop drinking. Maybe for good." He downed the rest of his beer in one gulp. "She gave up being queen, but she ain't afraid of anything. Or anybody."

"Yeah, then why'd she use the law on Heidrek?" a man said. "Hiding behind the pigs. That's not how we do things."

Mac hitched up his jeans a few times. "And why the hell are you defending her? Not like she's done you any favors."

Dan waved his empty mug at Arn, who nodded and moved back behind the bar as Dan said, "I'm not saying she was right. I'm saying she wasn't *afraid*. At least, not of any of you." Dan swapped his old mug for the fresh one Arn slid toward him.

Mal rolled her eyes at him. "Mom's afraid of everything. She tells us to be careful at least twenty times a day. And since when is my mom queen of anything?"

Men looked at each other, back and forth. Eventually, eyes settled on Dan. He sucked on his teeth, staring into the middle distance as he drank from his beer.

Eventually he lowered the mug and let out a long breath. "Long time ago, when your ancestors still lived in their own land, there was a king. He owned a sword called Tyrfing that was special, but it was cursed. Handed down from king to king. It came to America with your ancestors. Your mom's dad, your grandfather Angantyr, he owned the sword last. He never used it, because of the curse, but he was also the strongest and the fiercest, so he was kind of like a king to the berserkers around here. When he died, he didn't say who was supposed to be king after him. Your uncle was older, and popular. And a man. But your mom—she was wiser, you get me? She took the sword and hid it so Heidrek couldn't be king."

"Stole it, you mean," Mac said. Men murmured and nodded.

Dan flicked his wrist, sloshing the rest of his beer straight into Mac's face. "I'm telling this story. Not you."

Snorting and wiping beer out of his eyes, Mac surged forward, fist up, as the other men stepped back. Mal raised her glass like a club, heart pounding. Dan just laughed and caught Mac's hand with his palm. "You won't touch a frostie, but you think you can take me?"

Their eyes locked a minute, Mac still snorting beer out of his nose. Finally, he shook off Dan's hand and turned away, accepting the bar rag that Arn held out. Mac retired into the crowd as Dan nodded.

Dan looked over at Mal, her mug still raised. "Relax, kiddo. You hold your fists like that in a fight and you'll have a hand full of glass. Anyway, your mom, she showed up at the funeral wearing Angantyr's gold, with Carl and your dad and me backing her. Like a queen of her people. No one said a word about it during the funeral, but once everybody was back at the house for the wake, she told him that the sword belonged to her and she was in charge now." He drew a long breath and picked up a third beer. "She and Heidrek threw down right then and there."

"I remember that," Mal said. Dan had swung her off the bike and dropped her to the ground before tearing off into the house. She remembered the slam of the screen door. Standing in the front yard alone, sure someone was killing her mom, but her feet were nailed to the grass, unable to take her inside. Glass breaking. A neighbor lady had come over and pulled her away.

"I bet you do. You remember the cops coming?" She nodded. "It was a fair fight up to then. But she let the cops take her brother away. Wouldn't speak a word for him. And then when they wanted to charge him with attempted murder, she testified for the prosecutor. Put him away for a good long time.

All that to be queen. And then your dad died, and she walked from us away like none of us mattered. Wouldn't give any of us the time of day, not even Carl."

Angry muttering filled the room.

"That's...shitty," Mal said.

"Yup." Dan motioned for Arn to give him another beer.

"What happened to the sword?" Mal asked.

Dan shrugged. "She's got it somewhere. Nobody's seen it since."

"She's got a real heavy box with a lock on it in the back of her closet. She never let Caleb and me play with it or look inside. Maybe that's where the sword is."

Men nodded, slow thoughtful nods. Mac spat on the floor and said, "Figures. Take a thing, tell everybody about it, and then not use it, just to make sure no one else has it. That's the kind of cunt she is."

A few nodded and laughed in agreement, but others edged a little farther from Mac, their eyes darting back and forth between Dan and Mal. Two distinct groups formed—Mac and his backup singers and a larger, uneasier group that was not exactly on one side or another, just trying not to get caught in the middle. Mal gulped hard, Arn and Dan were closest to her, but she wouldn't bet much money that they still counted as being on her side. One elbow leaning on the bar, Dan cracked a peanut and looked at Mal, as if to say, "Your move."

Mal tried to force some spit into her mouth. She looked Mac dead in the eye and said, "You don't get to use that word about my mother. No matter what she did."

"That so?" Both hands on his belt, Mac tugged hard at his waistband, sidling towards her. His bunch of weasels giggled and nudged each other. At Mal's side, Dan crossed his arms and gave her a nod.

"Yeah, it is," Mal said, trying to keep her voice from shaking. She put her mug down, remembering what Dan said. "Now shut your mouth and sit down."

Mac grinned wider than she'd seen him do yet. All teeth, rolling up his sleeves and coming toward her. Men scooted farther out of the way, widening the circle around them. Some pulled up chairs and settled in to watch.

Arn reached across the bar, tugging at Dan's sleeve. He muttered in Dan's ear, but Dan shook his head at the bartender. Arn backed off, frowning and edging out from behind the bar, but not coming between Mac and Mal. Dan turned back to Mal and gave her a nod. He settled back on his heels, arms crossed. Whatever happened next, she was in it alone.

Mal's heart beat a mile a minute. The beer in her stomach soured, her palms sweating. This guy was big. Okay yeah, he had a beer gut, but his fists were like hams. He moved slow, but knocking him over would be like tackling a full beer keg. She clenched her own fists, trying to hide the tremor.

Mac shoved his sleeves back. "Okay sweetheart, let Daddy teach you some respect."

She edged sideways, trying to get her back away from the bar. Her fists wobbled between herself and Mac. Mac shot out his hand. She threw up her arm to block the punch. But he grabbed her wrist, jerking her toward him. She flailed like a fish on a hook, punching, trying to wriggle her arm out of his sandpaper grip.

The flat of his hand caught her right across the jaw. Stars flashed across her eyes. He slapped her again. She gasped, her knees buckling. But he held her up by her wrist. Her shoulder popped.

"You got anything more to say, sweet tits?"

She blinked, trying to get something smart out of her mouth, but all she got was a squeak.

"That's what I thought." He dropped her. A few men laughed. Someone whooped. It was the whoop that did it. She couldn't stop the tears in her eyes, but she didn't have to lie there and let him walk away. Sniffing back the tears and snot, she scraped her arm over her eyes.

Mac had his back to her.

Well fuck him.

Mal grabbed the nearest chair and swung it over her head. "Hey! You. Turn around."

Mac turned, a sneer on his lips. She brought the chair down on his greasy head. Somewhere on the downswing, the same red-hot power she'd felt before surged through her. *He's just another Taylor Padowski with a bigger gut.*

She brought the chair down square on his head and shoulders. The legs tangled around his head as he turned back.

She yanked the chair off him and swung again, catching him in the chest. Air *oofed* out of him and he wheezed, stumbling forward. Mac grabbed the chair with one hand, trying to yank it out of her grip.

Mal threw her weight into his pull and rushed him. The two of them went down in a tangle of chair and limbs. The chair caught her sharply in the chin, but she still dug her knee into Mac's groin as she scrambled to her feet. He groaned and she kicked, hitting him in the leg.

He lumbered to his feet, but she got the chair first. She raised it over her head for another strike when Arn stepped between them. His broom caught the chair on its downswing. A tangle of wood and a sharp pull and the chair went flying out of her hands.

"Hey!" She swung on this new opponent. *Let them all try if they wanted.* She'd take them. On the other side of Arn, Mac swung at her, but Arn's broom prodded them both in the ribs.

"That's enough now. *Enough* I said." Arn circled, keeping the two of them each at broom's length, no matter how she dodged. "You made your point."

Someone slapped her on the back. She spun on them, ready to claw, spit, kick, punch—whatever it took.

Dan shoved a beer into her hand and stepped back from her swing. "Nice work."

The red fog wavered in front of her eyes.

"Come on," Arn said. "We're friends here. No killing."

Other men clapped, hollered. She swayed on her feet. The red in front of her eyes faded to gray. Her cheek ached where Mac slapped her. It only took a nudge from Dan for her to flop into a chair. Mac and his friends were moving away, looking over their shoulders as they did. A couple of his buddies stayed, pulling up chairs near her.

"You got a pretty good swing for a girl," one said.

She glared and Dan snorted. "You remember what happened the last time someone said 'for a girl' to her mom, don't you?" Uncomfortable chuckles answered him.

She took a long drink from her beer while her eyes figured out how to focus again. These guys knew her mom, but they knew a whole different person than the one she thought she knew. "So," she said, "tell me about being a berserker."

TWENTY

In the concrete prison yard, Heidrek dug his hands into his pockets as he strolled along the fenced perimeter. Concertina wire and a double row of chain link fencing kept the humans in, but they couldn't keep out the wind or the ravens circling overhead. All around Heidrek, men played basketball, walked, or worked out on the outdoor weight benches, but they left a wide berth around Heidrek himself. Even the guards avoided making eye contact with him, preferring to watch him out of the side of their eyes. Heidrek pulled a piece of sliced ham from his pocket, offering it palm up to the sky. The dry, government surplus meat wasn't much of an offering, but it was the best he could save from his lunch.

A raven swooped down and snatched the food before circling in lazy loops above the yard as it cawed. The razor wire atop the fences left it nowhere to settle, but Heidrek still caught the bird's message.

"She runs. Alone. We see. We watch. She goes to the woods by the river. She seeks on foot near her house."

A sharp smile made its way across Heidrek's face. He tossed more food to the bird, which caught it and flew away to the west where the sun still hung in the sky. His shadow-walker failed, but another opportunity had come his way. No time to wait until dark. He tucked his right hand into his left sleeve, fingernails raking across the runes. Warm blood oozed under his fingertips. Winter. Water and bone. Revenge. Sister. Blood of my blood. He flicked his fingers outward, scattering drops of blood across the dirt.

Invisible lines of blood power flowed out of him and into the hungry ground. His breath came fast and shallow as he fought to control the flow. His heartbeat stuttered. The afternoon sunlight fought with the darkness he sought, but years of hard practice had taught him well. He dropped to his knees, palms grinding into the dirt. Damp seeped through his pant legs. Blood ran down his wrists, each drop tethering him to the ground, sending his spirit far beyond his prison walls.

He found the hidden streams and underground reservoirs, sought along the connections until he found the Niagara River flowing icy cold. *Wake up. Hunger. Hunt.* The response was slow, held back by the sun that filtered through gray clouds, but his will was stronger. *Rise. Rise and hunt. I command you.*

The cold at the bottom of the river answered his commands. Frost shards crackled under his fingers as hunger and winter and the desire for revenge joined into one and took solid form. Heidrek pressed his palms harder into the ground, feeding it with his own life's blood.

A hand gripped his shoulder and pulled him upward, breaking his connection with the ground.

"Hey," the guard said. "Time to go in. Move it."

Heidrek snarled at the man, blood thundering in his ears. "Take your hands off me!"

The guard's eyes widened and he took a step back, one hand clutching at his whistle. Still kneeling on the ground, Heidrek panted, every limb shaking, his breath rasping in his lungs. Darkness fogged his eyes. The taste of river water and damp earth filled his mouth.

"Do not. Touch. Me," he said.

"Get up. Get in line," the guard barked, but his wide eyes and the tremor in his voice gave him away.

Heidrek rose to his feet, his eyes still locked with the guard's. Slowly, deliberately, he brushed his knees clean and pulled his sleeves down over his wrists. Squeezing his fingers into his palms, he broke the connection with the earth and water. It was enough. What he had unleashed was on its way.

Rolling his shoulders, he turned his back on the guard. At his own speed, he strolled toward the waiting line of prisoners. Other guards watched with hate in their eyes, but none spoke to him as he fell into line. Inside his thin, orange prison jacket he shivered with cold and blood loss, but still he smiled. This time, he would have her.

TWENTY-ONE

ritting her teeth, Harvey ducked under the branches of an oak into the woods that edged Fisherman's Park. Mal still wasn't answering her phone two hours after she'd taken off. Odds were she was down by the river with some friends. Dodging underbrush and low branches, Harvey wove her way into the woods. Black water showed between the branches.

Soon she popped out of the trees onto the narrow dirt path. She picked up speed as her feet hit the open ground. To her right, waves whipped by the cold wind lapped the rocky shore a foot from the path's edge. They lunged forward, gripping the rocks before falling back.

Harvey breathed in the smell of hemlocks and wet, fallen leaves. It had been a long time since she'd dodged through the woods looking for trouble. She sniffed again. A campfire and a sweet, skunky smell. Sure enough, not far down the path a bunch of teens sat around a campfire a few feet from the water.

"Relax," she said as they scrambled to hide the beer and weed. "I'm not here to bust you." She looked around the group. A couple she recognized from Mal's track meets. "Brittnee? Tracy? Have any of you seen Mal?"

They drew further back, eyes wider.

A few shook their heads or looked away, afraid to meet her eyes, but Brittnee pointed down the path. "That way."

"Thanks. Was she...? Did she look okay?"

Feet shuffled in the dirt. The kids looked everywhere but at her.

Harvey shivered, cold in the shadows under the trees. Waves whipped up by the breeze grew on the riverbank. *No one is bleeding.* "Right, thanks. Look if you see Mal, tell her she's not in trouble, I'm just—Oh shit!"

She saw the frost demon before any of them did. Gray white, glistening like wet ice, it lurched out of the water behind Brittnee. Harvey charged, vaulting the fire to land in front of Britnee. Brittnee screamed.

Kids scrambled, most to get out of her way, but a stocky kid with a wrestler's build stepped in front of Brittnee. "Don't hurt her."

"Move, hero." Harvey grabbed him by his jacket and tossed him to the side as the frostie loomed over Brittnee. The girl looked up and screamed again, scrambling on her hands and knees to get away.

Harvey hauled back and landed a haymaker on the monster's face. Her fist skidded across ice, tearing her knuckles. The frost demon lunged at her and she grappled with it. They fell together, landing on the wet dirt inches from the fire. She kicked, gouged its eyes with her thumbs. Ice blue claws raked her face.

The berserk roared within her. She needed no battle cry, no ritual to work herself into the battle state. It was always there, always waiting ever since the first time she called it.

Harvey kicked hard, and the frost demon slid backwards enough to let her up. She popped to her feet into a fighting crouch. It hissed at her, flexing its clawed hands. They made a sound like old ice creaking and popping. Its naked muscles gleamed, slick with melting lake water.

They circled, sizing each other up like wrestlers. Even three feet away, Harvey could feel the heat being sucked from her body, the frost demon's hunger for warm life drawing hers into itself. She threw punches, dodging around the milk crates and logs. It grabbed at her arms, claws raking holes in her coat. On the edge of her vision, teens screamed and danced in a panic. The boy she'd called a hero hefted a tree branch in both hands.

The creature opened its mouth, jaws snapping. A sound like the hisses and gurgles of water under ice came out. She kicked it where its ribs should be. Kicked again and got a satisfying crunch. It screamed at her. For a second she thought it called her sister.

Then the hero swung his stick. The frostie ducked and the branch caught Harvey right across the face. Pain. Full of stars. She threw up her arm in self-defense and the monster knocked her to the ground, jaws snapping. They went down in a tangle of limbs.

Claws raked her face and neck. Lines of cold fire seared her. She grunted in pain, rolled and kicked. Her burned eye throbbed, hard and hot with her pulse. The thrum of battle joy grew inside her, but she pressed it back, even as she struck again. She clenched her throat against the war cry even as the frost demon drew blood. Mustn't lose control, not with the kids here. If one of them got in her way, the frostie might not be the monster that hurt them.

The frost demon grappled her to it, jaws snapping near her throat. She forced her arms up between her face and the frost demon, trying to break its grip, but the monster's jaws closed on her wrist.

Her feet slipped and skittered in the mud. The demon's teeth tore through her already-shredded sleeve, ripped away the gauze covering her burned arm. Pain laced through her body. She head-butted the frost demon straight in the forehead. It didn't let go.

"Don't make me do this," she gasped. It bit down, worrying at her wrist like a dog with a bone. With her free hand she punched her enemy in the jaw, once, twice, a third time, her jabs painfully weak at that close distance. The creature held on. Her own blood drooled down her face.

Its claws pressed Harvey's head back, digging into her collarbone. The demon chuckled, a noise like ice settling on the river in deep winter. It shook her from side to side, claws and teeth sinking deeper into her flesh.

She let the berserk out.

Pain gone.

Fear gone.

Nothing left but the battle joy and the closeness of her dear enemy. Heat flooded her limbs. She was invincible again, twenty years old and at the peak of her strength. The deep part of herself she had kept chained up for so long was finally free.

Roaring like a charging bear, Harvey wrapped her arms around the demon like a long-lost lover. Ice ribs crackled and snapped. It screamed. She rolled it into the fire. She met its face with her forehead again, shattering teeth like icicle shards. The demon screamed, letting go of her arm, but her war song drowned out its cries.

Nothing, *no one* could stop her. Never.

She rolled again, her enemy under her, black and red, its blood and hers. She pinned it in the mud beneath her knees and struck for its head, driving her fist straight at its eye. Eyeball and socket cracked together. Blood gushed over her hand. The demon let out a high, thin wail like branches breaking in the wind.

She beat its body into shards and pulp, chanting a war rhyme in the old language. "Die and be gone, water demon, black water's thane. Look on your death in me. Sing your victory song to the shadows and die." She laughed as she sang, full of heat and strength.

The enemy mushed under her hands.

Gone. No one to fight.

Cold crept in. Her war song faded, stuttered to a halt. She beat lifeless slush beside a dead fire, crouched on all fours and panting. Pain came back. Pain and cold, cold shame.

A circle of white faces and wide eyes stared at her. A few gasped with fear. She tried to say, "it's okay," but her swollen tongue clogged with weakness. She reached out a hand, but no one reached back.

She got to her knees, lurching, covered in mud and blood. "It's fine. It's gone."

They broke and ran. Left alone in the woods, wet and freezing, Harvey's burns throbbed. She yawned and wiggled her jaw. Painful as all hell, but not broken.

She tried to wipe one hand clean on her jeans. No use. She touched the back of her hand to her neck where it met her shoulder. Yup, bleeding, a slow ooze. Her wrist throbbed. She clamped a hand over the bite. Fog clouded her head. She leaned on a tree, breathing hard, fighting the urge to lie down and sleep.

"Not here," she said, unable to halt her shivering. "Get moving." Eyes half closed, she slogged forward. Follow the path, get out of the woods. Get to the truck.

She made it home with her fingers so numb she could barely turn the doorknob. Caleb sat at the kitchen table eating a pile of cinnamon toast—half the loaf by the looks of it. He'd put on red and green flannel pajama pants and his baggiest black hoodie. He didn't so much sit in the chair as perch in it, one leg curled under him, the other with his foot on the chair seat and his knee sticking up above the table. With his dark bangs hanging over his eyes, and his body hunched into the loose neck of his hoodie, Caleb looked like a giant crow that had landed on a Christmas package.

At the stove, Ivor, in fresh boxer shorts, a wife beater, and his ancient, brown plaid bathrobe, was cooking eggs. He hadn't shaved, but by the damp in his white mustache and the smell of Old Spice, he'd been up long enough to take a shower. As soon as Ivor saw her, he swore and dropped the frying pan of scrambled eggs onto the stove. "Who did this?"

"Frostie." He tried to pull her into a chair, but she waved him off. "Is Mal back?" she asked.

Ivor and Caleb shook their heads. Great. She turned to go back out, but she shuddered with cold so hard her teeth clattered together. "I'm—" *Food. Need food and warmth.* She dumped her keys and cell phone on the table and scrambled through the cabinets until she found the honey bear. She squirted honey directly into her mouth, the taste of concentrated sunshine spreading through her.

"You want some eggs?" Ivor said.

She nodded hard and turned on the hot water at the sink, plunging her freezing hands into the stream until they burned with returning feeling. Ivor poured her a mug of hot coffee. At the table, Caleb watched her with wide eyes and a full mouth.

When she had some feeling back in her hands, she struggled out of her wet and muddy coat. She hung it to drip onto the boot mat. Her fingers were too numb to wrestle with her bootlaces. She dumped half a cup of sugar into her coffee and tucked into the eggs.

Caleb asked, "What's a frostie?"

She waved him off with the fork and took another bite of eggs. Soon the plate was empty. The post-berserk fog crowded in on her and she slumped for a minute, head cradled in her hands. God, she wanted a beer and someplace warm to curl up. She scrubbed her hands over her face, trying to think. The late afternoon sun slanted through the window over the sink. The light made the wood of the table glow amber, warm and safe. But outside it would be dark in an hour. Sooner, if the clouds blew up.

She needed to get back out there, but her jeans were wet and coated with mud. Her long hair had come half unbraided. Loose strands of hair tickled her face and neck. She had to get changed before she went out again. And with the berserk gone, she could feel all thirty-eight of her years and more. As she slumped at the table, the pooch of stomach fat that had gotten bigger with each child reminded her that her days of flat abs and a tight rear end were well behind her.

Ivor put more coffee in her cup and began scrambling up another batch of eggs for himself. "Get yourself warmed again," he said, "and I'll go out with you. We'll find Mal." There was a catch in his breath as he said it, a hint of a wheeze. But she didn't have time to worry about that. The temperature outside was already dropping.

"Caleb, help me," Harvey said. "Where else would your sister go?"

He squirmed in his chair, peering out at her under his bangs with one stockinged foot up on the seat, his bony knee tucked under his chin. "I don't really know..."

"So help me, if you're covering for her, you're both grounded. This is serious!"

He gave her a wounded look, his pale blue eyes wide. "I'm not!" He pointed to the phone. "Why don't you track her phone?" He grabbed Harvey's phone and tapped in her passcode, thumbs flying.

Hope surged in Harvey's chest. But Caleb slouched back down, grimacing, and tossed the phone on the table. "No luck. She turned locations off."

"Can't you force it to tell you?" Harvey reached for the phone. "Lost mode or recovery or something, right?"

Caleb rolled his eyes at her. "I tried that."

"Great. So wherever she's gone it's somewhere she knows she's not supposed to be." Harvey gulped down her coffee and got up again, reaching for her coat. "I'm going back out there. Ivor, stay here." She held up a hand as he objected. "You need to protect Caleb. Call me if she comes back."

Caleb scrambled to his feet. "Wait. I'll go with you." Harvey's heart skipped a beat. The feverish glitter was back in his eyes so that they almost shone out from under the edge of his black hoodie. The red slash on his hand from the previous night throbbed red.

"No. Stay here with Grampa."

He huffed in frustration. "What is going on? The ravens are all talking, we got attacked last night, now Mal is missing and you're all beat up. Take me with you! I can help."

"No, you can't." Harvey pulled on her coat. The motion made the burns across her chest pull and sting. "I want you here where it's safe."

"Mom!" Caleb threw up his hands. "This isn't fair!"

"Life isn't fair!" she shouted back.

At that, Caleb kicked over a chair and stormed out of the kitchen. A few seconds later, his bedroom door slammed hard enough to rattle windows. Ivor and Harvey exchanged glances.

"Maybe you should take him with you," Ivor said. He scratched thoughtfully at the white chest hair that stuck up above the neckline of his tank top. His hands, widened from years of work and arthritis were almost as broad as they were long.

"Why? So he can get eaten? Or worse? He doesn't know the first thing about fighting."

"So teach him. Before it's too late."

Harvey grimaced. "I don't have time for this. Call me if Mal comes back." She grabbed her cell phone and went out the kitchen door. Ravens watched from the roofline and the trees as she climbed back into the truck to start the search again. She had to find Mal before darkness fell.

CHAPTER

TWENTY-TWO

In the garage office the phone was ringing. And ringing. And ringing.

Carl, elbow deep in an engine, yelled across the shop, "Someone answer the damn phone." It kept ringing. "Lars! Where are you? Dan, you here?"

No, Dan had gone out hours ago. He glanced at the clock on the wall. Lars' fifteen-minute break should have been over by now, but he was nowhere in sight. Chris, the other guy who worked at the shop, had come in early and already clocked out. "Lars!"

No answer.

Muttering and scraping his hands clean on a rag, he went to get the phone. It stopped ringing. Harvey's number blinked on the screen—four missed calls, one message. For a second he stared at the ceiling, imagining that he was going to put the phone down and pretend he hadn't heard it ring. Instead, he pressed play.

"Mal's missing. You have to help me find her."

"Would it kill you to say please, woman?" Carl muttered under his breath and hit the redial button. No answer, but the crunch of tires on gravel told him someone had come into the lot.

Five seconds later, Harvey walked in. Her chestnut brown hair was a wild tangle, as if the wind had followed her indoors. A new scrape showed over her eyepatch, but her good eye gleamed like lightning and her cheeks glowed red. All she needed was a sword in one hand and gold at her throat to be the queen he remembered. His heart swelled in his chest, bumping up against the knot in his throat.

He chucked the phone onto the desk and smiled. "Welcome to Carl's Classic Cars, stranger. How are you doing today?"

"My brand new teenage berserker is missing, that's how I'm doing. Have you got her?" She looked around as if she might start tossing cars in her search.

"You know, you used to have a sense of humor." A breathing silence answered him, Harvey's nostrils flaring.

Light dawned. "You're all wound up from a berserk, aren't you?" He shoved an office chair at her. "Sit down. Get yourself together."

"I need to find Mal!"

He held out empty palms to her, pitching his voice low. "Not like that you don't. You might hurt her. Come on, sit down."

Harvey's face fell. She nodded and dropped into the broken-seated, overstuffed chair by his desk. A tremor crept into her hands and she sat, pulling her arms in for warmth. The fevered glow in her cheeks was edged with gray.

Carl poured her a cup from the coffee maker and dumped in the last of the sugar. The creamer was gone. Probably none upstairs either. Even with creamer it was a far cry from bread and honey, beer and mead. "Here." He shoved the super sweetened coffee sludge at her. She curled her lip but gulped it down.

While she drank the coffee, he turned a desk chair around and sat across it, arms leaning on the back. The metal parts squeaked under him. "What happened? Who'd you beat up?"

Shoulders drooping, her head down over her mug, she said, "A frostie. It tried to eat a bunch of kids. I didn't have a choice." She sounded like an alcoholic confessing she'd fallen off the wagon. "And now I can't find her anywhere."

He scratched his beard. "Did you try Arn's?"

A hint of her mother bear growl crept back in to her tone. "How the hell would she know about Arn's? I don't even know where Arn's is these days."

"It's in the alley back of St. Lawrence Street."

"Oh. That empty area?"

He nodded, rolling his wrists. He didn't know if it was the cold or all the extra work or what, but his hands and wrists were always stiff these days. Or it could be that he was pushing forty. *Yeah, could be that too.*

Her face bent down toward her mug, she said, "How is everybody?"

"Pretty much the same. A little grayer, a bit fatter. Not many youngsters, except Lars. Arn's still the best brewmaster in the world, but he won't go get a loan and start a legitimate business because then he'd have to let the IRS know he existed. Mac's cock of the walk since there's nobody around to put him in his place."

Her shoulders sagged and she seemed to shrink in on herself. Looking up into his eyes, she said, "You could do it. Be king." It sounded like a request.

"I never wanted to be king."

"No, I suppose not," Harvey replied. "Are there... Are any of the girls left?"

"They all stopped coming pretty soon after you left. Kids. That sort of thing."

"Yeah. That makes sense." Still hunched over her mug, her voice sad and far away, she said, "There's not much time left to be a fool when you've got kids."

Carl banged his fist on the desk so hard its metal sides boomed. It sounded like thunder rolling in the background.

She flinched. "I didn't mean it that way."

"Yes. Yes, you did." He stood, breathing hard. "Is that what I am to you? Your fool?"

She shook her head, her eyes brimming. Wisps of her dark hair hung over her face, tangled like water weeds. "I'm sorry. I meant me, not you."

Snorting, his arms crossed over his chest, he propped his butt back against the desk, eyes on the ceiling, not ready to let go of the anger yet.

Harvey swept the hair out of her face and tried to put the mug down on the desk, but there was no room where it wouldn't leave a coffee ring on some piece of paperwork. Carefully, she set the mug on the floor. "Thanks for the coffee. I've got to get going."

He watched her go, his arms still crossed over his chest. As she got to the door he shouted after her, "We're not all fools, you know."

Her shoulders slumped. She half turned, one hand still on the door and opened her mouth. She shut it again, turning away. The door banged behind her.

He blew out a long breath and looked through the office window into the shop. There were ten cars lined up that needed work. Good, respectable work that paid the bills and kept his hands busy. But for a few minutes he let his mind's eye call the shots—a forge, bright with fire warmed the open garage. The stamp of hooves waiting to be shod in the yard outside. Apprentices working the bellows, learning weaponcraft from him. And a woman's voice calling the children—his children—to come and wash their hands.

He passed a rough hand over his eyes. He was, indeed, a fool.

He ought to get the plow attached to the truck soon—with the weather getting cold so early, the first snowfall wouldn't be too many days off. He glanced at the clock on the wall. Four-thirty and the last of the sun was already gone. It would be full dark in no time. *Shit.* Carl grabbed his keys and rolled down the garage doors with a bang.

"Lars! Get your ass down here. Now." He stood at the base of the stairs to the apartment and yelled again. If that boy didn't show in ten seconds, he was going up there and dragging him back down by his stupid hair.

At two seconds to go, Lars pounded down the stairs, his short blond dreads more askew than usual and his eyes still sleepy. "Sorry, boss. I laid down on the couch and kind of forgot to wake up." He yawned without bothering to cover his mouth. "What's up?"

"We've got to find a girl. I'll explain on the way. And Fisherman's Park has got more frosties in it. Come on."

Lars rolled his neck and shoulders, joints popping. "Man, I hate having to do things twice. That's why I always hated math. Double check your work. Double check your work. Blah blah blah." He followed Carl out to the truck, rambling about his high school years.

Before getting into the cab, Carl checked his box of gear behind the front seat. Chainmail shirt, oiled and ready. Heavy duty flashlights, two of them. Helmet. First-aid kit. And his axe in the gun rack. Ready for anything.

He flicked on the police scanner as they eased out into the road. "Focus. Keep your eyes open."

Lars leaned back, arms spread across the seat. "I can talk and look at the same time. You worry too much."

Carl let himself chuckle. Hard to stay irritated with Lars for some reason. Even his parole officer kind of liked him.

"What are we looking for anyway? Give me the 411."

"A girl named Mallory. She's white."

"With a name like that? You didn't have to tell me."

Carl rolled his eyes. "Have you looked in the mirror lately? Anyway, blond hair. Seventeen. Shit, I don't know how tall she is. I'm guessing tall. She's got to be—her dad was my height and her mom's five-ten. Runs track."

"Oh I get it. Yeah, I see how it is. Her mom's that queen lady with the man's name whose truck we tipped back on its wheels. She sent you out to go rescue her little princess."

Carl focused on the road.

Lars kept nodding. "Yep. Uh huh. I see how this works. She says jump and you say how high."

He tightened his grip on the steering wheel. "Mal's only berserked once in her life before and she doesn't know the first thing about fighting. If she gets caught by a frostie it'll kill her. Even her mom couldn't have taken on one of those before she'd learned a thing or two. Mal's been sheltered. Way more than Harvey ever was. Besides, I was friends with her dad."

"Yeah, but it's her mom you want to bang." Lars' voice was cheerful, matter of fact.

Carl white knuckled the steering wheel. "Just shut up and keep an eye out. Before I strap your ass to the hood."

"You got it, boss. Whatever you say."

He drove on, only the crackle of the police scanner making a peep. The last rays of the sun faded, leaving only the yellow street-lights to hold off the dark.

TWENTY-THREE

C arl's stomach growled as he eased the truck down another street in the gray twilight. His truck's lights shone on the growing fog, the kind that promises freezing rain later.

"I'm starving," Lars said, right on cue.

"Me too. But we need to find her."

"Why us? That's what I don't get. Oh hey," he punched Carl in the shoulder. "Like are you the real daddy? Is that it? You and the queen lady had some sort of hot and heavy thing going on way back when and then you broke up after her old man died 'cause she was wracked with guilt and so she wouldn't let you see the kid, but now she needs your help, so we're out combing the streets for your long lost baby girl."

Carl slammed on the brakes hard enough that Lars jerked forward against the seatbelt. "What the hell is wrong with you?"

"I dunno. Boredom. Just trying to bring a little romance to the situation."

"You're nineteen. Where do you get romance from?"

A blush spread over Lars's cheeks all the way to his ear tips.

"That's all they had in the library at juvie and we had lockdown a lot. It was better than being bored."

"Learn to live with being bored. It's a grownup skill."

"Meh. Growing up is overrated. Next thing you know, you're old. I'll skip it."

Carl had to laugh at that. "You should have been born a thousand years ago and been some king's *thyle*."

"What's that? Badass warrior?"

"Some of them were. But it was more like a professional smart ass."

"Sweet."

A driver behind them laid on the horn. Carl started and took his foot off the brake. "Look, Jon Otvar was the best friend I ever had. I wouldn't have touched his wife if she'd shown up in my bed naked. Which she would never have done. They were high school sweethearts and she loved him like crazy. Now look out the window and keep your crazy theories to yourself."

Lars shifted around in his seat, close enough to his window that his breath fogged it up. "What about after he died? Why didn't you make a move then?"

"She was in mourning!" Eight years ago. Carl sighed and turned down a new street. "We did talk...a bit about it. It was a few years ago. But, um, our lifestyles don't really match up. It wouldn't have worked."

Lars grunted. They continued to hunt in silence, their stomachs complaining from time to time. Eventually, Lars said, "This is stupid. We are not going to find jack like this."

Carl had to agree. They weren't looking for a lost dog that might be trotting along the side of the road. Mal was probably holed up in some friend's basement having a beer and bitching about her mom. But if she wasn't and he gave up... He couldn't risk it.

"Can we at least run through a drive through or something? Or, hey here's an idea, let's go ask for help. If we go to Arn's somebody there might have seen her. Dan's probably there. He could help us look. Come on."

Carl rolled his eyes. "You're not fooling anyone." But he smiled and turned the truck toward the river. Maybe Dan would help. And they'd pass a drive-thru on the way.

"I cannot drink that piss water they sell at the store anymore. Seriously, Arn's stuff is like..." He spread his hands, looking for the right words.

"Like the brew they drink in Valhalla."

"Yeah okay, whatever that is. It's good is what I'm saying."

The streets around Arn's were dark; only one in five streetlights still worked. The few remaining businesses and residents in this hollowed-out industrial wasteland probably generated so few taxes that in the city council's mind they basically didn't exist. And people who don't exist, don't need streetlights. As he got out of the truck, Lars stuffed the last of his drive-thru burrito into his mouth and tossed the wrapper into the gutter where it skittered away on the wind.

"Don't do that," Carl said.

"Why not? Who's it going to hurt?"

"Try not to be a complete barbarian, okay?"

Lars bowed elaborately and picked up the wrapper, stuffing it in his pocket. "Yes, my lord. I will endeavor to be on my best behavior as we enter this fine, um, place of drinking." He stuck his hands in his pockets and walked down the alley whistling.

For a second, Carl thought of taking his axe with him. But that was stupid—things never went beyond a punch and a tussle in there. No one in Arn's was out to get him. Besides, Arn had a rule against weapons. He locked the truck and headed after Lars. Still, walking down the dark alley unarmed made his shoulder blades itch.

Arn's was loud tonight, louder than it had been in a long time. Shouts and laughter came out the door the second Lars opened it. They exchanged questioning looks.

The tables and chairs were pushed back to make an open space in the middle. A crowd of laughing, cheering, jostling men three deep the center. Some stood on benches and chairs in the back. Others shouted bets and encouragement. And Mal stood dead center of it all.

Her face flushed with beer and exercise, she threw punches as fast as her opponent could block them. Battle joy lit up her face, sweat pouring off it. She landed a hard right hook on the guy's shoulder, missing his face, and followed it with a left jab that knocked the air out of him. He crumpled, knees buckling. A cheer echoed off the ceiling.

"I win! I win!" Mal danced around the ring, pumping her fists over her head and high fiving lucky gamblers. The unlucky paid up and cursed. With her hair in a rough ponytail and her eyes shining she was the spitting image of her mother.

Carl took out his phone and sent Harvey a quick text. The next second he was muttering, "Oh fuck no," and shoving men aside as she started to pull off her t-shirt Mia Hamm style. He elbowed, kneed, and pushed until he reached her. He caught the back of her shirt with one hand and yanked it back down just as she got it to her neck.

"Hands off, perv!" She wheeled around on him, fists up.

He held up his hands, palms up. "It's okay. I'm not trying to touch you. You remember me?"

"Carl!" She threw her arms around his neck, flopping into his chest. She reeked of beer. "I like you. You're a hero." She looked up at him, "Nice beard. Very lumberjack. You should wear more flannel."

"Okay, time to go." He tried to steer her toward the door.

She squealed and jerked away. "I have to fight this other guy, over," she flapped her hand, "over there somewhere. I'm winning." She tripped, hit the floor in a heap, and popped back up. "Who's next?"

Carl grabbed for her shoulders, but his grip was too tentative. The last thing in the world he wanted was to be manhandling his friend's drunk teenage daughter. Cold sweat broke out all over his scalp as he tried to shoo her towards the door, flapping his hands as if chasing a chicken.

Mal laughed and dodged. More cheers. Some boos and "Back off, Carl," from the crowd. The crowd surged closer.

"Yeah, back off, Carl," Mac said. "You heard the young lady." Eight of Mac's boys stepped forward as the rest of the crowd eased back. Mac and his crew formed a rough circle around Carl and Mal, blocking the way to the door. Lars did a quick sidestep and ducked away into the crowd, pulling Mal with him. That left Carl alone in the center of a slowly tightening circle.

He breathed deep, calling to the battle rage to be ready. The world narrowed to the lit circle in which he stood. Everything beyond was dim noise and shadows. Carl let out a long, slow breath and focused his attention.

"She's underage, Mac," he said.

Mac's hyena grin widened. "Won't be the first illegal thing I've done tonight."

Carl flexed his fingers, shifting his weight forward, wishing he had his axe in hand. If Mac put one greasy paw on this girl he'd split him in half, axe or no axe. "You know who she is, right? You know what's going to happen to every one of you if she gets hurt?"

Mac held up his hands as if pleading with heaven to witness his innocence, but his hungry smile said otherwise. "Who's talking about hurting her? This is just a little welcome party for Heidrek's niece. About time somebody brought her into the fold."

Carl took a step forward, towering over Mac. "Was that you? Because if it was, so help me—"

Dan's hand landed on his shoulder. "Relax. It was me."

Carl spun on his heel, ready to meet the attack. But it was only his friend. His heart thundered in his ears for a second, as he adjusted. Finally, he said, "Why? Why would you do that?"

"She needed to know. I'm not letting Harvey turn her into some weakling."

Inside Carl, the anger rose up higher and hotter than before. Mac had always been a shit stain of a human, but Dan—Dan was supposed to be his friend.

"What is wrong with you?" he shouted. His chest collided with Dan's, their faces close enough to feel each other's breath. "You think this is a joke?"

There was no laughter in Dan's brown eyes as he spat back, "You're the joke here."

The crowd around them edged back. Some part of Carl's brain told him to get it together, not to let this go any further, but out loud he said, "I am not taking this shit from you."

"No, but you'll say 'how high' every time Harvey tells you to jump." Dan's wind-beaten face was all harsh lines, his dark, unbraided hair falling forward to shadow his eyes. He stepped closer, shoving against Carl.

Carl put his hands up against his friend's chest and pushed. Through gritted teeth he growled "Back. Off."

Dan planted his feet, eye to eye, chest jutting. Carl took a step back and pasted him in the cheekbone.

In a split second they were rolling on the floor, punching, kicking, scrambling for a fingerhold. All around them men shouted and whistled, stamped their feet. They rolled through crackling peanut shells. Men skipped out of the way.

They rolled under a table. Carl's shoulder bashed into the table leg and he kicked Dan off him. The table splintered and fell on top of them. Both flailed, trying to knock away the tabletop and punch the other one at the same time. Dan's blows were wild, unfocused, but every one that landed was like being hit with a brick. Carl got him by the hair and kneed him in the stomach. Dan spat in his eyes.

Half blinded, Carl tried to throw Dan away from him, but his friend had him by the shirt and they both went down in a heap again, kicking and punching. Carl straddled him, raining punches on his face. Dan sat up and bit him in the arm, right where the stitches tugged at the skin.

"Knock it off! Idiots." Cold beer sloshed over them. Carl gasped, trying to wipe the beer out of his eyes. Underneath him, Dan started to laugh, a harsh and broken sound.

Harvey stood over them with an empty pitcher in one hand. Behind her Lars had pieces of a broken chair in his hands, raised like a weapon. All around the room, men stared from a safe distance. Toward the back, Arn stood guard over his kegs with a baseball bat in his hands.

TWENTY-FOUR

T he lamps flickered in the draft when Harvey walked in, but all eyes were on the room's center where Dan and Carl struggled on the floor. Men stood on chairs to get a better view; cash passed from hand to hand. Mac danced back and forth with the rolling men like an unrecognized referee, spittle flying from his mouth.

Harvey spotted Mal on the far side of the room, hair in a sweat-soaked rat's nest, her clothes torn. A rangy, blond kid with short dreadlocks and an ugly, homemade tattoo of a flaming skull on his arm was putting his hand on Mal's shoulder and talking into her ear. He had a bruise the size of a saucer on his right cheek and the marks of frostbite on his ears. And he had the berserker glint in his eye, the little extra dose of crazy she knew too well. Mal ignored him, her eyes focused on the fight.

There was no way she was getting Mal out of here unnoticed. Might as well make a statement. Harvey grabbed a full pitcher of beer of a nearby table and elbowed her way through the crowd until she was in the circle.

"Knock it off!" She flung the beer straight into both fighters' faces. The crowd froze. Carl reeled, and pushed back from Dan, pawing at his eyes. Dan choked and lost his grip.

"Idiots. What is wrong with you?" Harvey stepped over the two men and grabbed Mal by the wrist, pulling her away from the boy. "Get your hands off my daughter, blondie." She unleashed just enough of the berserk into her voice that the growl vibrated her breastbone.

The kid's eyes went wide and he stepped back.

"Come on." She turned her back on him and dragged Mal along, past Dan and Carl.

"No." Mal jerked away. Her wrist slipped in Harvey's grip, the tug strong enough to pull Harvey up short. "I'm not done here. Dan can give me a ride home."

"I wouldn't let him walk you across the street."

Laughs and jeers from the men. Arn had gotten out his baseball bat. *Shit. So much for making it out the door while they were all still wondering what was going on.* Harvey shifted her grip on Mal's arm and gave the circle of men a warning glare. "Come on. We're leaving."

"Harvey, stop." Carl struggled to his feet, hands out, imploring. Dan rose up behind him, popping his jaw and shaking out his hands.

"Get out of my way," she hissed. "You're supposed to be helping me."

Mac sidled into view, out of arm's reach. "Yeah Carl, you're supposed to be helping. Do whatever the queen wants, Carl. Get down on your knees, Carl."

The red in Carl's face deepened, but he didn't turn toward Mac. "It's too late, Harvey. She knows what she is. She needs to know what that means."

"She is my daughter, not yours," Harvey snapped. "I decide who tells her what and when."

"Then teach her yourself, goddammit!" Carl yelled in her face. "Before some jackoff like Mac does it for you."

"Hey!" Mal wriggled her hand out of Harvey's. "I'm right here. You don't have to talk about me like I'm a toddler."

Harvey's hand curled into a fist at her side, her eyes locked with Carl's. "You are on thin ice."

Carl took a step toward her. "You're threatening me? I'm the one who came down here and found your baby girl. You wouldn't have known where she was if it wasn't for me."

"Oh, I'm sorry. I forgot to say thank you." The grins on men's faces faded as her voice rose. "Thank you so much for bringing that motorcycle riding maniac back to town. And thank you from the bottom of my heart for giving my daughter a live demonstration of bar fighting. I'm sure that skill's going to look fantastic on her college applications next year. Maybe they'll let her major in finding trouble and you can be her internship supervisor."

A nervous laugh rippled around the room.

Carl breathed hard and his jaw worked, but no words came out. "I...you..." he stammered.

"I what?" Harvey said.

Instead of answering, he looked past Harvey to Mal. "You want to learn how to be a berserker? When you turn eighteen you come down to the shop and I'll teach you whatever you want to know."

White-hot rage flooded through Harvey like acid in her veins. It took all her self control not to grab him by the throat. "Don't you dare."

Their faces were so close she felt his breath on her cheek. "You're not queen around here anymore. You said so yourself. Ether step up and lead or stop expecting me to follow."

Men cheered and whooped.

"Hey, hot stuff!" the dreadlocked blond danced up. He flinched as Harvey turned on him, but that didn't stop him from talking, "From what I heard, you used to be the Queen of Finding Trouble. Before you got all fat and full of yourself."

A louder, more confident laugh spread around the room. Harvey took a deep, calming breath and grabbed him by the shirt front, yanking him toward her.

She let the full berserk resonate in her voice as she spoke. "Listen to me, young man. I did not find trouble; I made it. And I will make the kind of trouble for you that your grandchildren will regret if you open your mouth to me again. Understand?" She released him with a shove.

Eyes wide, the boy said, "Yes, ma'am."

"Mal, get in the truck. Now."

Mal opened her mouth and shut it again, nodding. Harvey stalked toward the door, barely missing Carl with her shoulder as she passed.

Dan moved to block her path, his hand reaching out to Mal. Faster than a striking cobra Harvey hit him in the temple. He fell backward, landing like a sack of potatoes. She charged out the door, shoving Mal in front of her.

Once in the alley, she took Mal's hand and broke into a run, dragging her daughter down the alley to the truck. She shoved Mal into the front and peeled out, tires squealing before either of them had their seatbelts on.

TWENTY-FIVE

The door to Arn's slammed behind Harvey. No one moved. On the floor, Dan rubbed his head.

Slowly, his eyes still on the door, Lars let out a long sigh.

"Yeah! That's right. And don't come back, bitch." Mac gave the door the finger and grabbed his crotch.

Carl turned on him. "Shut up, Mac. The only reason she didn't lay you out cold was you're too piddling small to matter."

An uneasy laugh spread through the room. With too much banging and rattling, Arn stepped between them, putting tables and chairs back to rights. Mac took a step toward Carl, thought better of it, and veered off toward the bar.

Carl's shoulders sagged. *I'm too old for this.* "Here." He held out a hand to Dan, who glared it away and got to his feet unaided. Dan stomped behind the bar, grabbed a bottle despite Arn's yell, and retreated to a bench in an unlit corner farthest from the door. Carl sighed and bent to pick up bits of broken chair.

"Eh. Throw 'em on the woodpile," Arn said, pointing to a box beside the iron stove.

"Sorry, Arn."

"Eh, happens all the time. I'll get some more next time I go down to Goodwill for glassware." Arn swept on, his broom knocking the feet of those still standing and muttering.

Carl turned toward Lars. "You alright? You're pale as a ghost."

Lars nodded, his short blond dreads shaking. "Did you see the look in her eyes? I thought she was going to eat my face."

"She saw you with Mal. Don't even think about it. You'd be safer trying to steal a cub from a mother bear."

Lars nodded dumbly. Carl patted him awkwardly on the shoulder and went behind the bar to get two shot glasses. He took them over to where Dan drank in the shadows.

"Fuck off." Dan took a deep swig from the bottle. The smell of clover and lavender distilled in a bee's stomach spread around them.

"I'm sorry."

Dan took another drink. They sat in silence, the rest of the room giving them a wide berth. Even Lars had the sense to stay away for once.

Arn finished his sweeping. Men paid their tabs or made their excuses and drifted out a few at a time. Eventually it was only the two of them. Dan fingered the bear claw that hung from his neck, the half-empty bottle dangling in one hand. "Women."

Carl laughed. "Love her or hate her, you'd have a hard time finding another woman like that."

"I suppose so." He handed the bottle to Carl.

"Thanks, man." The mead warmed without burning. The old stories said it was god vomit, the stuff that poetry and madmen were made of. He took another swig.

"You know Heidrek's getting out?" Dan said.

"I know he's up for parole. Harvey's going down to try to stop it. You?"

"They'd give him another ten years just for knowing me." He took the bottle back. Drank. "We going out tonight or what?"

"Yeah. Might as well. I figured we'd sweep around Fisherman's Park again."

Dan shook his head in disgust.

"We'll go somewhere else. North up the river?"

"Fine with me."

"Great." He stood, clapped Dan on the shoulder and finished the bottle before heading to the bar to pay their tab and collect Lars. If they got their work done quickly, maybe they'd be home before midnight.

Maybe.

As Harvey sped away from Arn's, Mal settled into a dark sulk, sliding down until her back was nearly horizontal with the seat.

"Put your seatbelt on," Harvey said.

Mal met her eyes in the rearview mirror and sat a little straighter, reaching for the seatbelt.

Harvey forced her foot off the accelerator, even if the streets around here were deserted. She breathed carefully, concentrating on little things—the stop sign ahead, the sound of the engine. Anything calm and normal. Still the urge to rage and punch things didn't let up. In this mood she felt like she could rip the steering wheel out of the dashboard if she wasn't careful.

Mal kicked the underside of the dash. Harvey tightened her grip on the steering wheel. Another kick.

"Stop it."

Kick.

Keeping her voice even, she said, "Mal, you do that again and I will dump you in the lake until you cool off. You are in so much trouble."

Mal turned toward her, seatbelt straining, "That's rich coming from you. How much trouble did you get into when you went out looking for fights in bars?"

Harvey kept her mouth closed and her eyes on the road.

"Or when you went drag racing?" Mal persisted. "Or when you got into a monster hunting contest with dad?"

Mal dropped back into her seat, arms crossed like she'd won the fight.

Harvey glanced down at the speedometer. She was doing sixty-five in a thirty-five zone, and they'd reached more populated streets. There were actually other drivers to look out for now. Harvey took a deep breath and eased back on the accelerator.

She drove in silence until she could find the right words. "Mal, I also had unprotected sex in the back of cars, drank myself stupid more than once, and ditched class so much I graduated with a C-average. I got in a lot of trouble. That doesn't mean any of it was a good idea."

"It all turned out fine." Mal said.

"No. It didn't."

Mal rolled her eyes. "You're alive. You've got a good job, a house, and two kids. How is that not fine?"

Harvey's voice cracked as she forced out the words. "I have no friends. My brother is in jail. My husband is dead. I'm working time and a half to pay the mortgage and keep food on the table at a job that could get shipped overseas any day now. Oh, and I'm raising two kids on my own and failing at it. Badly."

She pulled the truck up at a stoplight, the red circle swimming in her vision. Dammit, she wasn't supposed to cry for at least a week. She stared hard at the light, willing the tears to go away. Instead they slid down her cheek and under collar. Her burned eye stung with saltwater. Beside her Mal stayed silent.

The light changed and she shifted into neutral, letting the slight downhill slope pull her forward behind a grandma mobile going creeping into the intersection. Behind her horns blared. Rush hour in Buffalo.

At the next light, Mal said, "You're not a total failure as a mom."

"Well, I haven't beaten either of you kids lately, so that's something."

Mal half giggled, but her arms stayed crossed. "You're such a hard ass. You don't let us do anything, but you got away with doing everything."

Traffic moved again. Silence filled the car.

Eventually, Harvey said. "I wasn't allowed to run wild. I fought with my mom about it all the time. And I got away with a hell of a lot less than my brother ever did. Which was probably for the best, considering where he ended up. At least I have the same standards for you and Caleb. And my parents were a ton rougher on me than I have ever been on you. My mom even locked me out of the house a couple of times."

"Why?"

"Because I snuck out when she told me not to. Or came back drunk."

"See, that's what I'm talking about! You got away with it."

"I lived to tell about it. There's a difference."

"You stole your brother's sword."

"It was as much mine as his. And it needed doing."

"Why?"

Harvey looked over at Mal. "You really want to know? I'll show you." She jerked the wheel hard right, veering across three lanes of traffic and cutting off a minivan. The truck rocked on its wheels as she made the right turn onto a side street just in time to turn hard into the street's left-handed S-curve. Mal held on to her seat, eyes wide.

Harvey gunned it out of the next light and down the road, dodging cars, weaving like she was playing a video game until she made another hairpin turn and skidded to a halt in the St. Stanislaus cemetery parking lot, right in front of the open gates. The sodium streetlights cast a sickly yellow glow over the cast iron fencing.

Turning in her seat, she said, "You like living dangerously? Get out of the truck."

Mal didn't move. She crossed her arms over her still connected seatbelt. "I know Dad's dead, Mom," Mal said.

"Get. Out." Harvey reached across her daughter and flipped open the passenger side door.

Once she'd gotten out of the truck and slammed her own door, Harvey hopped the chain across the cemetery road and turned on the flashlight in her phone. She strode out toward the far corner plot near the creek, not looking back to see if Mal was following. If nothing else, her daughter's curiosity would get the better of her.

Stretching her legs felt good. It gave the lingering berserk somewhere to go. Tonawanda Creek curved around the small cemetery on its way to the Niagara River so the land was hemmed in on two sides with water. Wet sod squished beneath her feet. Behind her, Mal jogged to catch up, grumbling about getting her sneakers wet.

Harvey walked hard until she reached her husband's grave. A short, rough stone with one polished face marked the spot. It shone in the light from her phone. *Jon Otvar. Beloved Husband and Father.* Other stones dotted the grass in a wide swath. No rich monuments or burning ships full of gold for her people. Not anymore. For most of them, it was nothing but a piece of half-polished granite with a name and a date. To one side was a little mausoleum, no bigger than a garden shed, maintained by the Sons of Cnut for their own who couldn't afford even that much.

"Here's your dad." Harvey pointed.

Mal hugged her arms around herself, looking down at the plain stone. "You say that like it was his fault."

"It was." Her throat hurt again, but she kept her voice steady. "I loved him, but it was his fault."

"Lots of people get in car accidents."

"That's what I told you kids. You were too young, and I didn't want you to know the world had monsters in it. The truth is, he went out hunting frosties alone. Because he was bored. That's it. He was bored; and it killed him. The last thing he said to me was 'Don't worry. I'll be fine. I always am.'"

Mal hugged herself tighter.

Harvey pointed the light from her phone at another two graves. "Both your grandmothers died of heart attacks—probably caused by all those nights wondering if their men were coming home drunk or beaten half to death. Or not coming back at all. Mom barely made it past my high school graduation. Your dad's mom lived long enough to go to our wedding a couple years later. And there's your grandfather, my dad. And all the others." She swept her arm in a wide arc, the light flashing across the polished faces of the gravestones.

Harvey took Mal by the arm and moved again. She picked her way between the graves, careful not to step on them until she stopped in front of the standing stone, taller than her head. Rough cut outlines of dragons twined and knotted across the stone. Along their bodies carved runes ran, painted in rusty red like dried blood.

Harvey crouched in front of it, shining her light over the very lowest runes, translating out loud. *Here is Snorri Wulfgarsson. Here is Otvar and Carl the Swede. I, Wulfgar, did this.*

"This stone used to stand up in Nova Scotia, but my great-grandfather helped bring it down here. This is his name." Harvey pointed to a spot. She rose, following the red spiral with the light as more names were added. Initials appeared in cramped spaces. She pointed to a space on the stone's back. "And this is your grandfather. And this is your dad. Ivor helped us write out the runes correctly. Carl carved it and I painted in the lines once spring came."

Jon Otvar. He was mighty.

Harvey smiled as she read Jon's name. He was mighty.

Beside her, Mal reached out. She shivered as she ran her hands across runes like broken twigs. "It's powerful." Her words came out hushed.

Harvey nodded, tears pricking in the corners of her eyes. "Yeah."

She eased the eye patch up to press her cold fingers over the burning in her eye.

Mal got out her own phone light and walked around the stone, fingers tracing the curve of the dragon. "What are you trying to tell me? They were all dumbasses who got killed for nothing? Or that they were all heroes and here's their monument?" Mal's angry pout had faded to a sad, thoughtful look.

Harvey shoved her hands into her pockets. Her own angry scowl relaxed into tired slackness. "I'm trying to tell you that even the mightiest heroes die. And they leave people behind who needed them." She turned her head so she could see Mal's face, sunk as it was into her collar. "I need you. I need you and your brother to stay alive."

"You're still alive. And so's Carl and Dan."

Harvey laughed. "Fortune sometimes favors the bold, if his courage is good. That's what Carl would tell you anyway." The wind off the lake stung her exposed ears. The wind took on a colder edge with the loss of the light.

Mal rocked back and forth on her feet, her eyes on the ground. "I'm not trying to get myself killed, Mom. It's just...somebody has to beat up the Taylor Padowskis of the world."

"Does it have to be you?"

Mal shrugged, shoulders rising to her ears. "Maybe. Who else will do it?"

Harvey sighed and put her arm around Mal. After a second's hesitation, Mal relaxed against her shoulder. They stood together, their harsh phone lights casting sharp shadows into the darkness. Beyond the cemetery the city glowed under low cloud cover.

Still against her, Mal said, "If you were so set on staying home and taking care of us, why did you pick a fight with Uncle Heidrek? The guys said you made a big show at Grampa's funeral, said you were queen and everything. I don't get it. Why not let him have the sword?"

"Because it's cursed. If I'd let him have that sword, sooner or later he'd have murdered someone with it. Probably me. Or your father. Or one of you. It's a kinslayer, that sword. Every generation of our family, someone has killed one of their own kin with it."

"Get out." Mal pulled away from Harvey. A half smile quirked up her mouth. "Magic swords aren't real."

Harvey laughed. "You believe in monsters, but not magic swords?"

Mal rolled her eyes and laughed a little too. "I don't know anymore. I mean, something attacked the house, so I have to believe that. Back at the bar, they told all these stories that sounded so real, but—" She spread her hands helplessly. "It's like something on TV. It doesn't make sense. We're in a city full of people with cops and streetlights and everything! And you're telling me monsters wander around at night eating people, but nobody else knows about it."

Harvey nodded. "Remember that ribcage you kids found by the river one time? You got all freaked out and insisted we call the police, and then they laughed at you because it was only a deer that got caught in the river?"

"Yeah."

"That was probably a frostie's work. The police weren't wrong— the river did catch it—but they didn't understand how. Look, modern daylight people have all kinds of protections from the darkness they don't even recognize as protections. And people who live on the edges of the light or in the dark themselves—they aren't exactly going to run to the police and the evening news to talk about what they've seen, are they? Besides, normally there aren't that many frosties. The guys at Arn's probably made it sound like they killed dozens each, right? The truth is most of them have never fought a frostie in their life. Bar fights and mixing it up with other parents at little league games is more their speed. The glory days your grampa talks about are long gone."

Mal tilted her head. "What about Dan? Was he lying too?"

"No. He's never been one to brag. But he and Carl, and yes, me and your father, we used to go further than other people. Like I told you, we went looking for trouble. And we always found it."

Mal nodded, her eyes on the rune stone. She blew out a deep sigh and bit her lip as if thinking. "Okay, next question—if the sword is cursed, aren't you doomed to kill someone too? You can't get a cursed item and not get the curse too, right?"

"Do I look stupid?" Harvey said. She pointed back at her father's grave. "It was his sword, so I figured he should keep it. I only let Heidrek think I still had it."

Mal gave her a slow nod, finally impressed at something her mother had done.

Harvey held back the impulse to say, "See? I'm not a total idiot." Instead, she said, "Let's go. I'm starving and my rear end is getting frostbite." And staying this close to a body of water after sunset wasn't a great idea.

They walked back to the truck at a slower pace, each lost in their thoughts. Before she got in the truck, Harvey looked back one more time toward the corner where her loved ones lay. A faint blue flame hovered over the ground and lined the edges of the standing stone. She slammed the truck door and locked it.

TWENTY-SEVEN

The next morning Harvey levered herself out of bed and stood in front of her closet. She only had one suit, so it wasn't like she had a decision to make. Made of black polyester that itched and caught on her biceps, the jacket came with a knee length skirt lined in some awful fabric that made cricket noises if she walked too fast and bunched up around her thighs if she tried to cross her legs. She'd bought it years ago at JC Penny for Heidrek's trial because the prosecutor had told her to dress respectably. She'd worn it one other time—at Jon's funeral.

Eventually she told herself to stop being a baby and took the suit off the hanger. She wrestled her legs into nylons and slid on the skirt, tucking her tank top into the waistband. She stood in front of the mirror, tugging and picking at it. No matter what she did it looked stupid. And it scraped the edge of her burns.

She opened the jewelry box on her dresser and poked at the contents, searching for something to brighten her outfit. A few pieces of costume jewelry bought on a whim, a few bits from her mom that she never wore. A pair of hoop earrings with peacock feathers in the center. She'd bought them at the county fair twenty years ago—that probably meant they weren't respectable. Her wedding band and engagement ring, maybe? Jon had spent a whole paycheck on that diamond. She'd worn them for a year and a day after he died. She slid the two gold bands back over her ring finger. The cold metal felt strange, too heavy.

In the center of the box lay her father's neck ring. A torc, Ivor called it. Made of twisted gold bands and capped at each end with a bear's head. Each bear had tiny garnet eyes. The only piece that was probably worth serious money. Not that she would ever sell it. Not if she was starving in a ditch. She lifted the heavy ring in both hands, staring into the bears' eyes. He'd always said it went all the way back to the original Hervor, the one she was named for. The one they had made a song about. Heidrek would flip his shit if he saw her wearing their father's ring. Harvey settled it around her neck, the bear heads pressing into her collarbone.

Downstairs in the kitchen, Ivor and the kids sat around the table. Ivor was teaching them words in the old language, half of them insults.

As Harvey entered the room carrying her heels, Mal was saying, "So, if someone calls me a stupid dog, I can only punch them, but if they call me a stupid bitch, I can kill them because being a girl animal is worse than being just an animal?"

"Under the old law, yes," Ivor said.

Harvey put on her coat, pulling her hair out of her collar.

"That is some stupid, fucking, sexist shit! Mom, did you hear that?" Mal called.

"You keep that in mind next time you think the guys down at Arn's respect you," Harvey said. With one hand on the doorframe, she stepped into her heels. Her feet winced at the shift in pressure and balance. If she'd been wearing her steel toed boots the day of the funeral, she'd have done a lot more damage to Heidrek. Of course, then the cops might have seen it as a fair fight and not arrested him.

She took a deep breath and blew it out again, walking over to the table. She kissed Mal roughly on the forehead and said, "I love you.

You need to text Coach Wells and apologize for making her look for you. And you're grounded till hell freezes over."

Caleb snickered. "Technically, Hel is already cold, so does that mean she's not grounded?"

"Don't be a smart ass. And tomorrow you're going back to school. I don't need the truant officer after you. Stay indoors today, both of you. And, Caleb, don't talk to any ravens." Caleb muttered and scrunched down in his chair. Harvey kissed him on the top of the head.

"You sure you don't want me to come with you?" Ivor said.

"I'm sure." Harvey picked up her keys. "Stay in the house and keep an eye on the kids."

"Mom!" both kids yelled in unison.

"Fine. Then you keep an eye on your Grampa. Nobody get killed or maimed while I'm gone, alright?" She resettled her eye patch before going out the door.

It took her over two hours driving to reach the Pawtuxet State Prison. As she pulled into the visitor lot, the flock of ravens that had followed in her wake settled into the trees ringing the parking lot. Stormcrow dipped and wheeled above the prison.

She got out of the truck and flipped up the hood of her coat against the drizzle of freezing rain. Neatly clipped bushes and bright mums around the parking lot edges made the building seem like nothing but a storage facility with a bit of extra security. Maybe that made it easier for the locals to live with a fort full of criminals.

Inside there was no pretending. Double-walled bulletproof glass windows protected the guards from incoming visitors. After she'd shoved her ID into a drawer, she was allowed to step through the first door. The guard on the other side said nothing, but his eyes followed her as she put her purse on the table and stepped through the metal detector. A second guard pawed through the purse, rattling off questions about weapons, mace, drugs, sharp objects, projectiles or any other weapon. Eventually, they handed her a visitor's pass.

The first guard stayed behind as the second one took her into the windowless concrete maze. She shivered and dug her hands into her jacket pockets, trying to block out the smell of the place—the bulk cleansers, recirculated air and dark places underground. There was no daylight here, not even the thin gray light of November.

As they walked, she studied the guard in front of her. He carried a billy club, bear mace, taser. A key card on a zip string. He worked out, if his biceps and rolling walk were any clue. Probably into protein powders, by the bulk of his neck. But she'd seen Heidrek take down men who were bigger, meaner. If Heidrek was still here, it was because he chose to be.

"You don't have a gun," she said.

"No ma'am." He opened a cafeteria door and stepped aside for her. "Guns aren't much good in an indoor riot, especially if an inmate gets one away from you."

"That makes sense. Thank you." The cold of the place crept up her legs, making her shiver under her skirt and jacket.

He nodded once, a single sharp jerk of the head. "You wait here. You'll be called when your case is up."

"Thank you," she said again as the door closed on her. The white painted concrete floor made her tractionless heels slide so that she was forced to take small, timid steps. Around the cafeteria people sat at tables in clusters of two or three, not talking to anyone but each other. The round tables had attached round stools, barely big enough to fit one ass cheek on a grown adult. Harvey took a seat on a bench by the wall, away from the others where she could sit with her back covered and her eye on the doors at either end of the room. The walls were painted green up to shoulder height. After that they were painted white. One wall was broken by a serving hatch with a stainless steel shutter still locked down over it. The room might have been a school cafeteria, if there were finger paintings and class pictures on the walls.

"Mrs. Otvar?" A young man approached her, his hand out. "I'm Dr. Collins." He wore a brown plaid jacket with suede patches on the elbows, like a professor in an old movie. All he needed was a pipe and a busty blonde draped across a desk so he could announce the invasion of the ant-men or something.

"Mind if I sit with you? You go by Harvey, is that right?" He sat on the bench beside her. "I have to admit when Heidrek first mentioned 'Harvey' I thought giant rabbits."

She blinked. "I'm not a rabbit."

"I know, I know. Sorry old movie reference. Forget it. I can't tell you how glad I am that you've finally decided to come down here. It's a big step. A really big step. You know, we started this family reintegration program about six years ago and we've had a high level of success. Most politicians won't spend a dime on therapy for convicted criminals for fear of looking soft on crime, but we won a McArthur grant that funded the program's startup. I'm hoping that once we have a track record of success we can convince the general public that the cost of not doing this is much higher."

Harvey nodded as he talked, looking around the cafeteria, trying to find a reason for the crawling unease she felt, the sense of dislocation. It couldn't only be nerves, could it? The walls were the same soothing green used in hospitals and mental wards. That didn't help. But there was something else. Something worse about this place. Harvey's stomach gurgled unhappily around the hash browns she'd picked up on the drive down.

Dr. Collins was still talking. "The support of our closest community, our family and friends is a vital part of recovery and rehabilitation. Just by crossing the threshold, you've told Heidrek that you care. That you see him as a person. That gives a prisoner hope and hope..."

Threshold. That was it. This place has no threshold. No dividing line between the cold outside and the safe inside. Okay, there was a literal threshold. She'd walked over it. But the dark and the cold, the danger—those things were inside, instead of out.

Dr. Collins' words finally filtered through her thoughts.

"I'm not here to help," Harvey said.

He jerked to a stop. "But Heidrek has been writing to you, asking you to testify for him. He's a changed man."

"I don't believe it," she said.

His disappointment would have been easier to take if he'd been angry or sneered at her. Instead he looked like she'd kicked his puppy. "I know it can be hard to let go of the past, but it's been almost a decade. Don't you think your brother deserves a second chance?"

"I can't risk that."

"I understand you were the victim of your brother's crime. But he's done a lot of hard work on himself. When I first started working with your brother he told me getting put in solitary was the best thing that ever happened to him because it gave him time to think."

Her heart beat faster. Cold, violence, darkness. They were all here, concentrated in one place. And no family, no circle of firelight to counterbalance the night and keep it at bay.

"What's Heidrek been doing?" she said.

Collins's smile returned. "He's made remarkable progress this past year. Our program concentrates on the worst violent offenders. Would you believe, Heidrek had been in isolation for three months when I first met him, and he served another nine months in isolation after that? It took some work to convince the warden that the men in solitary were the ones I most wanted to work with."

"What had he done to get there?" Harvey asked.

The doctor froze, looked down, not meeting her eyes. "I believe, um, he was in a fight," he said. "It's unfortunately common here."

"How bad was the other guy hurt?" She kept her eyes on the cafeteria door. A couple was called and went out. The wife carried a picture of a smiling young man in a cap and gown. She hugged it to her like a holy relic, or a shield. The door closed behind them.

Again the doctor paused, running his fingers over the crease in his pants leg. He licked his lips. "He required hospital treatment. But that was several years ago, when he first started his sentence," Dr. Collins said. "He's a changed man. I really wish you could have some time to talk to him before the hearing. It would give you a much better basis for talking to the parole board."

"Really?" For a second she gave him her full attention. "That will be interesting to see."

"Oh, it will. I think you'll be really surprised." While they waited, Dr. Collins went on talking about his program, the meditation sessions, the personal inventories, and role-playing activities. He kept returning to the progress Heidrek had made, how Heidrek was a model inmate who'd earned the respect of other prisoners in the program. Harvey nodded along, but she kept her eyes on the room, watching for trouble. Another person left the cafeteria. An old man this time. His hands shook on his cane as he limped after the guard.

Collins reached out and took Harvey's hand. "I'd like you to consider joining our family reconciliation program," he said. "Inmates and their loved ones meet for family therapy once a month to make amends, ask each other's forgiveness, and practice new communication strategies. Together we learn to replace the dysfunctions of the past with the kind of relationships we'd like to have."

A surge of anger rolled inside her. Not the deep, bone level thrum of the berserk, but the good old ordinary human desire to slap a fool. She yanked her hand out of his. "Don't touch me."

"I'm sorry, I—"

"Shut up and listen to me. Heidrek told you his side of the story, right? Well, here's mine. I spent nine days in the hospital. I had tubes coming out of every part of me. I had to have surgery to let out the blood that was pooling under my skull. Are you listening?"

He shrank back but nodded, eyes fixed on her face.

"Good," she said. "Remember it. I don't. I had to be told about it later because I don't remember much of anything after he strangled me unconscious. In my own kitchen. At our father's wake. In front of my kids." She prodded Dr. Collins in the chest. "I do remember Caleb's fifth birthday party. That was the one we had in the living room because Mommy couldn't make it upstairs yet." *They'd had store bought cake and canned spaghetti for dinner.* "I got him a Harry the

166

Hospital Bear. The doctor said it would be therapeutic." She inched forward. "His sister had screaming nightmares for about six months. They both slept in my bed most nights for the next year. When their dad died a year later, right about the time you were holding hands with my brother and reciting the Serenity Prayer, her nightmares came back all over again. That I remember, all right."

Harvey sat back, hot anger pushing back the damp chill of the prison walls around her. "And you think it will all be better if I look deep in Heidrek's eyes and let him say he's sorry?"

Collins leaned forward, all empathy, as eager to help her as he was to help her brother. "It sounds like you have a lot of anger left. Have you ever considered getting some counseling for yourself?"

She looked away, finding a sparkle of light as the fluorescent bulbs gleamed off the metal fittings of the cafeteria tables. She stared at the light until she was calmer. "I didn't put Heidrek in prison because I was angry. I put him there so I wouldn't have to kill him."

"Hervor Otvar?" A guard called from the door. "You're next."

She got up and walked away from the doctor, heels clicking on the concrete floor.

CHAPTER

TWENTY-EIGHT

With Dr. Collins trailing behind, the guard led them into a room where a man and a woman in suits, and the prison warden, sat behind a table. Heidrek was already there, facing the panel from a single chair in the center of the room. The guard ushered Harvey and Dr. Collins to chairs at the side of the room. From her position, Harvey studied Heidrek.

His dark hair, the same chestnut color as her own, was slicked back into a small ponytail that made his forehead high and glassy under the glare of the ceiling lights. Roughly tattooed runes circled his wrist, half hidden by the cuffs of his orange jump suit. The ragged lines reminded Harvey of the skull she'd seen on the blond kid at Arn's. She squinted, trying to read the symbols without showing Heidrek she was staring at him. Runes for protection, runes for power. Repeated over and over again, the rune for blood. The ink was crisscrossed and broken by scabs. In places the rune was visible only as red, puffy lines carved into the skin over poorly healed scars. Harvey winced, imagining her brother carving the letters of the old language into himself over and over again. Her heart squeezed with sorrow for him, for her, for the family they never managed to be. Heidrek turned toward her and smiled.

Her jaw set, she met his gaze with her own. Dr. Collins was right —something about Heidrek had changed. The shadows along his cheekbones were deeper, the lines of his face leaner and sharper. His muscles bulged under the prison jumpsuit sleeves, but he was pale. He reminded her of a root, white from being buried in the ground. The tendons in his neck stood out with every slight movement of his head. His sunken eyes glittered like pools of water that had never seen the sun.

For a split second Harvey wanted to take his hand in hers, to warm his cold fingers, and feed him bread and honey. "What have you done to yourself?"

The warden coughed. "Do not address the prisoner. All remarks should be addressed to the panel. Are we ready to begin?"

The woman opened a folder and tapped the button on an old tape recorder. "Parole hearing for Heidrek Otvar, prisoner TW923548. Aggravated assault. Attempted murder. Prisoner has had no disciplinary infractions in the past five years. File includes a recommendation of parole from the prison warden. Prisoner has participated in the Community and Family Reconciliation Program under the supervision of Dr. James Collins. File includes a letter from Dr. Collins also recommending parole. Dr. Collins do you have anything to add?"

Collins stood up to talk. The longer he spoke, the tighter Harvey curled her fingers in her lap. Her heart pounded, but she kept her eyes fixed on Heidrek.

"Thank you for your time," Collins said. He sat back down.

Harvey lifted the edge of her eye patch, staring at Heidrek's wrists. His hands were flat on his knees, his eyes forward, but to her burned eye the runes around his wrist wriggled and shimmied. Blue grave fire burned around his hands.

The woman was talking again, her voice a rote monotone. "Since there are no other statements, are there any objections from the panel? No, then I move that the prisoner be paroled. All in favor?"

"Wait." Harvey stood hard enough to knock her chair over. The members of the panel turned toward her. Their eyes were vague, confused.

Heidrek's hands clenched on his knees.

"You have to let me talk," Harvey said. "He's not better. He's dangerous."

"Sit down, Harvey," Heidrek said.

"No." She walked up to the table. "What's wrong with you people?"

The rune's around Heidrek's wrists flared with blue light. The smell of frost and snow, fens and dark places underground filled the room. And all along the metal of the handcuffs, frost was forming. "I said sit down, sister," Heidrek said "Now."

Her knees wobbled. His words were like lead weights, pulling her down. Slowly, she lifted her hand to her face. Harvey took the patch away from her eye and looked him full in the face.

In a breath, the room stopped. Darkness flowed out of the prison walls, blotting out the lights, covering the guards, the prison warden. The walls became rough and dank like the uncut stone of a deep cave. Water dripped in hidden caverns that echoed far in the distance. Creatures, half-seen, writhed and flexed their claws in the shadows. Blue grave flames flickered on the hearth. Only she and Heidrek remained. She stood before him as he sat on a throne of twining roots.

He sat, raised above her, and though she could not see them, she knew his warriors were all around her. The shackles on his wrists became twisted iron bands that hissed and writhed with a life of their own. The runes etched into his skin glowed blue, as blood dripped from them down his fingers and spread in spirals at his feet. Beneath his feet, something white and fleshy crawled. Sparks flared from it, like the molten steel at the factory. Here Heidrek was king.

"Well, sister," he said in the old language. "How did you learn this trick?"

"What have you done?" she screamed at him. "What have you done to yourself?"

He rose and took a step toward her. "Give it to me. Give me my birthright and I will let you live." The moisture on the walls crackled into spikes of frost.

"Over my dead body." She dragged the patch back down over her burned eye, clamping a hand over it. The cave blinked out of existence. She was back in the prison under swinging florescent lights and Heidrek was only foot from her.

The guard from the side of the room hurried toward them, reaching for his belt. Dr. Collins was pleading with Heidrek to remain calm, but Heidrek was on his feet, grasping for Harvey's neck with both hands.

She stumbled back, her heels slipping on the polished floor. Heidrek lunged for her and she dodged, knocking into the parole board table. Heidrek caught her by the long mane of her hair, but his manacles around his ankles caught his stride and he stumbled, dragging her down with him.

She punched him in the throat as she fell, putting her whole weight behind it, and stitches popped in her jacket's shoulder seam. Heidrek gagged and let go. Harvey leapt over him, scrambled for the door. Her ridiculous suit skirt caught her, shortening her stride. Dr. Collins wailed, pleading with Heidrek to reach for his calm, to find his center. The parole panel shouted for guards.

She got to the door handle, but solid ice coated the door half an inch thick. She reared back and kicked it. Ice shattered and fell to the ground. She caught the clink of chain in time to half turn as Heidrek caught up to her.

He grabbed her by the hair again, dragging her head back. The link holding his wrists together snapped. Harvey spun, elbowed him across the face, stamped down on his soft prison shoes with her sharp heel. He doubled over groaning and she slammed her knee into his face.

The guard grabbed Heidrek from behind and got tossed across the room. A guard rushed into the room, taser out, shouting for help. Dr. Collins clung to the opposite wall. While Heidrek was distracted with the guard, Harvey slid away, skating her high heels over the floor. She needed a weapon. Something. She kicked off her heels for traction, but her slippery nylons only made the going worse.

Heidrek grabbed the first guard's ankle and twisted his leg, yanking the bone out of the hip socket with a sickening pop and crunch. The guard fell screaming as Heidrek lunged over his body toward Harvey. She scrambled into the mess of chairs, throwing them at Heidrek, but he batted them aside.

He leapt, tackled her and they went down in a tangle. His hands on her throat, he thumbs pressed into her windpipe. Harvey clawed at his face, nails digging into his eye sockets. The berserk rose inside her and she fought to control it, to keep it focused on Heidrek alone.

She kicked and writhed. She tried to knee him in the groin, but his weight held her down. He squeezed harder. Her lungs burned. Black sparks flooded her vision. Tasers popped and sizzled. Through her tunnel vision, Harvey barely saw the guards, batons raised.

Heidrek jerked, his hands loosened. The taser zapped again, and his body jerked in a crackle of burning ozone. More guards poured into the room, batons raised. They dragged Heidrek off of her and he disappeared under a mass of beige. Harvey slid backwards on her butt, nylons slipping on the linoleum. She made it upright and retreated to the wall. There she shoved Dr. Collins behind her, crouched and watching for Heidrek to emerge from the fight. Boots and clubs rose and fell.

She pressed her palms flat against the clammy cinderblock, clawing back the berserk. Not here. She couldn't lose it here.

Six guards carried Heidrek away, bound in half a dozen places and screaming curses in the old language. The taste of cold and blood filled Harvey's mouth as he went by. More guards came with a stretcher for the man with the dislocated hip. He moaned, only half conscious from the pain.

Ashen faced, Dr. Collins stepped away from her. She sagged against the wall, trying not to sink all the way to the floor. She should have run. The rest of them would have been safer if she'd drawn Heidrek away. Collins bleated about setbacks, a culture of brutality, her own fragility, apologies, should have realized they weren't ready to meet. She concentrated on the ceiling light over his head, breathing slowly through pursed lips and letting a little more of the fight go with every exhalation.

Papers from parole files were scattered across the room. The parole board scrambled to collect them as they shouted at each other over the siren going off. Harvey shoved chairs around until she found her shoes. She limped back to the door where Collins wrung his hands.

Her hair hung in tangles around her face. She shoved it out of her eyes and tried to tuck her tank top back into her skirt. "I need to go home. Can you show me the way out?" she asked. Collins nodded wordlessly and took out his badge.

It took forever. Every intersection had a door. Every door had a guard who had to double check with his superior if it was okay to let them pass. Eventually the siren was shut off. Without the sun or her phone to gauge by it was hard to tell, but the trip out must have taken over an hour. She and Collins didn't speak. Eventually they reached the final gate, where Harvey turned in her badge and got her purse back from an impassive guard.

As she dug out her keys, Collins finally said, "That language the two of you were speaking? I don't understand."

"You wouldn't. It's old. Norse, more or less." Her throat burned when she spoke, her voice rasping like a raven's.

He nodded. "May I ask...what was he saying as they took him away? It might help me to understand." He paused, frowning at his feet. He looked like Caleb when he got a less than perfect grade. "It might help."

She hitched her purse over her shoulder. "He said, 'I killed your husband. I can kill your children. Don't think these walls will protect you.'" His look of misery deepened. She patted him on the arm. "I'm sorry, Doc. I'm sure they don't all turn out like this. Heidrek's...were different. Good night."

Turning her back on the man, she hurried out to parking lot, keys clutched and ready. Overhead black clouds blocked what was left of the daylight. The yellow sodium lights made the cold fog look like sulfur. From the prison walls a black cloud of ravens rose to follow her. Stormcrow landed on the hood of her truck clacking his beak. Harvey shot out her hand.

Stormcrow screamed in her grasp. He flailed and pecked at her hand, but she gripped him with both hands, his wings pinned.

"Look at me, Stormcrow. Look at my eye!" she ordered.

Stormcrow calmed, his heart beating wildly against her fingers, but no longer struggling. He bobbed his head and stropped his beak against her wrist, peering at her with first one bright eye and then the other. "One eye," he croaked. "Yes. I see. I listen." The bird croaked once more and hunched his shoulders meekly.

Harvey spoke slowly and firmly. "Listen to me, bird. Tell every creature that flies or walks. Tell my own kind whether they understand you or not. My brother killed my husband in secret. He is a murderer and a warlock. I make him an outlaw—a wolfshead. If he ever brings his face into the light again I will kill him with my own hands. Do you understand?"

The bird flapped in her hand, tugging against her grip. "Oh yes, oh yes, oh yes, oh yes!"

The others in the oak tree echoed him, hurling themselves out of the branches and turning black somersaults. She flung the bird up and outward. He cawed once, bowed in the air to her, and wheeled off into the wet sky.

Harvey watched the birds go. Word would reach Heidrek sooner or later. He'd been warned and the declaration had been made public. It wasn't anything a modern court would care about, but she'd followed the old law. Drops of rain fell onto her coat. One found its way down her hair into her ear. She shook it off and climbed up into the truck cab. Maybe when she got home, Ivor could tell her how to ward off whatever Heidrek tried to send after her next.

CHAPTER

TWENTY-NINE

Outside the garage it was full dark already. The wind whipped and howled in the house gutters. The cold drizzle that had been pissing down all afternoon had turned into a freezing rain that coated the trees and roads in slick ice. In the garage, the space heater made a pocket of heat against the cold.

Carl reached deep into the car's transmission, ribs aching as he stretched to reach a bolt. Old Buicks were a beauty to look at, and a pain in the ass to take apart. But he'd promised the owner he'd have this baby done by noon tomorrow, and he did not miss deadlines.

With a few good whacks and some encouraging curse words, the broken solenoid came free. "There you are." He held the part up to the light. It was more rust than steel at this point. He chucked the broken part onto the scrap heap and went to look for a match in the storeroom.

In the unheated storeroom a cold draft snuck down his collar and he remembered the beer sloshing over his face, Harvey calling him an idiot. He had to admit she had a point. Pushing forty and he was rolling around on the floor of a bar, punching the snot out of his friend. He ran his hands through his red hair. He'd found another gray hair in his beard this morning. No use crying over spilled milk. If he really hated the gray he could start dying it blue or something.

Lars stuck his head into the garage. "Hey man."

"What do you need?"

"Uh—" Lars fidgeted. "You know when Dan is coming back?"

"Nope."

"So, like, does that mean he's gone for good?"

"No idea." He scanned the wall of parts, pulling open drawers until he found a new solenoid. Aftermarket, but acceptable. The owner wanted his baby ready for the Classic Cruise on the weekend more than he wanted the insides to be one hundred percent authentic. He gave the part a flip and caught it again.

Lars was still standing in the doorway. Carl spread his hands —*you going to move or what?*

"Is there...I mean, you doing okay?" Lars said. "'Cause you've been out here for hours."

"I'm fine," Carl said.

"Good. Great." Lars moved out of the way, barely. He trailed Carl back into the service bay. "You know she probably hasn't called 'cause she's busy taking care of Mal."

Carl yanked a wrench off the rack harder than he needed to. "She hasn't called because she doesn't need me for anything. Which is fine. I've got work to do." He dove back into the car's insides.

Lars's shadow loomed over him, blocking the light. "You coming in anytime soon?"

From underneath the car, Carl said, "When I'm done, I'm done. Leave the leftovers in the fridge for me."

"Yeah, see, that's the thing." Lars waved his hands vaguely in the air in front of him. "Dan ate all the rest of the stew and we're out of beer and you've got, like, five cans of sloppy joe mix in the cupboard, but no buns or hamburger, so uh, I was kind of wondering what you were going to make for dinner."

Carl's wrench slipped. His knuckles scraped across metal and the wrench disappeared into the car's insides. "Dammit!" He cursed again and shoved himself upright. "What are you, ten? Go to the store and get some food if we're all out. I'm your boss, not your goddamn mother. Now get out of my light. And there better be beer in my fridge the next time I want one." He shoved Lars out toward the door. "Go on, get out."

Lars's face twisted. For a second he danced on the balls of his feet, hands loose at his side ready to swing. Carl snorted and turned back to the Buick. A second later he heard Lars's Doc Martins scrape on the concrete as he slammed out of the garage.

Mal slouched around the house in her stocking feet. The house had a chill to it. Not quite enough to turn up the heat, but enough to make her shiver and pull the sleeves of her sweatshirt over her fingers. Her hands ached from yesterday's punching. Outside it had started to rain.

She reached into her pocket for the business card she'd tucked there yesterday. That blond guy, Lars, who came in with Carl had given it to her. *Carl's Garage. Tow, Repair, Classic Cars.* Below that Lars had written "Bad Ass Monsters Killed" and his number.

"We're supposed to be rescuing you or something," he'd said. "But you look like you've got it under control."

She twiddled the card between her fingers, thinking. Down the hall in his room, Grampa Ivor snored like a buzzsaw. Mal got a box of Pop-Tarts from the kitchen and wandered into the living room.

Caleb sat there, hunched over the computer, his hoodie drawn up over his head and a notebook full of chicken scratch beside him. "What're you up to?" she said.

He mumbled something about ravens and didn't look up. She peered over his shoulder, looking at the screen and his notes. "Hey, I recognize some of those twig letter things. They were on the stone Mom showed me."

Caleb whipped around so fast his chair back knocked the computer desk. "What stone?"

Mal gestured with her pop tart. "There's one in the cemetery. It's full of people's names including Dad's. Mom took me there yesterday on the way home."

Caleb glared up at her, shoving his hood and his straggling bangs out of his face. "That is so unfair. You run off for hours, get drunk, and she tells you all kinds of cool stuff. I do nothing and get a pat on the head and told to ignore it."

Mal shoved the Pop tart box at him. "Yeah. You're right. It's not fair."

Caleb grumped in agreement and took a Pop-Tart. "What happened last night?"

"Well, first this guy named Dan picked me up—" She told him the story from beginning to end, finishing off with "so that's why she and Uncle Heidrek got into that big fight at Grampa's funeral. But she didn't actually keep the sword. It was in Grampa's coffin the whole time."

Caleb shoved the last of his Pop-Tart into his mouth and reached for another one. Munching slowly, he said, "That would explain a lot. Do you believe her?"

"Why wouldn't I?" Mal shrugged.

Caleb broke off another piece of pop tart, chewed, and swallowed. "If you had a magic sword, would you bury it in the ground? And she's got that trunk at the back of her closet that's always locked."

Mal set the now empty cardboard box on the computer desk, nodding. Finishing his Pop-Tart, Caleb reached into the penholder on the desk and pulled out two paper clips. He unbent them, a wicked glint in his eyes. "Want to find out?"

Mal only hesitated for a second. Ivor's snores still echoed around the house. "Yeah," she said. "Let's go."

On tiptoe they ran up the stairs and down the hall to their mother's room.

179

Leaving the door open so they could hear if the snoring stopped, Mal dove into the back of her mom's closet and dragged out the locked army chest. Her fingers trembled. Poking through mom's jewelry box or playing hide and seek in her closet as a kid was one thing—Mom would lose her shit if she ever found this out.

On the other hand, she was already grounded forever.

Caleb knelt in front of the trunk. A few seconds of sawing back and forth with his little tools and the padlock clicked open. Mal bounced in excitement. Caleb opened the lid.

An old forest green sweater lay on top. Crap. Mom was going to kick her ass over a bunch of old clothes. For a second she was ashamed of herself. Maybe these were Mom's memories, her private stash of sentimental old junk she couldn't stand to let anyone else see. She leaned over the trunk and sniffed. Maybe it would smell like Dad.

Instead, it smelled like gun oil and old wool. Weird. Mom didn't own guns. She'd outright laughed at the last person who suggested she needed one for home protection.

"Go on," Caleb hissed. "What else is in there?"

Mal picked up the sweater. Underneath the sweater lay something wrapped in oiled silk. She peeled back the cloth. "Oh wow."

Chainmail, the rings close linked and shining, nested beneath. She picked it up—a full shirt. She shook it and the rings chimed.

Caleb put his hand out to feel the mail. He grimaced at the oily feel, but Mal held the shirt up against herself, measuring it on her body in the mirror. It was too small for her dad to have worn. The metal's weight draped down her chest and across her lap.

"Mom's going to kill us," Caleb said.

"Jesus Christ!" Mal's heart almost stopped as Caleb appeared in the reflection with her. "Don't do that."

He gave her his best "whatever" shrug. "What else is in there?"

Together they knelt by the footlocker. A plain sword, about three feet long lay at the bottom in a leather scabbard. Caleb made a face as Mal picked it up. "That can't be Tyrfing. It's not authentic."

180

"What do you mean, not authentic? It's not made out of plastic, doofus." She buckled the belt around her waist and drew the sword, trying to copy moves she'd seen in movies.

"If Tyrfing is this ancient Viking sword it's going to be *old*. That thing is practically new looking. The blade's too narrow at the base, it's clearly made out of modern steel, and it's got, like a weird, round pommel."

"Whatever. It's awesome." Mal planted her feet and wrapped both hands around the grip. Holding the thing made her feel powerful, ready for anything. She swished the blade through the air. "You think Mom will notice if I take this?"

"Yes!"

She slumped a little. Yeah, somehow Mom would know. She always did.

Caleb held out his hand. "Can I see?"

"No. You said it was crap."

"Come on!"

"Shhhhh! You'll wake up Grampa."

"I'll tell Mom."

She glared at him, letting the blade drop. "Seriously? Snitch." She handed him the sword. He sat on the end of mom's bed, the sword across his lap, and tested the edge with his finger. His gasp and quick move to stick his cut finger in his mouth told her it was as sharp as it looked. Served him right.

He held up the blade, glaring at it. "I think it's actually been used. See? There are scratches. There's even a little nick up near the tip."

Mal peered at the marks. "Yeah. I see it. I wonder what she used it on."

The crunch of tires on the driveway snapped them both out of their reverie.

"Holy shit." Mal lunged for the chainmail shirt.

Caleb rushed to the window to act as lookout. "Put it back. Put it back. Put it back."

"Shush!" She grabbed the blade from him and stuffed it back in the scabbard. The belt buckle stuck and tangled as she tried to yank it off.

"She's getting out of the car," Caleb hissed at her from the window.

"Shut up!" She tossed everything in the footlocker and stuffed the green sweater down on top. Mal snapped the padlock back in place and shoved the footlocker to the back of the closet.

Both of them dashed out of the room as Mom called from the kitchen, "Kids? Ivor? Where is everybody?"

"Grampa's asleep," Caleb shouted back at her. An answering "shhhhh" came up the stairs. Mal punched him in the arm and snickered. He grinned at her. From the kitchen the clattering of pans promised dinner soon. Caleb gave her the thumbs up and galumphed down the stairs, back to the computer.

She stood on the top landing a few moments longer with one hand dug into her pocket. She could go down there, help Mom with dinner, ask how the hearing went. She probably should.

Instead, she took out her phone and Lars's card. Her fingertips shivered with more than cold as she walked toward her room. She eased the door closed and locked it before hitting send.

A voice so chipper she could picture his mischievous grin answered her. "Mort's Mortuary. You stab 'em, we slab 'em. Discounts for bulk. What can I do for you?"

She hunched over the phone, voice barely above a whisper. "Um, Lars? It's Mal from the bar."

"Hey gorgeous, what's up?"

Her spine snapped straight up. "This is not a booty call." God, boys were gross. If he touched her she'd do the same thing to him as she'd done to Taylor.

But the cheer in Lars's voice didn't waver as he said, "That's okay, you're not legal anyway. What can I do for you? You need a tow?" From the beeping in the background he was in a grocery store checkout line.

"Do you have Dan's number?"

"Nope. I don't know if he even has a number. Lives in the wind, you know? I can tell him to call you from the garage later. If he shows up."

"Oh. No, that's okay." She swallowed hard and said, "If I wanted to hunt those frost monster things, where would I find them?"

There was a pause. Then, in a more sober voice, he said, "Now that is an interesting question. Let me get out to my car and I'll answer it."

"Sure. Okay." She sat on the bed to wait, phone cupped in her cold hands. Her stockinged feet tapped out a little rhythm, waiting while the sounds of groceries being bought came through the phone. She tried to think practically—*I'll need a weapon.*

THIRTY

Harvey tossed her keys on the kitchen counter next to her purse. Kids? Ivor? Where is everybody?"

"Grampa's asleep," Caleb shouted back at her.

"Shhhhhh," she hissed at him. The kitchen should have been warm and tasty smelling with the lasagna she'd put together last night and left for them to cook. Instead it was cold and dark. The note she'd left with exact directions for cooking the lasagna was still taped to the oven door.

She kicked her heels onto the boot mat and banged the lasagna straight from the fridge into the cold oven. Then she remembered it needed to warm up or the glass pan would crack. She pulled it back out, wrenching the oven knob over to start heating. Dinner wouldn't be ready for another hour at the soonest and she was already starving.

She looked in the cupboard for the Pop-Tarts, but the last box was gone. Unbelievable. Her phone chimed and she checked the new text. It was from Coach Wells.

"How'd it go? You all okay?" the text said.

Harvey texted back. "He's contained. For now. Thx for checking in." She got a thumbs up emoji in reply.

Stomach growling, she tossed the phone back in her purse and stalked into the hallway, muttering. "What have you three been up to all day?

She glimpsed Caleb hunched over the computer. A window blinked shut, replaced by Facebook. "I know that trick," she said to the back of his head. "And you're too young to be looking at that stuff."

His shoulders hunched guiltily, but he didn't say anything.

"Where's your sister?"

"Upstairs," he said without turning around.

"Where's your grandfather?"

"Mom!" He turned around to glare at her. "I told you he's sleeping. I'm working on something."

"Don't take that tone with me." But she said it more out of habit than conviction. "Dinner's in an hour."

Caleb was already back at whatever he had been doing, angling the screen away.

She closed her eyes and rolled her shoulders, trying to work some of the stiffness out. They hadn't relaxed any on the long, icy drive home. Salt trucks were already out in force on the highways.

Padding down the hallway to her father-in-law's room, she knocked softly. "You doing okay, Ivor?" From the other side of the door came a grunt and the creak of the old, iron frame bed as Ivor stood. His cane thumped across the floor and he opened the door.

He'd forgotten to shave that morning. The undershirt he wore tucked into his work pants showed the ropy scar that ran across his collarbone and into his armpit. He looked her up and down, then folded her into a crushing hug.

After a minute, Ivor let her go. "So, he's not getting out."

"No," she said. Tears prickled in her eyes, but she willed them away. Heidrek didn't deserve tears, and she didn't need them.

"Come on in." Ivor's room smelled like joint rub and peppermints. A bottle of liniment crowded the medicine bottles on his nightstand.

Harvey took the only seat, a high-backed armchair covered in giant roses. It and the bed were some of the only things Ivor had insisted on keeping when he moved in. The old man eased himself back onto the bed and hooked his cane on the foot before picking up his sword and whetstone again.

She rested her head on the roses and watched him stroke his sword's blade across a whetstone. The slow, methodical motion and the shushing sound of steel on stone eased its way into her shoulders. She took a deep breath and let it out again.

"He's become a warlock," she said. "I don't know how, but he became one."

Ivor grunted. He worked until the sword's edge gleamed. He set down the whetstone and laid the sword across his lap, drawing a piece of fine grit sandpaper across the edge.

"There's no threshold in that place," Harvey went on. "No hearth. I never thought prison would do that to him. I don't understand it. How did he learn to be a warlock in prison?"

"Where there's a will there's a way. Heidrek always did have more than enough will to go around." Ivor held the blade up to the light, turning it back and forth. "Maybe all he needed was time to think."

Harvey nodded. "He was in solitary a long time, they said."

"Makes sense. All the old stories I know, a warlock is always a man who lives apart, cut off. You remember the story of the deer-footed man?"

"He gave his brother blood to drink. Claimed it was animal blood, but it was his own. And then later he killed his brother and took his heart to eat."

Her mind went back to the runes around Heidrek's wrist, red and deep carved as if new lines had been laid down over old again and again. She shuddered.

Ivor wiped the blade down with a silk cloth, but he didn't lay his sword in its box. Instead he put it back in its scabbard and hung it up on the end of the bed before reaching for his nitroglycerin pills.

Harvey said nothing. Instead, she stood, tugging her skirt down as she did. "I've got to go change." She nodded at the sword. "You might as well do that in the kitchen. The light's better in there. The kids already know."

He smiled at her. "You're a sensible woman."

She patted him on the shoulder. He caught her hand, looking up into her eyes. "Sooner or later, you'll have to reckon with that sword. Your ancestor, the one you were named for, took it for her own. You will too."

"He's not getting out, Ivor. Let it lie where it is." She pulled her hand out of his. *Dinner.* She needed to get out of this damn suit and get dinner on. Just let her focus for a little while on something simple like whether or not the lasagna would cook in time. Heidrek and the grave could wait.

CHAPTER

THIRTY-ONE

The guards dragging Heidrek down the prison stairs didn't bother to be gentle. But it didn't matter. Every jolt, every bruise only stoked the berserk. How long it had been! Years and years he had held it down so he could seek power in another form. Now he fought, writhing in their grip, teeth gnashing. He snapped the plastic restraints around his wrists and ankles like they were cotton candy.

More guards piled on him, boots and fists pounding. He thrashed in their grip, suspended between heaven and earth. The door of the solitary cell clanged behind him. Heidrek hurled himself against it and the sound boomed through the underground.

He pounded at the door until his hands went numb and the berserk fire faded to cold ashes. Afterward, he lay on the rough floor for what seemed like hours, shaking with cold, gray waves of nausea rolling over him. Pressing his fingers to the raw scars around his wrists, he sought the power, but couldn't find the focus to call on the magic. His blood was spent and cold. She had buried him and this was his grave. He would never get out.

Footsteps and voices sounded in the hall. "This isn't a good idea, Doc."

Collins's stupid, bleating voice echoed in the hallway. "I am a licensed psychologist. That means he's my patient. I have a right to see him. Or do I have to file a complaint with the Prison Commission?"

The guard outside sighed and unlocked the door. "It's your neck." The door creaked open and Collins's sleekly polished shoes stepped into the cell. Heidrek lifted his head off the floor.

Collins crouched beside him, his voice gentle. "Heidrek? How are you doing?" The door closed behind the doctor. Heidrek raised himself to his elbows, forcing his eyes to focus on the doctor.

Collins said, "I'm so sorry this happened. I should have realized your sister would be too much of a trigger for you." He took a handkerchief out of his pants pocket and wiped at the blood dried under Heidrek's nose. As Dr. Collins brought his hand near to Heidrek's face, the blue veins in the doctor's wrist wormed their way under the pale skin. The human warmth felt like a candle on Heidrek's face. Heidrek closed his eyes, savoring the comfort.

Collins rose from his crouch and sat on the narrow bed attached to the wall. "This isn't the end, Heidrek. It's a setback. Remember that. You've come so far. You can come back from this. You're strong."

"Yes." Heidrek's word came out in faint whisper. "I will be."

"That's the spirit. Come on. Let's get you up." Collins put his hands under Heidrek's armpits, leaning close to lift him up. Heidrek wrapped his arms around Collins and bore him to the ground. He got his hands around Collins's neck, crushing the windpipe before the doctor could make a sound. He knelt on Collins's chest, knuckles white with strain, until the man stopped moving. His tongue bulged from his mouth, eyes bloodshot.

His heart racing, heat returning, Heidrek stripped the body and dressed it in his prison jumpsuit. He curled the body on the bed with its face to the wall and settled Collins's glasses on his own nose. He took his sharpened fork tine and stabbed it into Collins' jugular. The cooling blood oozed out. Bending over the body he lapped up the blood. The gray aftermath receded, leaving only cold and power. Dipping the tine in the blood, he scratched Collins's name across his forehead so that their bloods mingled. He had no mirror in which to check his work, but it didn't matter. He knew the spell had worked.

"Thank you, Doctor," he said. "You have no idea how much you've helped me." He drew up the single sheet, tucking the doctor in as if he were asleep.

Straightening his tie, Heidrek cleared his throat and rapped on the door with his knuckles, calling for the guard. A minute later he was striding through the halls, doors opening without hesitation as he flashed his badge. He emptied his pockets at the final checkpoint and watched Collin's belongings roll slowly through the scanner.

A heavy hand clapped him on the back and he turned, fist raised to pulverize his attacker. The warden backed up laughing, hands in the air. "Whoa there, Collins. It's me."

"Oh. Yes, sorry." Heidrek reached for his—Collins's— keys and wallet.

The warden, still smiling, said, "We're all a bit jumpy after this afternoon. Well, you can't win them all, eh?"

Heidrek tried to force an abashed chuckle like Collins used. "No. I suppose not. But where there's life, there's hope."

The warden laughed once. Together they walked out into the drizzling sleet, the warden thanking Heidrek for giving a statement earlier, making plans for a debriefing the next day. Heidrek mumbled agreement, throwing in a few of Collins's favorite therapeutic phrases, even as his eyes darted over the parking lot. Fear struck him as they reached the first rank of cars. He had no idea what Collins drove. He fumbled in his pocket, and sighed with relief. Of course, the man had an alarm remote. He clicked it and a Honda Civic chirped to his left.

"Well, good night, warden," Heidrek said. "Thank you for being so understanding."

The warden smiled and raised a hand in a goodbye wave. "You're doing good work. Have a good night."

The man walked off into the gloom. Heidrek's palms itched with the strain of staying calm. He waved once and walked toward the Honda. *Walk. Walk, don't run.*

It was an automatic. Of course it was. A weak desk jockey like Collins wouldn't have the brains to get his hands and feet coordinated enough to drive a stick. Heidrek's stomach growled. Time to hit a drive-through for the first time in nine years. Then he'd have a proper family reunion.

THIRTY-TWO

Propped up in bed with a running magazine, Mal checked the clock on the nightstand. Twenty minutes since Mom had gone to bed. She crept to the door of her room. No light coming from Caleb's room, though she heard a raven cawing. He was probably sleeping with the window open again. Weirdo. Grampa snored so loud she could hear him loud and clear upstairs.

"Yes!" She ducked back into her room and sent a quick text to Lars before she drew on her runner's leggings and insulated shirt. She pulled her hair back in a ponytail and slid on a fleece headband to protect her ears. After a glance at the frost ferns growing on the window, she added an extra shirt, hesitated a minute over her hoodie, and decided against it. Too bulky. Besides, she'd warm up running. Gloves in hand she slid down the carpeted stairs on her backside.

As she crept past the china cabinet in the living room she caught a glimpse of her reflection in the dark glass. In her slick black and neon green runner's spandex she looked like a superhero. She paused to pose and smirk at the girl in the glass before she hurried past. In the kitchen she laced on her sneakers and slipped the deadbolt.

Keeping her steps light, she jogged to the end of the street across from Fisherman's Park. Lars waited for her in the gravel parking lot, headbanging to something loud as he sat in an old beater covered in primer. She slid into the passenger's seat and stubbed her toe on a backpack sitting in the footwell. It clinked like it was full of metal chains.

"Sorry about that," Lars said. "You can move it." He hit pause on the music.

"Okay. Cool." Mal put on her seatbelt and lifted the pack onto her lap. It weighed a ton. A wooden stick with a spiked ball stuck out of the top. Mal slammed the car door, then had to slam it a couple more times to make it latch.

"Did you bring me a weapon?" she asked.

Lars stuffed the last of a Big Mac in his mouth and started the engine. "Crowbar. Works great and you can't cut yourself on it."

She fished the steel bar out of the footwell where it had also been bumping her feet. It didn't shine and flash like the sword in her mom's closet, but it had a solid, comforting weight in her hands and a nasty hook at the end. It wasn't hard to picture swinging this thing down on some monster's skull. She gripped it with both hands. "Awesome. Where are we going?"

"The St. Stanislaus Cemetery. Carl never goes there, but I figure it's got to have some fun for us and there's lots of open space. We can go nuts." He shot her a wicked grin.

She made herself grin back, in spite of the small thought that she was in a car with a stranger she'd met in a bar. This was pretty much the definition of the stuff your mother warned you about. But she'd gotten on Dan's bike and that had gone great. She eyed Lars. He was skinnier than Dan anyway, taller, but not as heavy muscled. She could probably take him out. She'd taken down Taylor, right? Besides, she had a crowbar.

"Cool tattoo," she said. A ragged pen line of a flaming skull with a snake crawling out of the eyehole covered his right wrist.

"Thanks. I did it myself with a paperclip. Didn't take very long."

"Cool." She tightened her grip on the crowbar.

He hit play on his phone plugged into the car's ancient CD player —metal she'd never heard before blared out. "These dudes are from Iceland," he screamed over the music. "Nobody rocks like they do."

She bobbed her head to the pulsing beat, bouncing in her seat. "Yeah. This is awesome. Let's go kick some ass!"

"Yeah!"

Lars spun the rattling car around in a gravel spitting circle and out into the road, whooping, and they tore off into the night.

The cemetery gates were chained shut so Lars parked under the trees by the road. He slung on the backpack and climbed the wrought iron gates, clambering up and over before Mal could ask how he was going to get in. He dropped to the ground on the other side, leaving her by the car, clutching her crowbar. He beckoned to her, a cheerful smile on his face.

"Oh, uh, okay," she said. She glanced side to side, to be sure no cars were coming, tossed the crowbar between the bars and leapt for the nearest piece of iron scrollwork. With a little scrambling, and a racing heart, she made it over the top and dropped down in a heap beside Lars. She popped back up, panting. "Cool. No problem." Mentally she kicked herself. She had to stop saying cool to everything.

Lars didn't seem to care. "Yeah. No problem," he said. He dug around in his backpack, pulling out a chainmail shirt. "You want it? Watch your hair. The links will yank it right out if you're not careful."

Tall as she was, the mail shirt went past her knees. She tried waving her arms and took a few steps. It was like she was being dragged down from all directions. "I don't like it. It's too weird."

Lars shrugged. "Figures. It's made for me. Probably too big for you." He helped her pull it back over her head and put it on himself. As the shirt settled into place he started, jumping up and down on the balls of his feet, dancing to the jingle of metal rings. "Wooh! Let's go! We're gonna kick some frostie ass!" He picked up the stick with a spiked ball at the end and strode off into the dark.

Mal grabbed her crowbar off the ground and stretched her legs to keep up with him.

After a few minutes, Mal recognized this portion of the cemetery. Lars was taking her in roughly the same direction her mom had gone the night before. The little shed-like mausoleum appeared out of the gloom. Not too far ahead the cemetery lawn dipped down a steep slope to a creek edged by trees. Lars pulled up and dropped his backpack by the mausoleum.

She could faintly see the outline of the rough stone her mom had showed her. Somewhere close were her Grampa and her dad. That felt right. He probably would have taken her on a frostie hunt, no matter what Mom said.

"This should be a good place to start," Lars said. "You want to be bait?"

"Fuck no." Mal glared at him. She knew dumbass hazing when she heard it. Next he'd tell her she had to take off her clothes. "You be the bait."

But Lars grinned and danced around some more, shaking his head so that his white boy dreads flew around his face. "Cool. Cool. Come on." He took off at a run toward the river at the far side of the cemetery, dodging between and over grave markers like he wasn't wearing twenty pounds of knitted metal. Mal took off after him, frost crackling under her sneakers as she ran.

Lars led her toward the water until they both pulled up at the top of the slope. Up at the top the ground was smooth mowed lawn, but below the drop off the trees and underbrush had been allowed to grow. It was darker down the slope. The city glow and the light from the cemetery's few security lights couldn't penetrate the thick leaves and branches, even this late in the fall.

Mal tightened her grip on her crowbar. "Now what? I don't see anything."

Lars pointed down toward the sound of running water. "Down there I bet. It's steep though. Too slippery to fight on. You wait here. I'll go get the frosties."

He took off again.

She reached a hand out to snag him, but it was too late. "Wait," she whispered. "How do I do the berserk battle thing?" But he was gone, disappeared in the shadows.

No owls swooped or small furry things skittered. Excitement ran up and down her inner thighs, shooting up her breastbone as she hopped from foot to foot, scanned the underbrush. Standing in the shadow of the grave house, crowbar in a death grip, her sweat cooled. Her breath fogged on the night air. She jogged in place, huffing to keep warm.

Something down by the river mewed—a stray cat, maybe.

The pit of her stomach filled with cold acid, worse than her first race. *Are you a cheerleader or a runner?* No, that was no good. Coach Wells's favorite rhetorical question wasn't what she needed right now. Running was bad. No running away. Dig deep, press on. *Fight like a girl. Yeah.* That was better.

She took the crowbar in both hands and pressed it over her head. Okay, she'd done this before. She just needed to get mad. Mal gritted her teeth and ran in place. Taylor Padowski grabbing your ass. The look on Brittnee's face when she told you to go away. Get mad.

Who gave a shit what Taylor and Brittnee did? Her feet were already cold and damp. She was alone in a cemetery with a guy with a tattoo a third grader could have done. And he wasn't even there anymore. He was probably back in the car laughing at her right now. She such was a dipshit.

And she had to pee. She looked back at the grave house. She would be pretty well hidden in its shadows.

"No," she said out loud. "I am not peeing on somebody's grave." Maybe in the bushes by the river though. No big deal. Every cross-country runner did it eventually. Mal hoisted her crowbar on her shoulder and started toward the river. The hurt cat was still down there, making sad sounds. She should look for it. She reached the lip of the slope above the river.

Her breath swirled out from her and over the water, joining the fog wisps that rose from it. It didn't disappear a few feet from her mouth as usual. The little cloud spun out over the water's edge and downward.

Mal tilted her head to watch and nearly squealed with excitement.

A rounded mass like the dome of a skull came up through the water. The whole body emerged, growing broader and bigger as it sucked the river into itself.

"Yes!" She danced, shaking out her numb fingers and legs. "Hey! Hey you, ugly!" She crouched in a ready stance, fists balled. "Come and get me, ice boy!" *This is going to be even better than kicking Taylor Padowski's ass.*

The ice demon waded toward her, white-gray in the dim light.

"Yeah, that's right," Mal taunted. "Come and get me."

Knee deep now, it picked up speed in the shallow water. Ice crystallized and broke on the surface of the water where it touched the monster.

"Whoo hoo!" She danced up and down. "Come on berserk. Come on invincible battle rage."

Nothing. No rush of power. No red vision narrowing the world down to her and her opponent.

"Come on!" she screamed again, hopping from side to side.

The next thing she knew Lars was running up the slope toward her, a white thing like a man chasing him. More white shapes moved on the water's edge. "Get back!" he yelled.

She dodged out of his way in time for him to hit the top of the slope. He turned and swung his spiked stick down on the frost demon's head. The head shattered and the body collapsed, sliding partway back down the hill. Lars raised his fists and bellowed. His eyes were fully dilated and he breathed hard, beating a fist against his chest.

More frost demons charged up the slope.

"What do I do?" Mal shouted.

Lars didn't seem to hear her. He swung his weapon, laughing at the frost demons. One of the monsters leapt at her. Clawed hands reached. Its mouth gaped, full of fangs like broken glass. It landed on her. It knocked her to the ground. Her crowbar skittered out of her hands and away in the dark grass.

Cold burned her skin. The monster's front claws held her shoulders and its legs shoved against hers, pinning her, grinding her hips into the icy mud. It bit down on her skull. She screamed in pain and confusion. She writhed underneath the icy mass, pounded at it with her fists. Pinned against the ground, she had no distance to punch. Her fists went numb beating its sides. She kneed it in the groin. Nothing.

For a second it released Mal's head and raised its face over her own. Her blood dripped from its mouth. She screamed again, trying to summon the battle frenzy, but there was nothing in her except fear and pain.

The demon shifted its grip, pinning her shoulders with both hands and lowered its head, mouth open toward her face. Mal met it with her forehead. Its teeth gouged into her face, but ice and bone cracked. Blood gushed out of her nose, but the demon's grip loosened. She wriggled, kicked against ice and mud and shot forward. Now her legs were bunched under the demon and she shoved, kicked again. She sat up and brought both her fists down on its head.

It half rose, clawed at her, but her shirt tore and she made it to her feet while the demon was still on its hands and knees. She kicked it in the stomach and the demon flinched away. But her foot slipped on the muddy ground and she fell, screaming.

The frost monster leapt on her again, mouth gaping. Mal curled into a ball, hiding her head. Ice claws raked down her back. She flailed at it, elbowed, kicked. It lost its grip and she scrambled to her feet. It dragged her down by her ankle. She kicked it in the head with her free foot, but its grip moved up her leg, hauling its bulk onto her body. She screamed and writhed. Clouds hid the moon. She was blind, fighting in the dark.

The ice demon pinned her to the ground with its body. It kneaded her shoulders with its claws. It rubbed its face across her exposed collarbone, savoring the warmth. It nuzzled its face between her breasts, down to her stomach. Cloth tore as it bit through her clothing. Its claws dug deeper into her shoulder and blood oozed out. They were both sliding down slick grass toward the water. Mal raised her head, struggling and it slapped her down.

Hot, humiliated rage flooded her. Pain numbed her fingers. Anger at herself, at the sheer stupidity of the world burned her. She was going to die a stupid, painful death because she was a stupid, stupid bitch who didn't listen to her mother.

"No! No." If she had to die, she was going to die fighting. She headbutted the demon again. The world inside her exploded. The cold, the wet, the pain disappeared. Only the fight remained. She would burn down the world, but she would not lie here and die.

Mal bunched all her strength into one hot ball of rage and threw the frost demon off her. She flailed to her feet and leapt on it as it rose. They rolled farther down the slope to the water's edge, the demon's claws tearing at her, her fists pounding it.

She straddled it and brought her head down again. Its face cracked. Icy ooze like river muck flowed out of the cracks. It wriggled out of her grasp and she stumbled after it. It fled into the river, splashing into the water, disappearing under the surface. She waded after it, fists flailing at the water that cheated her of her enemy.

River water swirled around her thighs. It pushed her down, trying to tug her under. She tripped on a rock and fell into the black water. For a second she lost all sense of direction. The shore was gone. Water all around her. The land rose under her feet. She tripped, fell, landed on hands and knees in the shallows, rose again, blundered into a bush that scratched at her face.

She clawed her way to her feet, fighting through underbrush. On the slope above her Lars was bashing frost demons. She ran up the slope but slipped on the wet grass. Her chin hit the ground and she punched it. She, rose, scrambled up, fell again. She grabbed a rock and lurched to her feet again, looking for an enemy.

Another frost demon grabbed her arm and she slammed the rock into its eye. It reeled and lost its grip. She kicked it away. More frost demons piled out of the water. She braced herself and screamed defiance at them. Lars pounded down the slope. He had her by the back of her shirt, dragging her up the slope.

"Come on."

"Get off me." She shoved him away and swung at a frost demon, crushing its jaw. Lars snapped another's knee with one kick. "Come on! High ground," he shouted.

"Come and get me, motherfuckers!" She charged the mass of frost demons pouring out of the water.

Lars wrapped an arm around her waist and tossed her over his shoulder. Above her the sky whirled. The clouds threatened her. She flailed at them, at Lars, at anything holding her back.

He dropped her at the top of the slope, pushing her forward. "Go. Go back."

She dodged him and headed back toward the frost demons, but he caught her sleeve dragged her along until they reached the shadow of the grave house.

He held onto her wrist, bent over gagging, trying to catch his breath. "Put your back against the wall and be quiet so they don't hear us. I'm going to call Carl."

Coward. There were enemies left to fight and he wanted to run. "I'll fight them then." She tried to yank his stick out of his hand.

He kept his weapon, but pulled a bowie knife out of his belt and handed it to her. Mal grabbed it and charged back around the grave house. Wind blew the clouds away and the moon shone. Gray-white shapes spread out through the grave, their heads weaving back and forth as if smelling for her. She charged straight for the nearest one.

Behind her she heard Lars shouting into his phone, "Carl, you have to help us."

Mal stabbed for the first frost demon's head and hit its shoulder. It screamed like branches creaking in high wind. She slashed at it again and again until it fell. She jumped over its body and lunged for the next one. She caught it in the neck.

More frost demons crowded around, arms reaching for her. She slashed wildly. The sound of ice cracking and splitting. They dragged her down, tearing at her clothes, her skin. She lost the knife. She choked, gasped, drowning in black water. She clawed and flailed.

The frost demons fell back. A scrap of moonlit sky shone above her. Lars swung his spiked stick like a baseball bat, catching the nearest frostie and knocking it off its feet. He stepped up, blocking the next one long enough for her to find the knife and claw her way back on her feet. She planted her back to Lars's and swung at anything that came near her.

Her lungs burned, her ears and fingers froze—some part of her knew this, but it seemed irrelevant. Every outgoing breath swirled away and down, absorbed by the gray demons. Only the space where her back met Lars's was still warm. They pressed together and fought on against the surging tide of hungry cold.

THIRTY-THREE

H eidrek parked Dr. Collins's Honda by the curb across from his sister's house. Such a quiet, tidy little place. So ordinary looking in the dark. His sister's truck was in the drive. Not a single light was on. But the rune lights showed on every door and in window.

She'd learned a thing or two from their mother after all. *Thank you Mother, for thinking only women should know such things.* That lack of information had made his first couple of years in the pen extra delightful. But there was always the internet in the prison library and Collins had encouraged "family heritage" research.

He sat in the driver's seat, rubbing a hand over his left wrist and studying the protections on the house. Something odd about these runes, familiar, but not. Some of them were written by two hands, one laid over the other, and the second was sloppier, but more powerful. And male.

He stepped out of the car and crossed the street to get a better look. The ravens stirred in the trees. He could break these barriers, but it would take time. Time and power he didn't have. Well then, he would get more now that he knew how. Heidrek took off Collins' shoes, digging his toes into the cold grass. He dug his fingernails into his wrist, drawing blood from the runes. He woke Stormcrow in the tree.

Following Heidrek's pressure on his mind, Stormcrow flew to the gable window and tapped on the glass. Rain rattled against Heidrek's face, but he kept his eyes fixed on the window. At last, Stormcrow's tapping was answered. The window slid up and a pale, teenaged boy peered out. So that was who had drawn the added runes. Heidrek raised a hand in greeting.

"Who are you?" the boy said.

"I'm your uncle. It's good to see you again, Caleb."

Stormcrow left the roof, swooping down on shiny black wings to land on Heidrek's wrist.

"You're supposed to be in jail," Caleb said. "What are you doing here?"

In answer Heidrek raised his hands so that the shirt cuffs fell away from his wrists. Rune light flickered around them. Caleb leaned farther out the window as if he had seen the answer to his prayers. "How do you do that?"

"Come down and I'll show you."

The boy hesitated. "Why should I trust you?"

"Why should you fear me? I've never hurt you. Now I'm offering you the gift of knowledge. I'm your own flesh and blood. Who else should you trust?"

Caleb snorted. "Really? I'm not stupid. I know what you did to my mom."

"The fight between your mother and me doesn't have to be between us, nephew." Heidrek held out his hands and made the runes flare in his palms, lighting the rainy night with blue fire. "Did you know that in the old days, a sister's son was sacred to a man? As precious as his own child. In elder days, you would have been my heir and I would have taught you everything I knew."

On Heidrek's wrist, Stormcrow croaked, laughing. Caleb tilted his head, as if he could half hear the bird, but not make out what he said.

"Do you want to speak the language of birds and animals?" Heidrek said. "You can if you're brave enough. You have the gift in your blood. I can sense it from here."

The rune fire lit Caleb's face in harsh shadows. He swallowed hard. "Okay. I'm coming down. But I'm not letting you in, got it? You can't cross our threshold."

"I understand." What did the boy think he was, a vampire out of an old movie? As if he needed an invitation to enter through a doorway. But entrance to the house wasn't what he wanted at the moment anyway. "Bring some food with you, raw meat if you have it, and I will teach you the first lesson in speaking the language of birds."

A few minutes later, Caleb, wrapped in a coat over his pajamas, came out the kitchen door. He eased the door shut and locked it behind him. Despite the rain, the boy pushed back his hood to look into Heidrek's eyes. He held a package of hamburger. "Okay, I'm here," he said. "What do I do first? Draw some runes with the blood, or what?"

Heidrek smiled, reaching out a hand to brush the freezing rain off his nephew's face. As his fingertips touched flesh, he felt their shared blood call out to him. His own blood, ready and waiting for use. "This first lesson will be easy," he said. "Open the meat. Hold it in your hand for the bird to eat."

Caleb obeyed him, holding a gob of ground meat out on a flat palm. Heidrek extended his arm and Stormcrow snatched the food. In the oak tree, other ravens woke, rustling at the scent of food. They swooped down to surround Caleb, settling on his arms and shoulders, jostling each other for a piece. Soon the Styrofoam tray was empty.

"Now speak to him," Heidrek said.

Caleb opened his mouth and tried to squawk. Stormcrow cocked his head and laughed.

"Stupid boy. I said talk, not make noises."

"Oh. Sorry. Uh, hi," Caleb said. "Can you understand me?"

"More food!" Stormcrow said. "More!"

"It worked. Holy shit, it worked!" Caleb yelled. "I understood that!"

Stormcrow spread his wings and cawed. "More? Mother woman does not feed us. You will feed us?"

"No, sorry. I don't have any more with me," Caleb said. Joy spread across his face and he turned to Heidrek. "I can't believe that's all it took. What else can you teach me?"

Heidrek tossed Stormcrow into the air. "So much more. But those lessons are more difficult. Are you sure you want to learn?"

"Hell, yeah! Anything. Teach me everything." Ravens fluttered all around them.

Drawing a pen out of the breast pocket of Collins's jacket, Heidrek said, "Give me your wrist."

Immediately, Caleb held out his hand, pulling back his jacket sleeve. Clicking the pen open, Heidrek drew the rune for *mine* over the place where the boy's pulse came closest to the surface. He dug in the pen nib, drawing and redrawing the rune. Caleb winced, but said nothing even as blood began to follow the pen's track. Tossing the pen aside, Heidrek pressed his fingers into the blood, then licked them. "Now," he said. "You are truly mine. You will do what I tell you."

Fear shone in Caleb's eyes, but he could only nod. "You know the language of the birds," Heidrek said, "but you cannot control them yet. If you want to truly understand something you have to join its blood to yours. Do you understand?"

Caleb nodded.

Calling on the berserk for speed, Heidrek shot his hand out and grabbed a swooping raven out of the air. He clutched the struggling bird to his chest, panting. Even that much of a berserk drained him now, all his power focused on the magic. He snapped the bird's neck and split its rib cage open, pulling out the warm heart. It pumped once between his fingers and lay still. "Eat this and you will know."

Caleb trembled. "You killed it."

"Everything dies someday. Few deaths are useful." He held out the heart. "Eat."

Caleb took it, cradling it in his palm. His mouth turned down, as if he were about to cry. Then all at once he stuffed the bird's heart into his mouth, chomping at it. Red blood smeared his lips.

Ravens rose up screaming, Stormcrow leading the flock into the air. The boy closed his eyes and tilted his head as if listening. "They hate me." His eyes shone wet with pain.

Heidrek smiled back and held out his hand. "We are already blood kin, you and I. Imagine the great things we can do together. Let me show you."

Dragging the boy's power into himself he spoke a word and the earth opened to him. They plunged farther, darker than he had ever gone before, past the boundaries of the mortal realm. Questing, he went out into the greater darkness. He followed the lines of power, touching them with his mind like intersecting threads that led through a blind maze. One thread, stronger, colder than the others led him downward, farther out, his nephew's eagerness fueling his own.

He pressed forward, following the thread as it grew toward the heart of winter. He came to a place, a crack in the world where fire and snow met. A place full of fogs and shadows. Powers clashed here, fire and ice in eternal conflict. It was a land of ice crags, jagged and broken slabs jutting upward. Great spouts of fire tore through the ice, melting it, only to have it fall and refreeze in new and fantastic shapes. Winds of chaos, fire born, ice driven seized them and they were tossed and battered, bowled over and beaten.

He scrambled for shelter, seeking some place to hide out of the wind, but there was none. There was no cranny in this place without conflict. The heat and cold did not cancel each other. Instead they intensified as they clashed. He thought he would split, freeze and crack like the glaciers looming overhead. He burned, his spirit form charring, but he held on to the power.

Wrestling with it was out of the question. All he could do was hold on. He clung with arms and legs to a pylon of ice that reared up beyond sight into the fog. The sheer power of the place threatened to destroy him. He would become a shadow on the winds, torn into shreds and eternally blown about, alternately frozen and burned.

But his nephew's blood fought the cold and the wind. All the drips and drops of power he had summoned in his concrete cell seemed like snowflakes lost in a blizzard compared to this. But there was no control, no direction. He bent against the winds, forcing the power through himself, creating a stable place for them to stand. He opened his eyes and bared his teeth to the cold. He let out a shout of triumph. It was lost in the wind's howl. He had found D`ragonheim, the heart of winter, home of dragons.

"I am your doorway," he told it. "I am your path out of your prison. Serve me and I will unleash you on the world."

A cruel voice laughed. Claws tore at him as they rushed passed. "I have no need of you," the maelstrom of fire and ice said.

Beside him, his nephew reached out to touch the dragon, stroking its crystal scales. "Beautiful."

"Serve me and I will feed you my own blood," Heidrek said.

The dragon raised an eyebrow and smiled. "You are a treasure seeker and your tongue is forked. Open the door into your world." It bent its sinuous neck so that Caleb could climb on, but Heidrek kept his grip on the boy's hand, drawing blood to blood. Together they rushed back into the world of men.

THIRTY-FOUR

arl jerked upright from a dream of white limbs reaching for him, grabbing him from every direction. He listened for a second, heart pounding. His phone rang again. He fumbled on the bedside table, looking for his phone but it wasn't there. He flung off the sheets and ran, clubfooted from sleep, into the living room. On the dinner table, the phone buzzed.

"Hello? Hello?" he shouted.

Dan jerked upright on the couch, a knife in his hand.

Lars, his voice broken by the blowing wind, said, "You got to help me. There's too many of them and she's nuts. You got to come get us."

Carl waved a hand at Dan to get up. "Where are you? What happened?"

"At St. Stanislaus Cemetery." The kid's teeth rattled over the phone. "I took Mal out...We were just going to hang—"

Bullshit they were just hanging out next to a river full of frosties at 2:30 in the goddamn morning. He took the phone into his room, cradling it between ear and shoulder as he pulled on his pants. "Where are you now?"

On the other end of the phone, Lars's voice cracked with panic. "At some little house. It's at the back end."

"Get Mal and get both of you up a tree or something. Get away from the river."

"I can't! She's...oh God, I can't even see her anymore. She's right in the middle of them."

Sweet suffering Jesus. If one of her kids died it might kill Harvey too.

"Carl, I don't know what to do!" Lars hiccupped. "I lost my berserk. Everything was fine and then it just went away."

Guilt like black water swamped Carl. He'd pushed too hard, asked too much. Even a young guy like Lars couldn't berserk all the time forever. If those kids died, he'd never forgive himself. Keeping his voice steady and slow, he said, "Take a deep breath. You're going to be okay. You can fight without the berserk."

"I can't!"

"Yes, you can. You're good, you know how to fight, you'll be fine. Have you got a weapon? Find a weapon."

"I've got a mace."

"Good. Dan and I are going to be there in five minutes. You can do anything for five minutes."

"Okay."

"You can do this. Go!"

The call ended.

Carl dumped the phone on the bed and stamped his bare feet into his boots and buttoned the fly of his jeans. No time for a shirt. "Dan! We are going. Now."

As they veered onto the I-190, he tossed his cell to Dan. "Call Harvey. Tell her to meet us there."

Dan snorted. "Like she'd come."

"For her own kid? She may kill us all when it's said and done, but she'll come. Now call her."

"Always giving orders," Dan muttered as he pulled up the number. Carl squinted into the night and drove.

Her phone woke Harvey out of rough sleep, full of dark caverns slick with ice and the sensation of being choked to death. She sat bolt upright, her heart pounding, throat raw. Her father's torc pressed down on her collarbone. "Just a dream. It was just a dream," she said.

Outside the crows screamed.

The phone buzzed again. Carl's number. She snatched at it. "What do you need, Carl?"

Dan answered. "You know where your kid is?"

Hot anger surged through her. "Dan, if you lured one of my kids out again, I will skin you alive."

"Relax. Your girl and Lars got themselves into a nest of frosties at the cemetery. Carl thought you should know."

In the background she heard Carl say, "Give me that." Then clearer, "Harvey, they're holed up by the mausoleum, but they can't hold out there forever. Look, I know you said you're done, but this is your own flesh and blood we're talking about and apparently there are a lot of frosties. We need your help."

Dark places underground, filling up with water. The fingers of the dead reaching for her throat. Darkness testing the windows and doors, trying to get in. Harvey shook away the images and red pain flared across her burnt eye. "I'll be there in ten."

Outside the yellow sodium lights turned the sleeting rain into yellow sparks. She knelt beside the bed and hauled the old footlocker out of the closet. She'd thrown the key into the lake years ago. She should have known she'd need it back.

Taking a deep breath, she wrapped her hand around the padlock and jerked. Wood splintered. The broken latch fell onto the carpet, padlock still closed. *So much for throwing things away.*

"Dammit, girl," she said, seeing the rumpled mess inside. "Next time take the chainmail." Hairs tore out of her head as she dragged the mail on, but she didn't have time for a braid.

"Hello, old friend," she said to the sword. Naegl—the Nail in the old tongue. Her nail file, Heidrek had called it. She'd given it one last sharpening before she put it away.

No time for thinking. She pounded down the stairs, sheathed sword in hand. "Ivor," she shouted. "Get up. I need you to watch the house." Someone had to stay home with Caleb. Not waiting for an answer, she ran into the kitchen. She paused at the door to stuff her feet into her boots. Ivor stumped into the kitchen behind her.

Through the window in the kitchen door, blue light like grave fire flickered. Harvey looked up, peering out into the rain. Caleb, dressed in a parka and pajamas, stood on the ice coated lawn. Her brother Heidrek stood beside Caleb, his hand on the boy's shoulder. Around them, a sinuous white fog coiled and flowed.

At Caleb's feet lay a dead raven. Blood smeared his lips. Behind her, Ivor gasped. Harvey put out a hand to stop him from charging forward. Slowly, she drew Naegl and unlocked the kitchen door. Stepping out, she called Caleb's name. He turned to look at her, as if she was a stranger. Heidrek turned with him, keeping his hand on the boy's shoulder.

"Hello, sister," Heidrek said. "This is a fine child you have. Is the other one as gifted as he is?"

Tightening her grip on her sword, Harvey ignored Heidrek and said, "Caleb, come over here please."

Slowly, Caleb answered. "Uncle Heidrek is teaching me things. He taught me to understand what the birds are saying. He taught me about the power in blood and darkness and cold. You should have taught me."

"I'm not a warlock, Caleb. I only know a few runes of protection."

Heidrek pulled Caleb closer to him. "I was going to kill them in front of you. I may still kill the girl. But this boy here," he looked down at Caleb, the freezing rain slicking his dark hair against his face. "He's far too useful to kill."

"Give him back and I'll tell you where to find Tyrfing," Harvey said.

"I know exactly where it is." Heidrek smiled at her. "Caleb told me all about it."

Keeping her voice light, she said, "Then you don't need him anymore. Get yourself a shovel and start digging."

"Do you really think I'm that stupid?" Heidrek's face twisted and his grip on Caleb tightened. "Do you think I spent all those months underground to be fooled by a trick like that? This isn't hide and seek, sister. You tried to bury me once and you failed. I won't give you the chance again. You're going into the grave, not me. And if you come back alive, you're going to kneel at my feet beside our father's bones and hand my sword to me as you should have done nine years ago."

"Never," Ivor said.

"Shut it, old man," Harvey snapped. She turned back to Heidrek. Mal was out there fighting frosties. But Mal had Carl and Dan already on the way to rescue her. Caleb was right here and he had no one but her to save him. To Heidrek she said, "I'll do whatever you want if you give Caleb back unharmed."

Heidrek looked down at Caleb, hugging him closer to his side. "That seems a fair trade."

Cold wind blew spatters of icy rain in Harvey's face. "And Mal? You'll leave her alone too?"

Heidrek smiled, a cruel curve of his lips over his teeth. "We'll see if she takes after her mother. Now, go get me my sword."

The wind blew harder, freezing rain turned to needle-sharp snow. The sinewy white fog around Heidrek and Caleb swirled upward, carrying them into the sky and they vanished from sight. Harvey lunged after them, vainly trying to catch Caleb, but they were gone.

"I'll get my things," Ivor said from the kitchen door.

CHAPTER

THIRTY-FIVE

As he drove into the St. Stanislaus Cemetery's parking lot, Carl switched on the tow truck's top lights to full power. In the glare the ornate cemetery gates loomed, chained shut. His bolt cutters were in the rear toolbox. He could be through the chain in three minutes. But Lars and Mal were out there, the cold closing in. He jammed down on the accelerator, plow fixed in place. Beside him Dan whooped. They blew through the gates, links off the chain pinging through the air.

Bouncing and swaying side to side, they tore through the cemetery, ignoring curves and fishtailing over patches of glare ice. Ahead of them the mass of frosties surrounded the mausoleum. Mal and Lars were backed up against the little building's wall, fighting for all they were worth.

Dan leaned out the window, a length of chain wrapped around each fist, and screamed a war cry that reached all the way back to the days when his ancestors drove Leif Ericsson's men from their shores.

Carl threw back his head and howled with him. He gunned the engine and lowered the plow, driving straight into the melee. Bodies crunched under the tires. Frost demons flew up and over the windshield. The wheels slewed sideways, catching and grinding on the mass of living ice. He threw the tow truck into park and grabbed his axe, the motor still running, the orange top lights blazing across the field.

Dan lunged out of the truck, arms churning, and disappeared into the murk. White arms reached out of the dark, and Carl knocked them back with the truck door. He slid out of the driver's seat, feet kicking, and braced himself against the truck's side, axe swinging. Ice crunched. He lunged into the attack, swinging the axe two handed. A frost demon's head went spinning away into the brush. He waded into the fight, headed for the mausoleum.

"Hang on," he shouted. "We're coming."

Ice crackled and snapped underfoot. Through the distant trees the river glittered, black and silver in endless motion.

More white shapes piled over the top of riverbank, an army of them. Two rushed him and he struck with the axe, catching the second one on the backswing from the first. He danced aside, dodging a blow and struck off the demon's hand. Keeping the light from the truck beams at his back he wove and ducked, slashing at glittering death.

From somewhere off to his left Dan laughed, a howling cackle underpinned by the snap of monsters being torn limb from limb.

Framed in the headlight's glare, Mal and Lars fought with their backs to the mausoleum. Lars's swings were weakening, his eyes wide with fear. But Mal fought like a lunatic, her blows striking fast and strong at anything that came near her. Every third swing or so, Lars had to dodge.

"Lars! Mal!" Carl shouted. "Get over here!" He sidestepped, spun, and buried his axe in a monster's back. More were coming from the river in the distance. Dan was already well ahead of him, meeting the flow of river creatures head on. The only problem with that was it left a large space between Dan and the rest of them and that space was full of monsters.

One lunged into the light straight for Lars. He threw up his hands, clumsily blocking the attack as he stumbled backwards. He and the demon went down in a tangle of limbs. Lars flailed at the monster on top of him. Without missing a beat, Mal spun on her heel, hacked the creature on top of Lars to pieces with her knife, and swung back around to stab the head of one coming at her from the left.

Carl dodged the snatching claws coming at him. The fight was too close, too tangled for him to chop at the creature with his axe, so he laid into its rib cage with his steel-toed boots. A frost demon caught Carl in the leg and he stumbled, almost falling on the mess of limbs. He recovered, landed another blow that cracked the creature's back, and kicked it into the nearest attacker.

He swung again, burying the axe in a frost demon's chest and kicked out at a second one, using the first as leverage. He wrenched the axe free and waded into the scrum of bodies, swinging the axe, back and forth, a pendulum of death in the midst of the reaching claws. Slowly, slowly he advanced toward the mausoleum.

"Dan!" Carl shouted. "I need you over here."

Lars yelped in pain, but there were still too many clawed hands and gnashing mouths between them for Carl to reach him.

"Lars, you still with us?" Carl shouted.

"Here, boss." A hand and then the rest of Lars appeared above the fray.

"Come toward the truck," Carl called. "Don't let them pull you out of the light."

"Can't—" Lars said in a gasp. "Busy...here."

Carl slashed and kicked and elbowed his way toward the sound. Slowly, slowly the number of frost demons started to thin out, at least in his immediate area. In the middle distance, Dan began making his way back toward them, but his progress was slowed by the creatures at his back.

"Hang in there, kids. I'm coming," Carl yelled.

Inch by inch, he cleared a path from the truck to the mausoleum, clawed hands catching at his legs. At last he reached Lars, burying his axe in the back of a frost monster as it dug its claws into Lars's chainmail.

Mal swung wide with her knife, nearly catching Carl in the arm. Her eyes were wide and unseeing, not registering friend or foe. Carl pulled Lars away, ducking around the mausoleum's corner to avoid becoming her next targets. Turning, she ran toward the knot of frost monsters around Dan.

Back to the truck while you can," Carl panted. "There'll be more along in a minute".

"We can't leave Mal," Lars said.

"I'll get her." He shoved Lars toward the truck. "Go while you've got a clear shot. Make a stand there until we get to you. Now!"

He shouted Dan's name, made the wooded cemetery ring with the sound, but got no answer. The air was filled with the sound of ice breaking. Lars put his head down and ran, dodging the frosties already surging into the space Carl had cleared.

"Mal!" Carl shouted. He ran after her, catching up to her as she joined the fight around Dan. Carl called her name again. No response.

"Sorry, kiddo. Have to do it." He reached past her knife swing and punched her hard enough to get her attention. She swung on him with a snarl and he ducked, dancing backwards. "That's right! Come and get me." He feinted at her with his axe. She shrieked and charged at him.

He turned and ran back to the truck, Mal close on his heels. But the sound of her feet behind him faded. He risked a glance back. *Shit.* She'd veered off toward the river, running at a mass of frost creatures that had come up the bank.

Lars, bleeding and cursing, still stood in the headlight beams' glare, swinging the mace like a baseball bat. "Get up in the back!" Carl shouted at him and took off after Mal. *Where the hell was Harvey?*

Mal was halfway to the river and twenty yards ahead of him when she met the wave of frost demons. The first one went down under her knife, but the rest of them swarmed over her and she disappeared.

One jumped Carl, landing on his back, sinking its teeth into his shoulder. He roared and spun, slamming the frostie backwards into a gravestone. He threw himself backwards again and again, beating at the fanged mouth that clung to him until the creature lost its grip and fell to the ground. He took off its head with one blow and charged into the pile swarming over Mal. Even with four frost demons piled on her, she was still kicking.

Carl heaved the last one off her and jerked back. "Don't hit me. I'm your friend!"

Recognition fought with the battle rage in her eyes and she hesitated for a split second. He caught Mal by the forearm and pulled her to her feet, swinging her in an arc toward the truck like a dance partner. "Go that way!"

She took off running, knife raised over her head to stab at the demons swarming toward Lars.

"Dan! We need you," Carl shouted again. The muscles in his arm burned. Every breath stung. The ground was slick with freezing rain that soaked down through his collar, through the layers of wool and flannel. He threw back his head and shouted, stoking the battle fires. But the berserk was running out of him like sand in an hourglass.

"We can't do this," Lars shouted from the truck.

"We have to," Carl called back.

The frost demons were endless as the river. For the second time, Carl pushed out into the dark, away from the sheltering light of the truck's beams, looking for Dan. He came to the downslope leading to the river and plunged over.

He forced his legs to move, but it was impossible to run through the brush on the steep, slippery ground. His thighs stabbed and quavered like jelly. He stumbled as he waded through the underbrush, slashing to the left and right.

He pushed deeper into the dark woods. A frost monster lunged at him, caught his arm. He shook it off, sliced it in half with his axe.

Another leapt on his back, but he slammed backwards, crushing it against a tree trunk. He took out a third with a kick and forged onward, calling Dan's name.

Carl came to a grove of pine where the thick carpet of orange needles padded the bare ground. Overhead the canopy blocked what little light there was. Here even the freezing rain couldn't reach the ground. He spun in the empty, silent space, surrounded by bare black tree trunks, all sound absorbed by the carpet underfoot. Chains clinked.

"Dan! That you?"

He was answered with a howl.

Dan emerged from the pine scented silence. He foamed at the mouth, and as he walked he lurched back and forth, chains swinging in erratic slashes. His leather jacket hung off him in tatters. He saw Carl and charged.

"Not me! I'm your friend." Carl dodged, sliding past Dan. He dodged again, but a link caught him in the ear. Too cold tell if the blow had drawn blood or not. Carl dodged and wove, some saner part of him wondering if he still had an ear. He kept his axe low, his empty palm open.

"Dan, it's me. It's your friend." Light began to dawn in the man's eyes. He stumbled and wove, still coming forward, but with a dim hesitation in his eyes. "We have to go."

"But...Harvey."

"I don't know where she is. But we're going to die out here if we don't go."

The berserk light flared in Dan's eyes and he snapped the chains taut between his hands. "Good."

Carl closed his hand over the chain. "I know, old friend. But die another day. The kids need us."

Lines of pain deepened around Dan's eyes. "Jon's kids." Carl nodded, silently. Dan dropped the chain and reached out his hand, gripping Carl's. In the silence of the pine grove, the two men pulled each other close, leaning forehead to forehead.

"It's just us," Dan said. "We're the only ones left."

Between their clasped palms, Carl felt his heartbeat matching with Dan's, finding their pace again. The last of the berserk faded inside him, the fire leaving behind its ashes. But there was still work to be done.

"Come on," Carl said. "We have to keep the kids alive."

Dan heaved a deep breath and stepped back, his mouth set in a line. His eyes were clear and focused. He raised the chain, snapping it taught again. Carl struck himself over the heart with the flat of his axe.

"Let's go," Dan said.

Together they charged back up the slope.

THIRTY-SIX

Harvey drove hunched over the wheel, peering out into the driving rain and heavy winds that battered the truck. Overhead lightning crackled through the clouds. Glare ice covered the road. "You kill me in a ditch and you're not getting your sword back, asshole," she shouted, not knowing if Heidrek could hear her. *Naegl* slid and clattered against the gear shift.

In the passenger seat, Ivor hung on by his fingers. "What's your plan when we get there?"

"We do exactly as he says until the children are safe."

"That's insane," Ivor said. "If the grave doesn't keep you, he'll kill you the minute you come back. And then he'll have an invincible sword."

She downshifted for traction and forced herself to slow the truck down. "My will and insurance policies are all in the safe in my room. The combination is my wedding anniversary. You do remember that date, right?"

Ivor's jaw worked for a moment. "Let me go. I'm old. Death doesn't scare me anymore. Who knows, I might meet some old friends."

Her eyes pricked and a knot formed in her throat. "Thank you, Ivor. But it has to be me. You know that."

"It's not right. The old shouldn't have to bury the young."

"I'm not that young anymore." She eased the truck into the cemetery parking lot.

The gates were wide open, battered and twisted. Harvey swung the truck down the winding narrow service roads, skidding around corners meant to be taken at a hearse's pace. Her high beams picked up swirling gray twists of river fog. The freezing rain turned into snowflakes that melted on the wet ground. In the light, tree branches and underbrush stood out stark and black, clawed fingers reaching for the truck. The slick gleam of ice coated each branch and twig.

Between her and the river, the cemetery was a mass of white bodies. Carl's truck was skewed sideways across the grass, the mausoleum a few dozen feet beyond. At the truck, Mal and Lars stood in the headlight beams, striking anything that moved toward them. In the distance, Dan and Carl tore a ragged path through the crowd, fighting to rejoin the young ones, but their movement was slow. And at the center of it all, the standing stone glowed bright with grave fire. The tall, rugged stone her ancestors had brought down from Nova Scotia and generations had carved with their names, shone like a beacon in the night.

White flakes swirled heavily around the truck, blocking out her view. For a few seconds Harvey could swear the writhing snow took on a shape, a lithe, scale covered body and grasping claws swimming through the snow.

"Do you see it?" she said to Ivor.

"Aye. A winter wyrm."

Their eyes met. Swords drawn, they leapt from the truck, a battle cry on their lips. As soon as her feet touched the ground, the whiteness swirled up around her, hemming her in. Somewhere in the storm she heard Caleb laughing.

"Do you want your damn sword or not?" she shouted.

Heidrek walked out of the snow, his hair and clothes coated in white. "Remember what you're here for, sister. I wouldn't want you to get distracted." He waved his hand and a tunnel of wind opened before her. Beyond, out in the falling snow, the others fought.

Dan went down again. Carl's axe swung tirelessly, his mouth chanting a battle song she couldn't hear. Ivor was lost to sight. Heidrek stood at her back and the wind hemmed her in. No way but forward to the standing stone. On either side, frosties stilled and turned their eyes toward Heidrek, leaving her an open path. She walked through them untouched, Naegl dangling from her hand.

"See, Mom, he's protecting you," Caleb said, emerging from the snow. His eyes were bright and his cheeks glowed as if he'd come in from a day of sledding. But a line of blue fire extended from his wrist to Heidrek, like a shackle. She glared over Caleb's shoulder at Heidrek, but she put her hand on Caleb's cold cheek. "It'll be fine, honey. I'll be right back." She set her jaw and walked toward the stone.

At the end of the wind tunnel, she laid her hand on the stone. Cold. The grave fires did not warm it. Beyond her the sounds of fighting were muffled, like a dream. She glanced at Heidrek once again and raised Naegl, slicing across her palm. Blood welled as soon as the slick edge pressed skin.

Warm blood pooling in her cupped palm, she held out her hand and tipped it over the stone. The red dragon etched over the stone's face writhed and hissed, blood running along all its lines. "Open," she said. "Let me in."

The stone cracked. Blue fire welled from the gaps.

Harvey raised her voice, gripping the stone. "I am Hervor Angan-tyrsdottir. I fear no dead men's fire. I fear no open grave. I am Hervor Angantyrsdottir and I come to claim my own. Open, earth, and let me in." Blood oozed out from under her palm, filling in the names of men long gone.

The center of the stone opened like a wall receding into an

endless, unlit drinking hall. She raised Naegl and stepped across the threshold. Dirt underfoot. Stone walls on either side, the roof invisible.

Benches lined either side of the hall and a fire pit ran down the middle of the floor, but the cold flame in it gave no light or warmth. Weapons, notched with use or pitted with age, lined the walls. But none of them was Tyrfing.

As she went, she counted each heartbeat, matching her echoing footballs to the beat in her chest. "I am the living," Harvey told herself with every thump. "This is not my hall. I have not come to stay in the hall of the dead." Only the trail of her damp footprints told her where she had been and where she had yet to go.

After a thousand steps, her mother's voice called to her from the darkness. "Hervor's daughter. Go back. Leave the dead alone or they will consume you."

"No. I fear no cold ghost. No grave hunger threatens me."

Her mother Anna appeared, long hair white around her face. "I see you chose swords over bread after all. Where are your children?"

"Heidrek has them."

Her mother sighed and closed her eyes. "Then they will be with us soon. Come. Leave your sword on a bench with all the other useless tools of men." She turned away.

Harvey tightened her grip on Naegl. "Where is he?"

Anna's ghost laughed. "Your father? How should I know? I make no loaves here. The grave is a cold and hungry place." She beckoned again. "Come. We'll wait for them together."

"No!" Her shout echoed down the hall. Grave flame flickered with the sound. "I did not come here to be patient. Now help me, Mother, or get out of my way!"

Her mother's shade faded from sight. "You always were a stubborn girl."

Harvey snorted and raised Naegl higher. "Damn right about that." She marched forward, making the stones echo, breathing low and slow through her mouth to calm herself. When no one else appeared, she shouted into the darkness. "Dad! Get out here, old man. I don't have time for this shit."

But it wasn't her father who came toward her.

"Harvey! Harvey baby," a voice shouted joyfully out of the dark.

Jon, his hair a golden storm around his face, ran out of the shadows and seized her in his arms. "Oh Harvey, Harvey, Harvey," he murmured, his lips hungrily seeking hers. "Lover. Wife. Mine." His hands on her ass held her tight against him, his mouth already moving away from her mouth, down her throat to her open collar brought her an ache and a want deeper than any food hunger.

Harvey meant to push him away, but she dropped her sword, tangling her fingers in his hair and holding him to her. She meant to say that she had not come for him, but his name came out in a sigh that remembered all the other sighs she had breathed for him.

His cold fingers pushed up under the warmth of her layered shirts as he kissed her and she remembered it all. That first urgent, giggling, half-hysterical fumbling in the back seat of his Mustang. Her crumpled satin wedding dress on the floor of the second-rate hotel where they never did get to the beach. The long rainy days when the factory was off work and all they had to do was make love to the sound of rain drumming on the roof. The fierce, still half-angry make-up sex that had brought Mal into the world.

Mal. Mal and Caleb were still in the land of the living.

"Jon," she said, "let me go." She struggled in his arms, not sure if she was holding him to her or pushing him away. "Please, let go. I have to save Caleb."

"Yes," he said and laughed, but he held her in a grip so tight she gasped for air. "My son. My wife."

"No!" Harvey wrenched away from him. "I loved you. I will always love you. But I'm not your wife anymore." They faced each other, panting in the dark. She ripped the gold wedding band off her finger. She shoved it into his hands, closing his cold fingers over the yellow gold. "You are dead. And I can't stay in the grave with you."

He closed his free hand over hers. Pale tears that glimmered with the dead man's fire ran down Jon's face. "I'm sorry."

"You should be." She held his hand tighter, her own tears hot and stinging. "I forgive you. All of it."

The light around him glowed golden; he smiled and his face aged. The cocky smirk of his twenties became a gentler, wiser smile she had never seen before. "You deserve to remain long in the land of the living." He leaned in, his lips pressed one last time against hers. "Kiss the children for me. Be well. Farewell." And he was gone, taking the light with him.

Stumbling, shaking with cold she went forward, counting and losing track of her heartbeats, breathing in ragged gasps.

After another thousand footsteps in the dark she heard other feet. Her father stood there, as still as stone, his body outlined in grave fire. They had buried him in his only suit, the one he wore to weddings and funerals. But now he wore the clothes of an ancient warrior. A round shield brooch held his cloak at one shoulder. Rough wool breeches were laced up to his knees and a wide gold buckle in the shape of a tangled dog biting its own tail clasped the belt around his waist.

His face still had the same grim look it had worn in his coffin. "Are you here already?" he said. Angantyr looked her up and down, mouth set in a grim frown. "What foolishness is this?"

"I've come for Tyrfing," Harvey answered. "Give it to me."

His face did not move, but his hand went to his sword hilt. "You have come to rob your own father in his grave?"

"Tyrfing is mine and you know it, old man. The dead don't need swords."

The furrows on his face deepened. "Why should you have my sword? What makes you the deserving one?"

Her eyes narrowed and she shouted into the dark. "I buried you. I took care of the mess you left."

"You're only a woman. A father's sword should pass down to his sons."

Your son sent me into the grave for him. He's not coming."

"You hid behind the law. Cowardly."

"You're calling me a coward? I've given birth twice. No man in our family can match that feat." Harvey raised her voice, gaining strength with anger. "Heidrek gives other men's blood to the darkness, but only I dare risk my own body. He sent me here because he feared the grave, but I am here alone in the hall of the dead and I am unafraid. Give up the sword!"

She thumped her chest with her clenched fist. "I have killed more monsters than you can name. I have passed through the grave fire. And I will kill the Winter Dragon." Harvey shouted so that the stone hall rang with her voice. "Do you hear me, you dead? I, Hervor Angantyr's daughter speak. Give me my sword or I will put a curse on your bones. I will leave your memory unspoken, your home untended. No one will remember your names."

Her father's ghost sighed, a wind of sorrow. His eye glistened in the dark and his voice pleaded, a soft note she had never heard from him alive. "Must I put a sword in the hands of my son's killer? Find another sword for your use."

"There is no other sword." She held up her bloody palm. "You call me a kinslayer, but what would you call the man who would kill his sister's son? What will you call the man who lets him do it?" She nodded at the ghost's silence. "Give me the sword."

Angantyr groaned like ice cracking on the river. "You and your brother were born to kill each other. Take it if there is no other way."

She took a step forward, held out her still bleeding palm. The blood fell in three drops between them, each making a red jewel in the soft dust. "By my own life and the lives of my children, I swear," she said. "There is no other way."

The ghost's voice was thin, like a distant echo. "Save your own life and the lives of your children. I will wait for my son to join me." He unclasped the sword belt and handed her Tyrfing, still in its scabbard.

She accepted Tyrfing with her free hand. "I miss you, Dad."

But she said it to the darkness.

The hall was empty again. Harvey spun on her heel and ran.

CHAPTER
THIRTY-SEVEN

Harvey burst out of the tunnel, a sword in each hand. The standing stone slammed shut behind her. Gray, pre-dawn light filled the cemetery. The blowing snow and crashing of frosties from the night before was silenced. A thin layer of snow lay on the ground under her feet. Even the ravens in the far trees were silent.

Harvey looked around, seeking her bearings. What seemed like a low wall of snow encircled her and the standing stone, but it moved and breathed. The white dragon raised its scaled head, blinking a reptilian eye at her. Caleb, smiling lips blue with cold and his eyes half closed, sat with his arms wrapped around the dragon's neck. Standing over Caleb, one hand possessively on his shoulder, Heidrek smiled at her.

"Welcome back. I was starting to worry," Heidrek said.

Panting, Harvey nodded at him, but didn't come any closer. She held Tyrfing close to her side in her left hand, Naegl at the ready in her right. "Where's everyone else? What happened to them?"

Heidrek lifted his free hand and gestured past the dragon. Frosties, at least two dozen of them, shuffled in a restless half circle around the truck. So that was how a frost demon had been able to appear in full daylight to attack her. Now Heidrek held these frosties under his control, using them to pen in Mal, Carl, Ivor, Dan, and Lars. The men stood in a ragged clump in front of the truck, their weapons at their feet. Ivor sat on the bumper, his hand pressed to his chest. Dan and Carl were poised, faces fixed on Heidrek as if looking for an opening to rush him. Beside them, Lars shivered uncontrollably. Mal swayed back and forth, eyes red and glaring through draggled hair.

Holding up Tyrfing, Harvey said, "Let everyone go and I'll give you Tyrfing."

Heidrek licked his lips and smiled. "Kneel and offer it to me."

"Fuck you. You want it or not?" She eased a step to the right, trying to get closer to Caleb. The dragon snorted at her. Lightning flared in the clouds overhead.

Caleb shifted on the dragon's neck. "You don't have to be so angry all the time, Mom. It's his sword. Give it to him and nobody will get hurt."

She swallowed hard around the lump in her throat. Under the dragon's watchful eye, she drove Naegl point first into the ground and knelt, holding the sheathed sword out on open palms. "You promised you'd give him back to me."

"I did." Heidrek strolled toward her. "And I will. Eventually."

He reached for Tyrfing.

Harvey closed her hands around the sheath as Heidrek did. She threw herself sideways, wrenching Heidrek towards her. He staggered, off balance, before he jerked back, both hands dragging on Tyrfing, and kicked her square in the ribs.

Then everything happened at once.

Heidrek's kick drove the mail mesh hard into her side.

Roaring like a wounded bear, Carl dove for Heidrek, Dan right beside him. Heidrek shouted in the old language and the frosties surged forward.

Still wrestling for control of the sword, Heidrek loomed above her. Harvey squirmed in the freezing mud, trying to drag herself up or him down with numbed fingers. The berserk slept inside her, the fire damped by the gray quiet of the tomb. But she hung on.

"Stupid bitch." He kicked her again. Air rushed out of her lungs. White sparks tunneled across her sight as she fought to breathe. Her bleeding hand slipped on the hard leather scabbard and the next moment she had lost it.

She rolled away from the next kick, reaching for her own sword. Her cut hand closed around Naegl's hilt and its point came out of the ground in a spray of slush and mud. She swung Naegl up to block the downward blow. Tyrfing, shining like lightning, sliced through Naegl. The broken blade went flying into the melee. She stabbed down at Heidrek's foot with the jagged end of her sword, but he slid his leg back and her broken blade struck a rock. The impact sent a shock up her wounded hand and she lost her grip on Naegl.

Heidrek stabbed down at her and Harvey rolled straight into his legs. She wrapped herself around him, tangling his legs together and sinking her teeth into his calf. Howling, he pitched forward. Tyrfing spun out of his hands into the churned mud and snow. Somewhere nearby others were shouting, but Harvey's world was compressed down to Heidrek's hands and face, his body pinned between her and the ground. She had to keep him from reaching Tyrfing. Nothing else mattered.

They writhed through the mud, clawing, punching at each other. The runes on Heidrek's wrist oozed blood and he shouted a word she didn't know. The next second the dragon's head loomed over her, mouth wide. She threw herself sideways, pulling Heidrek up between herself and the gaping jaws.

Heidrek landed another punch right across her temple and she sagged, fingers losing their strength as if all the nerves in her body had suddenly disconnected from her brain. Heidrek stood, pushing aside the dragon away as if it were hungry dog.

"Let me have her. I'll feed you later." Angry sparks of lightening crackled along the dragon's length.

"No. You said you wouldn't hurt her!" Caleb kicked and pounded on the dragon's neck to no effect.

Her head cradled in icy mud, her good eye struggling to focus, Harvey saw Caleb slide off the dragon and rush toward his uncle. Heidrek stooped to pick up Tyrfing. "Caleb!" She had to get up. Had to get between them.

But Heidrek pushed Caleb back with a shove to the chest. The dragon's head curved between them and she lost sight of the boy. Ribs aching, she tried to roll upright, hand groping in the muck for Naegl.

Heidrek planted one foot on her arm and ground into it with his boot. He raised Tyrfing in both hands, reading to plunge the blade straight down into her chest. Gray dawn clouds swirled above him and he filled up the sky.

This is it. This is my last sight of the world.

Glittering, Tyrfing plunged down.

Shouting a war cry, Ivor tackled Heidrek. They went down in a tangle of limbs and glittering metal. Harvey rose, but the sword stabbed up as Heidrek fell. It pierced through Ivor's body and out the other side. Ivor jerked once and fell still. Heidrek rose from the ground, shaking Ivor's body off the blade. He raised Tyrfing again and stabbed down, pinning Ivor to the ground.

Screaming, Harvey threw herself on her brother. The bear spirit inside her roared into full life. Weaponless as she was, she beat at her brother with her fists so fast he couldn't raise his sword. Heidrek faltered under the rain of blows, losing his grip on Tyrfing. She drove him away from the body, cursing.

His wrists bleeding, Heidrek turned and ran. Behind her, Tyrfing stood upright, buried in Ivor's chest.

"Don't you run from me!" She reached behind her for the sword, racing after her brother. But she was too late. Heidrek scooped up Caleb and threw him across the dragon's neck. The dragon's tail swung, knocking her through the air, even her full berserker strength unable to match the blow.

Heidrek rode astride the dragon with Caleb pinned down in front of him. Blood streamed from his nose where she had hit him, but he was laughing. "Goodbye, sister. Take good care of my sword for me until I come for it."

The coiled dragon leapt like a column of snow and disappeared into the clouded sky. The next second the frosties were on her.

Harvey tore through them as if they were an army of snowmen. Limbs snapped and heads crunched blade. The last of the frosties ran for the river. Mal and Dan ran them down and crushed them.

Her breath coming in ragged gulps of air, Harvey let the berserk go. Her legs and arms like rubber, her head threatening to fall she turned, slowly taking in the battlefield. Everywhere the grass was torn and gouged, snow beaten into slush. The door of the little mausoleum hung from one broken hinge.

Ivor's body lay trampled in the mud.

Harvey knelt beside him, Tyrfing still tight in her one good hand. She called his name, shook his shoulder. CPR. Chest compressions. She had to do something. But he was already dead. A trickle of half frozen blood trailed from his mouth.

Harvey laid Tyrfing across his chest, folding his hands over its hilt. With one mud caked hand, she reached out to close his eyes.

A choked sob above her. Carl, one arm clutching his ribs, dropped to his knees beside her. "Oh, God, Ivor, I'm so sorry. Harvey, I'm so sorry." Sobs wracked his body and he bent forward, covering his face with bloody hands.

Words crowded together in her throat and choked her. *Yes. All of it. None of it. I told him to come. I should have killed Heidrek when I had the chance.* Nothing came out. All she could do was lean against Carl and let her tears fall across his back.

A shadow fell across her face and she looked up. Dan, brass knuckles still on each hand, stood above her, his face a mask of grief, but his eyes dry. He struck himself across the chest, once, twice, three times, but still no tears came. The ravens rose into the sky shrieking.

Harvey closed her eyes and breathed hard, holding each breath in until she could hold back her tears. "We have to go." She shook Carl and he nodded. As she took Tyrfing back, he lifted Ivor's body, cradling him like a baby. Dan bent to help him.

Getting to her feet, she searched in the mud for the scabbard until she found it at the base of the standing stone. She rammed the still bloody blade into its sheath and wrapped the belt around her waist.

The curse had worked once again. Anyone the blade touches will die. Whoever carries Tyrfing will kill one of their own before they die. And now the sword was hers.

Stuttering a little, Lars said, "Shouldn't you clean that?"

"No," Harvey said. "Tyrfing can only go into its sheath still warm with blood."

His mouth made a silent O. A little behind him, smeared with black blood, her hair wild as water weeds, Mal stood trembling, hands clutched in front of her. Harvey pushed past him toward her daughter. "Mom...I—"

"I know." She threw her arms around Mal and hugged her. All the tears threatened to break out of her again, but she held them back.

"Is he really dead?" Mal said.

"Yes." Harvey held Mal tight while she cried. After a minute, she pushed Mal back, tears still running from both their eyes. "Can you walk?"

Mal nodded.

"Good. Because I'm too old to carry you." Mal hiccupped. A giggle-like sob broke out of Harvey and she held Mal tighter with one arm around her shoulders. "Come on. We have to go home."

"What about Caleb?"

"We'll get him back. I promised your father. And mine."

She nudged her daughter back to the truck where Ivor's body lay covered in a silver emergency blanket. She led the two-truck cortege out of the cemetery as the dawn stained the clouds pink and ravens flew behind them.

THIRTY-EIGHT

Heidrek flew over the roofs of the city, the dragon undulating beneath him. With one arm he held Caleb tight in front of him and with the other he still held the boy's hand, pulling blood and power from him, funneling it to the dragon. With every drop of blood that passed the dragon seemed to grow more solid. Heidrek breathed deep and hard, savoring the freedom of the open air.

No more bleeding his life away for scraps of power. Never again would he have to look over his shoulder, constantly watching. With this boy for power and his dragon for might, he could rule far more than a handful of men. Heidrek whooped for joy. Caleb barely stirred.

The storm above them grew.

Below him, a twinkle. A flicker of rune light sparkled in a dark and empty portion of the city. *Beer.* He nudged the dragon with his mind, and it dove.

They plunged down so fast into the square, he thought for sure the dragon would nosedive straight into the asphalt. But at the last second it curled around like a cat and settled into the loading yard with its head on its tail.

In front of him Caleb laughed like a drunk. He flopped forward across the dragon's neck, hand patting the scales. "Good dragon."

"Wait here," Heidrek told the dragon. He grabbed Caleb by the wrist. The dragon stared at him with dark amber eyes.

"Don't worry. We'll be back. Let go," Caleb tried to pull his hand out of Heidrek's, but he tightened his grip and dragged the boy along toward the loading dock. Caleb stumbled up the steps behind him. This hand holding wasn't going to work for much longer. But Arn or someone was sure to have a knife. He kicked open the locked door.

"Where are we?" Caleb said.

For a second, Heidrek wasn't sure. The setup was familiar. But the place was empty, the stove cold. The only light filtered in from a few dirty skylights above him. Where were the men, the laughter, and the firelight? Then he remembered. Of course. It was still early. People had jobs. He laughed.

A shout came from his left. "I don't know who you are, but you've got ten seconds to get the hell out of here!" Arn, Louisville Slugger raised high, stood in a back doorway.

Heidrek held out his arms. "Arnie! Don't you remember me?"

Lowering the bat, Arn said, "Well, I'll be dipped. They paroled you after all." Arn looked from him to the boy and back again. "Is he okay?"

Caleb stood still, his head cocked as if he was listening. His eyes were distant.

"He's fine," Heidrek said. "What have you got for me?"

Arn cleared his sinuses and moved toward the bar, leaning the bat against one of the sawhorses. "You're lucky—I've got a brisket smoking in the back and it don't do to leave it untended, so I spent the night. What's your pleasure? Beer, mead, or moonshine?"

"Mead. And a knife."

"Okay." Arn pulled down a bottle of mead, setting it and a cup on the bar. He took a jackknife from his pocket and handed it over. "The parole board didn't listen to Harvey after all, huh?"

"Where there's a will there's a way." Heidrek flipped open the pocketknife. He shoved the kid against the bar and sliced open his shirt above the heart. Behind him, Arn shouted. Caleb struggled, but Heidrek braced his arm against Caleb's neck, cutting off his air. Ignoring Arn, Heidrek carved runes into the boy's chest—Ownership, Dragon, Blood, Mine. He took the bottle of mead Arn held and poured it over the wounds.

The magic snapped into place. *Nice. Now he didn't have to bother holding onto the boy every second.* He let go and Caleb slumped to the floor, blood and honey liquid seeping through his fingers.

Caleb looked up, eyes struggling to focus. "You promised to teach me."

"You're learning aren't you? Now be quiet." He shoved the kid to one side with his foot and swigged the mead from the bottle. Arn edged toward his bat. "Don't even think about it, Arn."

Arn wiped his hands on his apron. He gulped hard. "You want something to eat? That brisket should be ready about now."

"That's a great idea. I'm starving."

Arn backed toward the door he'd come through. "Whatever you want."

From the floor, Caleb said, "The dragon's hungry too."

Heidrek kicked the boy, who curled in on himself further, but didn't make a sound. Draining the bottle, Heidrek set it down with a sigh. It was good to be home.

CHAPTER

THIRTY-NINE

They laid Ivor's body on his bed. Carl offered to stay, but she gently pushed him out of the room. For a long time, she sat on the edge of the bed and held Ivor's hand. Outside, heavy snow fell, thick fluffy curtains of flakes that promised to go on forever. Gradually the room lightened as the sun rose behind the clouds. For once, she couldn't hear the crows.

It is your duty to weep for the dead. One of the other things her mother had tried to teach her.

I'd rather laugh with the living, Mom.

And now she couldn't do either. The knot of tears in her chest clogged her throat and strangled her heart. Her grief was like a lead blanket pressing her down.

You're just like your father. You and your brother. You'll both come to bad ends.

Alright then, Mom. If that's what I'm destined for. But I'll go down fighting.

Without waiting for a reply, she went into the little side bathroom Ivor had used and washed her face and hands. She combed out her hair and put it up in a braid, wrapping it around her head into a

237

dark crown. No point in giving the enemy something more to hang on to.

She rung out the washcloth and used it to wipe away the muck from Ivor's face and hands. She rummaged through the coin jar on his bedstead until she found two gold dollar coins. Not real gold probably, but close enough. Sacagawea with her baby on her back looked expectantly from the coins' surface. The coins' back showed a man walking a steel beam. That seemed fitting. She placed them face up over his eyes, holding the lids shut.

"Sleep well, old man. Say hello to your son for me." She kissed his already cooling forehead.

Then she opened the cedar chest that always stood at the foot of his bed. It had been her mother-in-law's pride and joy, one of her wedding presents. In most houses it would hold an old wedding dress and pillowcase lace tatted by someone's great-grandmother, or baby linens and sepia toned family albums, maybe a fading corsage pinned to a satin prom dress.

In this house it held a treasure trove of swords and axes, mail byrnies, and leather bracers, all oiled and wrapped in silk to keep off the rust.

She stripped off her wet and filthy clothes, wiping away the mud. One by one, she took new clothes from the chest. Wool pants, lined against the cold. Heavy socks, hand knitted and carefully darned. A quilted shirt, tailored to keep the wearer warm under cold steel. She left the mail shirts for the time being, but she strapped Tyrfing around her waist.

One more set of things in the chest—Jon's lovely swords. The ones she hadn't been able to make herself bury with him because then he would be truly, finally gone. She selected the best of them, weighing it in her hand. It was longer than Naegl and had a narrower blade. Its edge was bright as ever. It would do nicely for Mal.

The others were gathered in the living room. Dan sat on a kitchen chair staring into the beer bottle in his hand.

Carl just sat. Tears ran thickly down his cheeks. His axe lay on the floor by his feet.

Lars and Mal were nursing their wounds on opposite ends of the couch, lying under blankets in separate piles of misery. Mal wept with her face buried in the couch cushion.

Beside Mal, standing at the ready with one hand laid protectively on the girl's shoulder, stood Coach Wells. Her clothes were nothing extraordinary, but at her waist she carried a long, curved sword with a wicked hook in the end. A polished wooden club was tucked into an orange sash around her waist. Around her neck she wore a double row of cowrie shells interspaced with deep orange beads.

Harvey and Coach Wells's eyes met. "Mal texted me what happened," Coach Wells said. Harvey's throat tightened. She nodded once and mouthed "thank you."

It took her a second to clear her throat so she could speak. When she did, she addressed Mal.

"Mal," she said. "Come here, please." Mal lifted her head off the couch, red eyes puffy. Hugging her blanket around her she got up and came over to Harvey. The others watched them silently.

Harvey wrapped her arms around her daughter and kissed her on the forehead. "I'm sorry, sweetheart. I should have prepared you instead of hiding you." Mal dissolved into tears again. Harvey stood there in the doorway, rocking her back and forth in her arms until the sobbing stopped. "Alright. I have something for you."

She held up Jon's sword. "Hold out your hands."

Mal obeyed, letting the blanket drop to the floor.

"This was your father's sword. His favorite. Carl made it for him as a wedding present. He had it with him when he died."

Mal took the sword in both hands, cradling it gingerly across her palms. She sniffed hard. "Shouldn't this go to Caleb? Like, father to son?"

"No, honey. This sword was always for you. I put it away because I was afraid of what might happen to you, but your dad always planned on giving it to you someday. Besides, I think Caleb has a different destiny."

Mal hugged the sword. "Is Caleb going to be okay?"

"I don't know. But we're going to try to get him back. I promise you."

Looking down at the sword, Mal said. "Does it have a name?"

"Bunny Killer. Your dad had a weird sense of humor."

Mal's face cracked into a watery smile. She giggled, then snorted, then she and Harvey were both laughing so hard they had to lean on each other for support.

When the laughter had finally died down into weak giggles and sore sides, Harvey gave Mal another squeeze. "Come on. We've got work to do."

She led Mal to the kitchen where she first got a packet of stew meat out of the fridge and put it on the counter. Then she climbed up on a chair and dug in the back of a high cupboard for an unlabeled bottle sealed with cork and wax. She cut open the seal and poured the heady gold liquid into a ceramic goblet. A smell like drunk bees filled the kitchen. "This is the very last mead your grandmother made before she died."

Mal sniffed it. "Wow."

"I know. Come on. Bring the bottle."

Holding the cup high, Harvey walked to the center of the living room. All the men's eyes were on her. "I am going to war against my brother," she said. "One of us, at least, is going to die." She took a long drink from the cup.

Then she handed the cup to Carl. "I shunned you, when I should have honored your courage. Please forgive me."

He stood, his hands closing over hers. "Welcome back, my queen." New light shone in his eyes as he drank from the cup.

Next she went to Dan. "You lost a brother when I put Heidrek in jail and another when Jon died. But his children still live. For their sake, forgive me."

Dan stared down into the depths of the cup, his jaw working. "You turned your back on us." She nodded. "I did. I'm sorry."

"I don't know if I can trust you, Harvey," Dan said. "But he's got your kid. It's not right." He took the cup and drank from it. "Right," he said, handing it back to her. "You tell us how we're going to stop this winter. I'm already sick of snow."

Next she went to Coach Wells. Before she offered the cup, she said, "Are you sure you want to be here? You have everything to lose by getting involved with us. I have no right to ask for your help."

Coach Wells studied Harvey's face for a few minutes. "I know that," she said. She took the cup, saluted Harvey with it, and drank. As she handed it back, she said, "You can call me by my first name."

"Thank you, Lily," Harvey said. "I won't forget this." Lily nodded her head to one side, as if to say "we'll see."

Finally, Harvey approached Lars, who sat on the couch, eyes wide and his mouth in an O.

"Pretty weird shit, isn't it?" she said to him. He nodded, looking up at her from the couch. He seemed younger at that angle, all his cockiness drained out of him. She took a long look at him, remembering what Carl had said about Lar's past.

"I need your help," she said, her voice gentle. "But I need to know I can trust you."

He nodded mutely, his mouth quivering. "I'm sorry," he croaked. He swallowed hard, licking his lips and looking over at Mal. "I'm real sorry about taking Mal out and about what happened in the cemetery. I didn't mean to get anybody killed."

She put her hand on his shoulder. "I forgive you about Mal. It's not your fault Ivor died."

Lars sniffed hard and swiped his sleeve over his face.

"The killing isn't over," she said "Someone else is going to die today. Maybe even a lot of people. Are you ready for that?"

Lars pulled his shoulders up, sticking out his chest. He held out his hand for the cup. "I drink this and I'm in?"

She nodded.

241

"Okay then." He scrunched his face as if he were about to swallow cough syrup and took a giant gulp, choked, turned beet red, and finally managed to swallow. Everyone else in the room burst out laughing. Harvey laughed and patted him on the back until he stopped coughing.

"Hey," Lars said, still sputtering a bit. "That stuff's good. Is there more?"

"Later. A little of this goes a long way." Harvey turned to face the rest of the room. "Come on. We're going to feed the crows."

Mal and the others fell into line behind her, following her out through the kitchen. She grabbed the meat off the counter as they went. Out in the yard, the snow was already shin deep. Only a scrap of black feathers peeked out where Heidrek had tossed the crow he had killed. Harvey stopped in front of the dead bird. Mal and the others fanned out around her, a half circle of protection in the falling snow.

Harvey ripped the plastic off the meat. "Stormcrow!" She held up the plastic tray. The largest raven swooped out of the tree and snagged a chunk of meat. Twice more, he flew past, snatching food and away before she could touch him. On the third pass he flew back and landed on her outstretched wrist.

"Raven killer!" he screamed at her. "Your brother killed mine. Your child drank my brother's blood."

"I am sorry for your loss," said Harvey.

Stormcrow pecked at her wrist hard enough to draw blood, wings flapping.

Harvey winced, but didn't shake the bird off her wrist. She said, "Listen to me, Stormcrow. I am going to feed you." The flailing and cawing stopped. In the tree, a hundred ravens held their breath. "You remember my vow at the prison?" she said.

"Yes, One Eyed."

"My brother and I are at war. I am coming to hunt him down and kill him with my own hands. Do you understand?"

"Yes, One Eyed." Stormcrow stropped his beak against her wrist, peering at her with first one bright eye and then the other. She ran a finger over the top of his head and down his back.

"But my son is not for you. You and your kind may not touch him."

The raven ruffled its feathers angrily. "Food?" it croaked.

"Tell me where he has gone with my son. Lead me to him." Harvey flung the rest of the meat into the air. In an instant, black wings filled the yard. Not a drop of meat touched the ground.

Stormcrow rose up in the air, his flock close behind him. The mass of birds whirled together, a spiral of living black in the falling snow. "He waits by the river. In the place where your kind go to drink," Stormcrow called.

Cawing, the birds settled back into the oak tree, shoulders hunched against the snow. The sound of their caws echoed off the surrounding houses. Harvey drew a deep breath and turned to her little warband. Dan cracked his knuckles, sucking on his teeth. Coach Wells—Lily—had a hand on her club, her eyes watching the birds overhead with suspicion. Mal's eyes were wide with fear, but she held her father's sword tight in both hands. Beside her, Lars stared up at the crows, his mouth pursed in a silent whistle. And Carl—he was as he always had been. His red-gold beard bristling, the blue dragons on his forearms rippled as he flexed his hands for action.

"Come on," she said. "Let's get inside and make our plans. I want my son back before we're up to our ears in frosties." She put an arm around Mal's shoulders and led them back into the house.

CHAPTER

FORTY

Outside Harvey's kitchen the snow fell in thick, slow clumps, the kind of snow that threatened to last all day and into the next. The sun had hardly reached full brightness but arguing had already broken out around the table. School was canceled due to the heavy snow falling over the city, but the factories were still open. They wouldn't shut down unless the entire city did, but she wasn't due back to work for weeks anyway.

Harvey stood against the counter, a coffee mug in her hand, watching Dan and Carl circle each other, debating strategies for getting into Arn's. At some point her mom brain was going to kick in, she was sure of it, and she'd care that the bathroom floor was covered in filthy towels and drying socks, that her fridge was half empty by 8am. But right now, all that mattered was getting Caleb back. She sipped her coffee and thought.

"He's at Arn's," Dan said. "We get our gear together, we go down there, and we kill him. It's that simple. The faster we move, the less time he has to protect himself. What the hell are we waiting around for?"

"An army," Carl said. "We barely made it last night. Arn's is right on the river and it's protected on every side even without a goddamn dragon. Getting through that alley would be like laying siege to a castle. Do you have a siege weapon somewhere on you, because I left mine back in the thirteenth century."

Lars scooped the last of the oatmeal out of the slow cooker and shoveled it down. "How about the guys under the bridge? We could ask them."

Mal rolled her eyes. "You want to ask a bunch of homeless junkies to rescue my brother? How stupid can you get?"

"Hey!" Lars said. "Sarge is a badass. And I'm not hearing any smart ideas from you, Miss Junior Varsity."

Mal glared at him. "Why aren't we calling the cops? Somebody kidnapped my little brother. That's what cops are for."

A chorus of "No" broke out from the adults.

Harvey scowled. "A man on a dragon stole my kid? They wouldn't believe us. And they'd come down here asking questions."

At the kitchen table, Lily gave Mal a stern look. "Cops do not make things better. Or did you forget how it went the last time you were in school?"

Mal hunched down in her seat.

Lars laughed. "Excuse me, ma'am, did you know you have a dead body in your back room? We're going to have to take him downtown for questioning. Somebody call CSI: Ghosttown."

Mal punched him in the arm. "That's my grandfather you're talking about, you fuck!"

Harvey reached out and snagged Mal's fist. "That's enough. We're not here to fight each other."

Lily drummed her fingers on the table. "What you need is some bait. Something that will lure your brother out. Or his dragon. Too bad we don't have a huge pile of gold."

A smile spread over Harvey's face. "I'm an idiot," she said. Putting down her coffee, she pushed off from the counter. "He has a hostage, but so do we."

She patted Tyrfing, still strapped to her side. "We're going to get our weapons together and we're going to make him come out of his hole to get Tyrfing."

Carl shifted his feet. "Harvey, he has a dragon. Even out in the open he's pretty much invulnerable."

"But he's proud. He's wanted Tyrfing ever since he was a boy. He's not going to let me call him out in public and get away with it, and he's certainly not going to let me destroy his sword." She clapped her hands together. "I know what we need to do. Get yourselves together in ten minutes. We're going to work."

She stepped out onto the concrete kitchen steps, calling, "Stormcrow! Go down to the river. Tell Heidrek to bring Caleb to the factory if he ever wants to see his sword again. If he doesn't show up or Caleb dies, I'll drop Tyrfing into the hottest arc furnace we've got."

Gliding through the snowflakes on wide, black wings, Stormcrow circled over her head, cawing. The rest of the flock rose up with him into a spiral of fluttering wings before soaring away under low clouds toward Arn's.

They geared up in the living room, their pooled resources spread out across the floor and draped over chairs. Lily accepted a light mail shirt after proving to herself that she could still move as nimbly as before in it. Carl shoved a helmet into Lars's hands and, for once, got no argument about it. Even Dan agreed to put on chainmail in place of his destroyed leather jacket, though he absolutely refused to put on a helmet or pick up a weapon other than his brass knuckles.

"You aren't mixing it up with the cops this time," Harvey said. "Please, use an edged weapon. Or at least a helmet."

Dan shook his head. "I never have before. Now's not a good time to learn."

"Your ancestors did," Harvey said.

He narrowed his eyes at her, his voice descending into a growl. "Don't tell me about my ancestors."

Harvey's shoulders slumped. "I'm sorry."

He quirked a corner of his mouth at her, his version of "apology accepted." He flexed his wrists, the silver bands he wore flashing. Each one was etched with an eight-pointed star. She laid a finger on one. "You didn't have these before. What are they?"

"Mi'kmaq. Ask me about them another time. If we live."

"Right. If we live." She slapped him on the shoulder and turned away, swallowing hard. In the corner, Carl was schooling Mal and Lars on how to ride the berserk without killing your nearest and dearest.

Harvey bent to lace up her work boots, the leather still curled and charred over one toe where the flash had hit it. She wriggled her chainmail on over her head and strapped Tyrfing on over it. Then she led them out into the snow, already ankle deep and piling higher. The ravens spiraled up into the air chanting of war.

FORTY-ONE

They drove in caravan toward the factory, Carl's truck leading the way with the snowplow down. The flock of ravens met them there, landing on the wires and fence tops as Harvey's little war band arrived in the parking lot. There were a few more open spaces than there should have been, but from the number of cars and trucks it was clear the factory was working and full of people. Wind off the lake whipped the falling snow horizontal across the train tracks separating factory from water.

"No helmet?" Carl said to her as they gathered out of the wind in the lee of her truck near the entrance. She tucked a wool cap down over her ears and pointing to the eyepatch. "I'm blind enough as it is."

She scanned her little group. Dan, Lily, and Carl stood still, arms loose, but Lars was bouncing on his feet, a heavy bass beat coming from his earbuds. Mal had her hands white knuckle tight around Bunny Killer's hilt. *The kids shouldn't be here. They really shouldn't.*

"Right, we're going in through those doors," Harvey said, pointing to the doublewide loading doors that led onto the train tracks. Even in the falling snow, the loading doors stood half open.

Shimmering waves of heat billowed from them. "You guys flank me. We're not going inside until we see the dragon coming. I want him to see me and Tyrfing. Don't berserk until you absolutely have to, especially you two." She gave the youngest pair a look. "I don't want you wearing out too soon or hurting an innocent bystander."

Mal nodded and swallowed hard. Lars gave her the thumbs up, though she doubted he could hear her over the music.

"Everybody remember, I'm carrying a cursed sword and it doesn't really care who it kills. Don't get too close to me. Let me handle Heidrek. Carl, you've got the most control, so you're in charge of grabbing Caleb if you can. The rest of you," she paused, her stomach tight, "you tackle the dragon. Lars, stick with Dan. Mal, you're with Lily—Coach Wells. I want both you kids to listen to them. You got it? Even if they tell you to retreat. Especially if they tell you to retreat."

"Follow Dan and Lily's lead, but give each other space." She looked especially hard at Mal, holding her very first sword with only five minutes of practice under her belt. "It's a big dragon. Be sure you're not stabbing someone on your side."

As she finished speaking, a sound like a tornado tore through the clouds overhead. The ravens erupted into the sky, shrieking and retreating for the top of the factory. They'd have full view of the battle. All the better to scope out their meal. Where humans fought, ravens ate well.

"Here they come!" Harvey shouted. She drew Tyrfing, and it gleamed silver-white, lighting up the falling snow. With the sword held in front of her like a torch, Harvey ran for the factory doors. At the doors she turned, waving Tyrfing over her head at the dragon that circled above the factory. The dragon itself was white, winking in and out of visibility against the gray cloud cover and the heavy flakes that fell from the sky. But the winter wyrm was low enough that Harvey could see her brother riding its back, her son clutched in front of him.

"You want this?" she screamed. "Come and get it!"

Behind her the others fanned out, crouching and shielding their eyes against the gusts of snow.

The dragon folded its wings and stooped, plunging out of the low clouds over them. It landed a dozen feet from her. Snow billowed up around it, blinding everyone. Harvey took a deep breath and pulled the patch off her eye. Now she could see the dragon even more clearly. It was bigger, more solid than it had been before. But it flickered, like a light bulb with a bad connection. In front of Heidrek, blue grave light tied Caleb to the dragon. When it flickered, he did. Cold acid flooded through her veins, but she tightened her grip on Tyrfing.

"What are you waiting for?" she shouted into the snow.

As the snow settled, Heidrek shouted, "Give it to me, Harvey. Do it now or I'll kill him in front of you." Caleb slumped, his head not rising to look around.

"Nice try, murderer!" she shouted back. "We did it your way once. Now we do this mine. Are you afraid to face me? Is that it? You're weak. All you've got are some pretty lights on your fingers and a big lizard. And you can't even control that without Caleb's help. Where's your berserk gone? Did you leave it behind in prison?"

With a scream of rage, Heidrek spurred the dragon toward her. It reared up, wings beating, and charged. Harvey turned and ran onto the factory floor.

A dozen feet inside the double doors, she turned to face the dragon Snow, driven on blizzard winds, plastered her. All around her men shouted. Snow landed in the two hundred-ton ladles of molten steel and exploded in a shower of steam and sparks. Alarm bells and horns went off as the line ground to a halt.

The next minute the outside light was blocked as the dragon thrust its head and shoulders through the doors. It lashed its long neck as its wings caught on the doorframes.

"Now!" Harvey yelled.

From either side, her war band attacked the dragon. The berserk roared to life within her, stronger and fiercer than ever, but she forced herself to run away from the fight. She ran straight for the two-story arc furnace, legs pounding up the stairs to the top. Loads of steel scrap and coke lay ready to be shoveled into the heat below. She ducked under the safety guards toward the glowing furnace mouth. Her feet struck up clouds of cinder dust.

Men in silver heat suits shouted at her to stop, but she held Tyrfing as close to the fire as she could bear and shouted, "Give me back my son. Give him back or I swear I'll drop it in the fire and you can fish for it. Tyrfing might survive, but you sure as hell won't."

"Enough!" Heidrek's voice echoed through the factory. Even the dragon froze at his command, laying its head on the ground. Below her, Carl threw an arm around Dan, holding him back.

"Well?" she said. "You want it, come get it."

Heidrek slid off the dragon's back, dragging Caleb behind him. He stalked toward her, the runes around his wrists glowing blue. Even at this distance she could see his mouth working, though cursing or calling on his power she couldn't tell.

In her burned eye, the line between Caleb and the dragon stretched, thinner but still very much there. The dragon moaned and Caleb looked back to it. But Heidrek dragged him forward by the wrist. Harvey's heart thundered in her chest. Maybe she wouldn't have to kill her brother after all.

A man's weight hit her from behind, knocking her to her knees. Mac wrapped his arms around her throat and she flailed, arms windmilling. She thrust back with her elbow into his ribs even as she gasped for air. His heat suit dug into her throat, crushing her windpipe. *Must not let go of Tyrfing.* Whatever she did, she couldn't let go of the sword.

She summoned the berserk and rolled forward, flinging him over her head and landing on top of him. The air went out of his lungs with a groan and his grip relaxed for a split second. She rose, but he dragged her back by her arm. She turned and fell with her full weight, elbow driving into his throat. Mac choked and gagged,

251

losing his grip on her. Harvey leapt to her feet and kicked him hard enough to lift his body off the ground.

But the berserk was on him as well and he grabbed her leg, hanging on with his arms and teeth. Tyrfing hummed with power in her right hand. *Kill him and be done.* But even in her full berserk, she held back. With her left arm she knocked the hard hat off his head. With her right hand, she slammed the sword's pommel into the top of Mac's skull and he fell back, eyes rolling. Dead or unconscious, she didn't know or care. She kicked him out of her way.

Behind her footsteps rang on the steel stairs. Harvey turned and Heidrek charged at her. Whether he still had Caleb, she couldn't tell. And then he was on her and there was no time to look.

She swung Tyrfing around for a killing blow, but Heidrek threw out his hands at her, runes alight. Wind and snow rushed off him, in a blinding attack that cut her face like a thousand razor blades. Instinctively, she turned sideways, shielding her face. Behind her the snow hit the arc furnace and flashed into boiling steam. She and her brother were enveloped in choking, cinder-filled fog that clogged her nose and mouth. Her good eye squeezed shut. Even through her burned eye, Heidrek was a cloudy shape, a black void marked by flickers of grave light in the heat and fog.

Harvey didn't dare stab at Heidrek. What if she hacked at her brother and killed her child as a result? "Caleb, where are you? Caleb!"

Harvey backed toward the furnace mouth, watching her brother's shape. "You let him go, you hear me? Do it, Heidrek, or I'll drop this into the fire."

Her brother's outline wavered and split. She swung wildly at a dark shadow but cut only air. She stumbled against Mac's body. Below her men and the dragon shouted in pain, but she edged ever nearer to the fire, trying to watch all sides at once.

FORTY-TWO

A t the far end of the factory floor, on the platform above the little war band, Harvey, Heidrek, and Caleb disappeared in a cloud of steam and sparks. For a heartbeat, all of them, dragon, berserkers, and workers, stayed frozen, their eyes locked on the fight.

Carl tightened his grip on his axe. It wasn't the plan, but he should be up there helping Harvey. He glanced out of the corner of his eye at Mal, her face blotched white and red with heat and battle. Her hair was wild, her eyes wide, going from dragon to furnace and back again.

The dragon, released from whatever had held it, made Carl's decision for him. It raised its head, roaring, and swung toward the nearest ladle of molten steel. From its mouth, snow and wind came, freezing the ladle. The giant bucket cracked and broke, spilling liquid fire across the floor. Steam exploded. Workmen scattered, screaming.

"Move!" Carl grabbed Mal by the arm and dragged her away from the billowing steam clouds. But she shook him off and ran at the dragon, screaming a wordless war cry. The dragon whipped its head around at this new attack, mouth wide.

"Take that, you scaly bastard!" Lily rushed in from the other side and swung at the dragon's head. The first blow bounced off the dragon's brow, but the second one struck the soft eye. The dragon screamed and swatted at her, but Lily flipped herself backwards over the reaching claws and landed on her feet. The dragon pawed at its injured eye, momentarily distracted.

Taking their cue from Lily, Dan and Lars rushed the dragon's eye on the other side, stabbing for the soft tissue. Lily renewed the attack, darting back and forth as they worked to blind the dragon. Carl swung his axe and hit the dragon square in the ribs. He might as well have hacked at a brick wall. The axe bounced back in his hand, sending a shock all the way up to his shoulder. To his left, Mal flailed at the dragon's hide like a squirrel attacking a tree.

Carl stabbed with the pointed tip of the axe's curved blade, aiming for the dragon's armpit, and the steel bit into softer flesh. The dragon screamed in pain and wrenched away from him.

"Mal! Over here!" Lily shouted and Mal raced forward to join the attack on the dragon's face. The dragon moaned and shook its head, claws flailing as it tried to guard its face and fight its attackers at the same time. It shuffled backwards, head swinging.

"That's it!" Carl shouted. "Drive it out the door."

All four of them renewed the attack and the dragon backed farther.

Lily dealt a rain of spinning blows that never left her feet in the same place twice, while Mal planted her feet and screamed, hacking wildly at whatever dragon part she could reach. On the opposite side of the beast, Dan bellowed and beat on the dragon's face. With a whoop, Lars vaulted onto the dragon's knee, leapt from there to the dragon's back. Like a kid scaling a jungle gym, he climbed up the dragon's side and wrapped himself around its neck, stabbing at its throat under the jaw.

The dragon belched snow and ice at them, but Carl ducked into the lee of its elbow and chopped away. The dragon bellowed and backed farther out the door, beating its wings.

FORTY-THREE

"Where are you, Heidrek?" Harvey shouted. Her breath came tight and fast, every nerve begging her to charge blind into smoke and steam. But the platform was small and slippery, with only a basic handrail for safety.

"Mom!" Caleb's voice echoed in the fog and was cut off. The blue line of his connection to the dragon shone in the fog.

She swung Tyrfing with a flash like lightning and snapped the magical tether. Caleb screamed and in the distance the dragon echoed him. Heidrek loomed out of the mist, a piece of rebar in his hand. He brought it down on her arm.

Even in her berserk state the blow numbed her hand. Her grip on the sword loosened. Heidrek swung the rebar again, but this time she brought the blade up, slicing clean through the metal in his hand. With a snarl, Heidrek lunged at her, stabbing with the sharp iron piece left in his hand. Harvey ducked, slipped on the wet platform, and fell. Tyrfing fell out of her numbed hand and skittered away from her.

Both she and Heidrek lunged for the sword, his foot stamping down on her hand before she could reach the sword. He ground his heel into her palm and stooped to grasp Tyrfing. As he rose, sword in hand, she flung sharp cinder dust upward into his eyes with her one free hand. He gasped and swung blindly.

As he stumbled backward, she wrenched her pinned hand free. On her hands and knees, she hugged herself to his legs, sending them both into a pile of coke. Heat from the furnace edge frizzled her hair.

Harvey gripped his clothes, hauling herself up his body. He swung at her, but she caught his sword arm and pushed the blow aside. She tried to batter his hand against the pile of coke and rubble, but he reached up and grabbed her throat. His nails dug into her neck, choking off her air. Darkness edged her vision, a darkness that had nothing to do with the sight in her burned eye. She kneed him in the groin, but the berserk was on him, too, and he laughed at her and pulled her closer. With no space to swing the sword blade, he beat at her head and shoulders with Tyrfing's heavy pommel and she dug her nails into his eyes, sank her teeth into his neck.

He pushed her away and air rushed back into her lungs. Heidrek kicked at her, knocking her back so that he had room to swing again. He got to his feet and swung, but Harvey ducked under his sword arm and tackled him. She caught him by the waist, landing her full weight on his chest and the air groaned out of him.

She straddled him, knees digging into the sharp coke pile and grabbed his sword arm with both hands. She would snap his arm, shatter his hand against the ground.

Words in the old language came from his mouth, words promising blood and darkness for help. Harvey's fingers burned cold, numb and stiff. Even through the power of the berserk she felt the pain, smelled her own burning skin and hair from the nearness of the furnace. And yet everywhere she touched Heidrek the warmth drained from her body.

He flung her off him, kicked her so that she rolled until she landed against the furnace control booth. Too much. She was too tired. Too weak after all these years.

The black cold around her seemed to fill her lungs. For the first time in her life, Harvey's berserk failed her. The bear spirit inside her faded, leaving her trembling and weak in the midst of a battle. Her hands shook as she struggled to rise to her knees.

On the opposite end of the platform, Heidrek spun the sword in slow arcs as he took slow, deliberate steps toward her. He always did like to play with his food. She crawled away, sharp cinders cutting into her palms. Her eye hurt. Her ribs hurt. Everything hurt. Exhaustion hung lead weights on her tongue, on her thoughts. Her hand touched a bare foot. Caleb's.

He was ghostly pale, gray as if he'd been bled dry. He lay huddled against the handrail, a hair's breadth from falling off the platform, a hand pressed to his bleeding chest. His eyes were open, but unseeing.

She shook him. "Caleb, baby, you have to get up. Get up and run."

His eyes met hers. They were dark and empty pools like Heidrek's, but in their very deepest depths a flame leapt. "He's so hungry, Mom. I can't feed him enough." She tried to pull him to his feet, but his eyes closed and his head lolled forward. Behind her Heidrek's soft shoes crunched in the cinder dust.

Harvey turned, shielding her child with her body.

"How convenient, sister," he said. "I'll kill the cub with its mother." With both hands, her brother raised Tyrfing high.

A weapon. Harvey needed something, anything. Her hand closed on one of the six-foot iron smelting bars used to push steel into the furnace. She braced herself, crouched over Caleb to meet his rush. She had no berserk left, no real hope that she could stop him. She could only buy Caleb a few more seconds of life.

Harvey gripped the iron rod like a club and rose, swinging the iron rod up to meet the blade.

Quick as lightning, Heidrek parried her blow, sliced through the tip of her weapon as if it were a thread. She swung again and another piece of the forge rod flew away into the darkness, leaving only a sharpened stub in her hand. Heidrek laughed and stabbed at her, caught her in the shoulder.

He reared back, swung again, sliced a line on her upraised arm. She stabbed at him with the remnant in her hand, but he kicked her hand aside. He laughed and stabbed again, catching her in the hip. The sword tip ground against bone and she fell, groaning through clenched teeth.

He yanked the blade out and stepped back, still laughing. Harvey reached for him, struggling to get up, but her hip wouldn't hold, and she fell again, sprawled at his feet. He laughed and kicked her, rolling her over. She caught at his leg and hung on, but blood slicked her hand and her grip failed.

He planted a foot on her breastbone. Still she struggled, but his weight held her. Slowly, methodically, he reversed his grip on Tyrfing, the tip poised over her heart.

"Hold still, sister," he said. "I owe the darkness another life." He raised the sword high over Caleb's body.

Harvey screamed. She stabbed once with the iron remnant in her hand straight through Heidrek's stolen oxford shoes, through the flesh and bone. She pinned Heidrek's foot to the ground. He screamed and his knees buckled.

He screamed again and raised Tyrfing to strike, but she jerked the iron stub out of his foot and stabbed him again in the thigh. Harvey seized the front of his shirt with her free hand and hauled herself up his body. Blood pumped from the wound in his leg and Tyrfing fell from his hand.

She plunged the iron stub into the side of his neck, yanked it out and stabbed again into his windpipe. Air rushed through the hole in his throat, made a ragged, whistling, bubbling sound as his blood poured out over her face. The last of her strength left her and she fell forward onto the platform, bearing his body down under her.

Harvey landed with her burned face against the greasy, slush-covered steel plates of the platform, her head pressed into Heidrek's side. His heart pumped once more and stopped. He was cold already. She lay there, her fingers tangled in the blue cloth of his shirt.

Wind howled. Water trickled in her ear before silence deafened her. Her thoughts scattered and swirled.

Dying. She wasn't allowed to die. Caleb. Frostbite. Mal and the others. Doctors. Someone call 911. She should call 911.

Her fingers scrabbled at the floor, pushing, too weak. Blood seeped out of her wounds and mingled with Heidrek's rapidly cooling puddles.

Kinslayer. I was born to be a kinslayer.

Harvey slumped over his body and her tears joined the blood on the floor.

FORTY-FOUR

S lowly, slowly they drove the dragon out into the blizzard. As its wings and neck cleared the doorway, it reared back, twisting like a wounded snake. Its tail lashed and knocked Mal head over heels. Carl jumped at the last second, narrowly avoiding getting knocked off his feet.

Dan charged in, mouth foaming, and flung himself on the dragon's wing. It flapped and shook him high into the air, but he hung on. Lars, shaken loose from the dragon's head, tumbled forward and fell under its claws.

Carl slashed at its snout. He buried his axe in its nostril, twisted and yanked the blade out for another blow. Acid-hot blood splattered down on him, eating into the metal of his helmet. To his right, Lily screamed in pain. The yard was a thrashing mess of trampling dragon feet and spraying blood.

Carl swung the axe again, only to have the edge bound off the dragon's tougher hide. The monster batted him aside like a plastic toy. He rolled, ass over teakettle, to land on his back yards away. Head ringing, he sat up. His axe was gone, slipped out of his hand. He groped in the muck and slush of the loading yard for his weapon. Above him the dragon's mouth loomed, teeth icicle sharp.

Lily leapt between them, her hooked sword in her hand. She rammed it into the dragon's mouth, burying the barbed end in the dragon's soft palate and yanking as if she'd hooked a fish. Squealing, the dragon flailed away, clawing at its mouth.

As the dragon reared overhead, Lily abandoned her sword and grabbed Carl's arm, hauling him to his feet. "Come on, lumberjack. You're going to get squished if you stay here."

He stumbled away with her to the far side of the loading yard. Lars and Mal still darted back and forth, stabbing at the dragon's sides before darting away again. And Dan hung on to the writhing tail, weighing it down.

"I'm out of weapons," Carl said.

Lily drew her knobbed stick out of her sash. "I don't know how much damage this is going to do against Godzilla there."

"You go low, I'll go high?" Carl said.

"No, this is stupid," Lily said. "You distract it, I'll grab the kids. We have to get them inside before they get its full attention. Then we close those doors."

Carl frowned for a second. "Yeah, that's a better plan."

He raised his fists over his head and charged straight at the dragon, screaming a war cry. From the corner of his eye, he saw Lily veer off to the left, running straight for Mal.

Even wounded as it was, the dragon was far from done. It saw Carl's charge and screamed back, ice and wind billowing from the rush of its wings. It raked him with its claws, and the chainmail shredded like paper. The blow rolled him over and over in the snow, but he popped back up, screaming again. The shreds of his chainmail shirt jangled as he taunted the dragon.

"Come and get me you overgrown newt!"

Wide open, the dragon's mouth plunged toward him. He raised his fists high and prepared to punch his way down its throat and out its stomach if that's what it took.

A brown blur on his left and Dan knocked Carl clear of the dragon's mouth. His head slammed into pavement and he saw stars. The dragon's jaws snapped on empty air. It screamed, twisting its neck back and forth, trying to see the two men between its feet. Dan leapt back to his feet with a laugh and screamed back.

And the dragon vanished.

Dan was left screaming at empty air, fists raised to the gray sky. The last of the whipped-up snow fell in utter silence in the sudden vacuum.

Panting, Carl struggled to his feet, not sure he believed his senses. Dan turned toward him, hands still balled into fists, but confusion in his eyes. Lily turned from herding Mal and Lars toward the factory doors, her wooden club at the ready.

"It's gone," Carl said, more to convince himself than anyone else.

"Did we beat it?" Lars yelled to him.

"Someone beat it," Carl said.

Dan shook his head, clearing the berserk. "Harvey," he said, his words clotted and heavy. He pointed back to the factory.

"Oh God, Mom!" Mal said. She took off at a run, Lars close behind her.

Berserk gone in the sudden loss of his enemy, Carl ran after her. Every step jarred his side. He put a hand to the rip in his chain mail and felt warm blood oozing. His lungs burned in a way they never had before. Panting, he slowed his steps, but pushed on. *Harvey is in there.*

"What are you, old?" he said to himself. He held the wound in his side shut and kept his feet moving.

Harvey lay with her face against Heidrek's side, the tears leaking from her eyes, as grief and the gray aftermath of the berserk rolled over her.

"Mom, Mom, are you okay?" Caleb whispered from the slag heap.

He crawled toward her on his hands and knees. "Please don't be dead."

She dragged herself upright and caught him in a fierce hug. "I'm okay." Pain stabbed through her hip and shoulder even as she said it. Probably going to need stitches. She wiped at the cuts on his chest, but her hand only left filthy black marks streaked with red.

"I'm fine." Caleb balled up his torn t-shirt and pressed it against her hip. "You're bleeding a lot though."

"I know." Harvey pushed him away. "Got one more thing to do." She tried to rise, but her hip wouldn't carry any weight. The slightest movement sent pain screaming up and down her body. "Help me up. Please."

But Caleb was too weak to support her. She clung to him, dragging herself upright against him and they both fell down in a heap. "Fine," she said through gritted teeth. If her legs didn't work, her arms would have to.

Crawling on her belly, she dragged herself to where Tyrfing lay, shining still in the coal dust. "Damn you, you stupid piece of metal," she said and dragged it with her toward the edge of the furnace. Below them on the factory floor alarms still blared. Men shouted at each other.

She heard Ken giving orders to shut down the ladles, shut down the furnace before an explosion happened. "And somebody call the goddamn police."

Not much time. And she had one dead body here and another in the back room of her house. She hauled herself as close to the furnace's lip as she could bear, until the heat baked the skin on her face tight and her eyes burned. One-handed she flung Tyrfing as far as she could toward the furnace's center. The sword dropped through the air, clanged off the furnace's side, and disappeared into the blinding yellow glow.

Harvey rested her head on her arms, shielding her face from the heat. She tasted ash on her teeth. Feet rang on the iron stairs behind her. People put their hands on her, dragged her back from the furnace. Ken was shouting her name. Other voices she knew.

I have the right to remain silent. But there's no point. I killed him. She didn't have enough blood or water left in her for more tears. A sob rose up in her, almost splitting her chest in half. She shut her teeth against the dry sobs, her cheek cradled against the diamond ridge steel plates, until someone heaved her onto a gurney.

Someone nice put their hand on her shoulder. "Hang in there, ma'am. You're going to be okay." Someone slid a needle into her arm. Cold flooded into her, spreading toward her shoulder.

Now would be a great time to be unconscious. But she was awake for every jolt and bump as they strapped her onto the gurney and carried it down the steep stairs.

There was Ken, yelling at a policeman. "You heard me. A goddamn dragon." He was a nice man. Even if he was a manager. She'd really fucked up his safety record though. She rolled her head to the side, eyes struggling to focus. *Where are the others?*

She tried to lift her head off the gurney, but they'd strapped that down too. "My kids." Her voice came out like a raven's croak.

"They'll be fine, ma'am. They're in the other ambulance."

Another needle in her other arm. This one stung and then warmed, spreading faster than the cold on her other side. She tried to focus on the EMT with her burned eye, expecting what? A Norn? A harbinger of death?

But she saw nothing. Her good eye told her he was a clean-cut guy in pressed white clothes. And then the warming drug reached her body and she saw nothing at all.

FORTY-FIVE

T he emergency room lay strangely empty. No hurrying feet beyond the curtain, no patients shouting. Machines beeped.

Harvey lay in the white bay, under a white sheet and blanket, waiting for someone to come back and tell her what happened. The drive to the hospital had been nothingness, intercut with blurs. Slow rolling through the silence of empty roads, empty world. No one but them in their warm, silent truck, rolling through the cold.

Then a flurry of people. A stretcher. Voices shouting. Someone stuck her with a needle again. Now she was alone in the whiteness. It covered her. Her feet were cold. Maybe if the blanket were a nice warm yellow she wouldn't be so cold. She grinned lopsidedly to herself and flopped her head to one side.

Slowly, her eyes traced the clear plastic tube down to her arm and the taped-in needle. Whatever was dripping into her vein must really be working. Except her arm still throbbed. And her hip. It didn't matter as much though. If the cold whiteness would go away. She tried to listen to the voices outside, but they blurred and washed together with beeps and passing feet.

"Hello?" she called. "Somebody?"

Harvey rolled her head to the other side. No water in sight. She should get some. "Silly," she said, the word slurring. "I am being silly. I am not that high." She tossed back the blanket with her good hand. It took her two tries.

"Stupid," she said. Caleb was probably freezing to death in the lobby. He didn't even have any shoes on. And where were the rest of them? Had the dragon eaten them? She had to go find out, go help.

Her feet were still on the bed. "Come on, feet!" Harvey told them. They didn't move. "I am getting angry with you."

No movement.

She giggled and slapped a hand over her mouth, even as tears sprang up in the corners of her eyes. Not a time to be goofy. People were hurt.

Harvey wrapped her fingers around the bed's railing and hauled herself upright. Hot pain shot through her hip and into the rest of her body, pain too strong to be contained in one part of her. She fell back panting. She squeezed her eyes shut and pushed back against the pain, holding it in place.

"Bullshit," she said to the pain. This wasn't as bad as pushing out Caleb's giant head. Or Mal, ass first. She gritted her teeth to try again.

Lily, in socks and a hospital gown, poked her head into the bay. "You awake? What are you doing? Hold still." She pushed Harvey gently back on the bed and poured her some water. She held the straw up, so Harvey could drink. It stung on her parched lips and swollen tongue.

"My kids," Harvey said, "are they okay? And Lars and Carl?"

Lily drew up a rolling stool and perched on it. "Your kids are doing fine. Mal's getting treated for a concussion and acid burns. Don't freak out—they're not that bad. Caleb is resting. They've pumped about two pints of blood into him and he looks much better. Your friend Carl is in surgery right now. This place is half empty. I

266

think they're really shorthanded with the blizzard, so they had to take him first and make you wait, but you're next."

"I need surgery?" Harvey giggled and then bit down on her lip. It was just a funny word—sur-ger-y. She tried again to be sober. "How do you know?"

Lily smiled. "I work in a high school. If I wasn't an inveterate eavesdropper, I'd never survive."

But Harvey persisted. "Why me? Why do I need surgery?"

"For your arm and hip. The damage is pretty deep—more than they can repair with just stitches, so they're sending you upstairs in a few minutes."

"I am really drugged up, aren't I?" Harvey said.

That made Lily smile. "You are a little. But you're also coming out of shock. It's pretty normal for trauma victims." She rolled her stool closer, and said, "The police are going to want to talk to you later. I convinced them not to talk to Caleb and Mal without you present, but they are looking for answers and they are not happy. They already grilled me up one side and down the other."

The giggles broke like a bubble and tears sprang out again. *Stupid tears.* This was not a good time to cry, not in this cold white room, with her kids somewhere else, in other cold, white rooms. The morgue where they put Jon had been cold and white, full of steel doors. And the prison where they'd kept Heidrek.

She gripped Lily's wrist. "Make sure Mal and Caleb are okay after they take me away."

"Pffft. You're not going anywhere. I told them your psychopath brother broke out of prison, killed your father-in-law, and kidnapped your son for some sort of Satanic ritual. They started to believe me when they saw the cuts on Caleb's chest. That kid is going to need some serious counseling, by the way."

A little sliver of hope broke through the numbness and pain. It wasn't a lie, just the truth told in a way that made everything come out right. She'd never been good at that.

"Thank you," she said. "Do you need a new queen? Because I really need a *thyle*."

Lily laughed. "Girl, no. I'm my own queen. And I don't know what a thyle is, but what you need is friends."

Harvey smiled in spite of the tears and pain. She reached up and took Lily's hand. "Thank you," she said.

Lily squeezed her hand and smiled back at her.

CHAPTER

FORTY-SIX

The police, strangely, were on Harvey's side. They didn't so much ask her what had happened as tell her and ask her to sign a statement. She and her kids were the victims of a dangerous criminal, a psychotic mastermind who had murdered his own therapist and a harmless grandfather, kidnapped and tortured his own nephew, and somehow induced a mass delusion in a factory full of solid union men, all of whom had perfect drug test records.

When the police asked to see the testing records the union threatened to sue them, the city of Buffalo, and factory management. No one ever connected Heidrek or the rest of them to the vandalism at the St. Stanislaus Cemetery. The cemetery company apologized repeatedly and profusely to Harvey for the desecration of her family graves by vandals and promised to put in better security.

Dan was not so lucky. The police ran a background check on him that turned up several outstanding warrants, including a few in Canada and South Dakota connected to First Nations protests. By the time Harvey came out of surgery, he and his motorcycle were long gone. Mal told her about it, sitting on Harvey's hospital bed eating her Jell-O.

"Where's he going exactly?" Harvey asked.

"Maine. Maybe farther north. He said he had friends up there, but he'd be back eventually. If he felt like it." Mal held up her wrist, turning a silver cuff engraved with an eight-pointed star. "He gave me this."

"It's pretty. I wish I could have told him thank you."

Lily kept the kids fed, including Lars, until they let Harvey out of the hospital the next day.

"Don't you have a parole officer?" Harvey asked Lars. "Are you in trouble?"

He kind of shrugged and grinned, rubbing the back of his neck. "Coach Lily talked to him. She...um... she made it all okay." He blushed beet red. "She called me a hero."

"And you are," Harvey said, wrapping her arms around him in bear hug. When he tried to go home, she insisted he stay. "You can barely feed yourself two-handed," she said, pointing to the cast on his left arm. "What are you going to do with just one?"

She put him up on the living room couch. When the doctors let Carl out of the hospital, she brought him home too and put him in her bed.

It made good sense. He was too hurt to go back to his apartment. And Lars was a big goofball, fun to have around, but not the person you wanted taking care of a sick man, even when his arm wasn't broken in two places. And there was nowhere else for him to sleep, since Lars was downstairs on the couch. No one suggested using Ivor's room. Lily went back to her own place but promised to come back for suppers.

When Carl tossed and moaned in his sleep, she shook him awake. And when Harvey pressed her face into the pillow in the dark, trying not to wake him with her tears, he pressed his cheek against her back and stroked her hair, holding her as best he could. During the day they did small, ordinary things around the house, went to doctor appointments, or sat quietly resting together on the couch.

Lars and Mal played video games and talked about weapons,

endlessly rehashing the fight with the dragon and what they would do if it came back.

Lily came over for supper most nights, happy to report on whatever the going gossip in the teacher's lounge was. "I can't cook for crap," she said. "As long as it's not Lean Cuisine, I'll eat whatever you're serving."

Caleb was another story. He barely came out of his room, even for meals. "I'm just tired," he said, anytime Harvey asked how he was doing. He refused to talk about any of it.

"Give him time," Carl said. But Harvey worried. At night, when his light was out, she traced a sign of blessing and protection on Caleb's locked door.

On the morning of Ivor's funeral, she eased her black nylons over the stitches in her hip. She drew her new black dress over her head, wriggling it into place and propping one hand on the bureau for balance as Mal pulled up the zipper.

Harvey considered herself in the mirror, the long brown hair rippling around her face and down her back. The dress was plain, long sleeved and without ornaments. She smoothed the skirt and picked up a star-shaped brooch, set with pale blue glass gems that had belonged to her mother. She held it up against the black material where it flashed and sparkled. *Not today,* she decided, and put the brooch back in its place. Instead she settled the golden torc around her neck. The bears' garnet eyes flashed red in the light.

Mal peered over her shoulder. Her burns from the dragon's blood had healed well. Shiny pink streaks of new flesh splashed across her cheek and down her neck. Harvey reached up and cupped her daughter's face, their heads leaning together for a moment.

"Do you want me to do your hair?" Mal asked. Her own hair was back in a neat ponytail. She'd borrowed a black skirt and a pair of heels from a friend, pairing them with a dark gray sweater.

Harvey combed her fingers through the locks again. The wind would make a horrendous tangle out of it, but that was the point. "No, leave it," she said. "It's traditional for funerals."

In the mirror, Mal nodded. She tilted her head to one side, studying her mother's reflection and then tugged the elastic from her own hair, shaking it out into brown waves that just brushed her shoulders. "Like this?"

Harvey smiled at her daughter. "Alright. Time to go." She gave Mal a little push. "Go on," she said. "I'll be down in a minute."

In the hallway, she knocked on Caleb's door. "It's time to go," she said.

"I'm not going."

She grimaced and turned the handle. The handle turned easily, yet the door wouldn't budge. Blue ghost light shone around the lock. She let go of the handle, wiping her hand on her skirt. "Please let me in."

A long silence and then a sigh. Caleb muttered something on the other side of the door and the lock opened. Caleb sat on his bed in the dark, curtains drawn to block out the light. He had a raven feather in his hands, stroking it through his fingers over and over again. The quill was tipped with dried blood.

Harvey sat down beside him, trying not to groan too loud as she dropped the last three inches onto the bed. "Grampa would want you to go to his funeral."

His eyes were hollow as he said, "I killed him."

"No. Your uncle killed him. Big difference."

"But I helped." Caleb drew the raven feather through his fingers again and again. "I made it possible."

Harvey didn't have any words for that. She slipped her fingers into his hand, stopping him from playing with the feather. She held his hand tight and said, "He was ready to die. And he had the kind of death he wanted. That's more than a lot of people get. Please come."

Caleb shook his head.

She gave his hand one last squeeze. "I have to go. I love you."

He nodded without looking up from the bloody raven's feather. She kissed him on the cheek and eased off the bed, hurting in more than just her hip. "I love you," she said again from the doorway.

He didn't respond.

Downstairs in the kitchen the rest were waiting in various levels of funeral clothes. Lily was neat and professional looking in black pants and a suit jacket, Lars not so much in a Metallica "...And Justice for All" t-shirt and spiked leather wrist cuffs.

Carl had actually gone out and bought a tie. It looked ridiculous on him, but she smiled. The color had come back to his cheeks, replacing the gray pallor that had lingered after his surgery. His arm and shoulder were still in the sling, but the slit in his back where the surgeons had repaired his spleen was healing. She'd peeled the last bandage off this morning, kneeling behind him as he sat on the bed. The red-gold of his beard shone, an echo of the gold at his throat. She took his good arm and let him help her down the steps and into the limo sent by the funeral parlor.

Despite the deep cold, more like January than the last week of November, the ground hadn't frozen yet. At St. Stanislaus Cemetery the snow was shoveled down to the grass and mats laid in a path to the standing stone. A small table draped in purple had been set in front of the stone and Ivor's ashes placed on the table.

It was a short ceremony. Ivor had never had much use for Christian religion beyond attending the kids' Christmas pageants. The minister shivered in his vestments, gloved fingers holding down the pages of his book as he read from Psalms. Men and women huddled together, heads sunk into coat collars, ears turning red in the open air. There were more jeans than suits. Arn brought his wife and kids. Mac didn't show his face, but a few of his boys did, hovering shame-faced at the back of the small crowd.

Harvey stood bareheaded despite the cold, her shoulders back in the sunlight, beside the table. It seemed impossible that such a solid man as Ivor could fit inside a wooden urn no bigger than a tissue box. The flowers laid on the table shone bright against the pale wood. The green herbs woven into the wreath gave off a sharp, earthy scent to mingle with the flowers' sweetness.

"Amen," the minister intoned for the last time and the congregation answered, "Amen."

Leaning on Carl's arm, she stepped forward. She laid her hands on the smooth wood and bent her head over it until her hair fell forward, draping over the box like a veil. Her tears dripped down to land on the flowers. This was her last duty to the dead.

Her hands braced on the urn, she raised her face to the sun and let out a cry, a long drawn out wail between a song and a scream. "My father-in-law is dead. Receive him, oh earth."

Then, in the old language, Harvey sang about Ivor, father and friend, wise counsel, battle hardened like oak smoked in the fire, a man of courage, he faced death and did not flinch. She held her hands high and sang until she ran out of words.

She let her arms drop, shivering like the aftermath of a berserk. The tremor ran up her thighs and through her core. The wind whipped her hair around her face, tangles catching in her mouth, stinging her eyes. But she stood still and erect as the other mourners filed past. Each murmured something, a memory, a word of comfort. Few of the men could meet her eyes.

They shook her hand instead, muttered that she'd done Ivor proud. It was a good funeral. A few could only squeeze her hand, harrumphing and swallowing before they hurried off. Women she hadn't seen since her father's funeral hugged her. They said things about getting together soon. She hugged them back.

Beside her Carl stood, tall and sturdy, blocking a little of the wind. At his open collar the gold torc gleamed. He shook each man's hand with a sharp downward snap, and met each of their eyes, his mouth set. They bobbed and bowed as they stepped away.

As the last mourner left, the funeral director handed her the wooden box of Ivor's ashes. She tucked it into the corner of her arm and took Carl's good elbow for balance. Lars, Lily, and Mal hovered for a minute and, seeing that they weren't moving, headed for the limo, leaving the two of them alone.

They stood a few more minutes in front of the standing stone, sheltering each other from the wind. "We should get going," she said. "The wake at Arn's will already be in full swing."

Carl nodded, but neither of them moved. The day around them was bright, the clear sky too cold for clouds. The wind tossed the empty branches of the trees, black against the bright blue.

"The ravens are gone," Carl said.

"Yes," she agreed. She let herself lean against his side, her hip resting just below his. He shifted, twining his fingers into hers. "When spring comes," she said, "I want to carve his name into the stone." She drew him closer, so that his side pressed against hers. She turned her face up to his. Her cheekbones came just to his shoulder. "And I want you to stay. Please."

He turned to face her. "Do you love me?" he asked. "Because I love you too much to stay for anything less."

She stretched up, taking his face in her hands and kissing him. "Do I love you?" she whispered between kisses. "How could I not?"

THE END

ACKNOWLEDGMENTS

First and best thanks go to Emily Lavin Leverett, my writing partner and friend for over twenty years. Without her willful optimism and excellent wit, I would have given up long ago. In the case of this particular book, I also have to thank her for suggesting a modern urban setting when I became obsessed with turning the *Hervararsaga* into a novel. Of course, I dismissed the idea out of hand the minute she said it. Shows what I know. Emily, you were right.

Next, let me thank the extremely patient editors at Falstaff Books who worked with me through personal crises, missed deadlines, and major plot changes, not to mention my erratic relationship to the em dash. John Hartness, Melissa McArthur, and Jay Requard - thank you for believing in this book even when I didn't and thank you for all the ways you made this a better book.

I must also thank my dear friend and college roommate, Jackie Monkiewicz, who routinely took me and the rest of our scruffy bunch of college friends home with her to Buffalo, NY for Thanksgiving and Spring Break. Jackie, I hope you don't mind how many of your high school stories I mined for story material or how I have played fast and loose with the geography of your hometown. I would have a *Star Wars* marathon and shoot imaginary blasters at hecklers again with you any day.

And of course, that means I owe a debt of thanks to Jackie's parents, Audrey and Kim Monkiewicz. Thank you for welcoming me into your home and family over so many holidays that would otherwise have been spent alone in a dorm.

Finally, my thanks also to the scholars Christopher Tolkien and Peter Tunstall whose translations of the *Hervarar saga ok Heiðreks* first introduced me to Hervor, the woman who gathered a viking crew and won a cursed sword from her father's ghost.

ABOUT THE AUTHOR

Sarah Joy Adams is a writer, editor, and medievalist. She teaches at Wake Tech and lives in Garner, NC, with her son, a dog, and three cats. She is the author of three fantasy novels with Emily Lavin Leverett and this is her first solo novel. You can find her at https://sites.google.com/view/sarah-joy-adams/home or on Twitter @SarahJoyAdams

FRIENDS OF FALSTAFF

Thank You to All our Falstaff Books Patrons, who get extra digital content each month! To be featured here and see what other great rewards we offer, go to www.patreon.com/falstaffbooks.

PATRONS

Dino Hicks

John Hooks

John Kilgallon

Larissa Lichty

Travis & Casey Schilling

Staci-Leigh Santore

Sheryl R. Hayes

Scott Norris

Samuel Montgomery-Blinn

Junkle